# How to *Fail* at Flirting

# How to *Fail* at Flirting

## Denise Williams

JOVE    *New York*

A JOVE BOOK
Published by Berkley
An imprint of Penguin Random House LLC
penguinrandomhouse.com

A JOVE BOOK, BERKLEY, and the BERKLEY & B colophon
are registered trademarks of Penguin Random House LLC.

Library of Congress Cataloging-in-Publication Data

Names: Williams, Denise, 1982- author.
Title: How to fail at flirting / Denise Williams.
Description: First edition. | New York: Jove, 2020.
Identifiers: LCCN 2020012255 (print) | LCCN 2020012256 (ebook) |
ISBN 9780593101902 (trade paperback) | ISBN 9780593101919 (ebook)
Subjects: GSAFD: Love stories.
Classification: LCC PS3623.I556497 H69 2020 (print) |
LCC PS3623.I556497 (ebook) | DDC 813/.6—dc23
LC record available at https://lccn.loc.gov/2020012255
LC ebook record available at https://lccn.loc.gov/2020012256

First Edition: December 2020

Printed in the United States of America
1   3   5   7   9   10   8   6   4   2

Cover art and design by Farjana Yasmin
Book design by Elke Sigal

For my husband. If I were rearranging the alphabet, I'd put U and I next to each other.

# One

The student in the fourth row glanced left then right as his friends stared in other directions and the bravado drained from his face. My question still hanging in the air, he muttered, "I don't know."

I itched to call him out for not doing the reading, then texting during class. Disengaged students didn't usually bother me this much, but it had been a long semester and I was tired of this room. Someone crinkled a bag of chips a few rows back, and the clock on the wall ticked away. The ticking brought back a flash of memory, but I pushed it aside.

*Not now.*

His expensive-looking shoes caught my eye. Boat shoes. They coordinated with his plaid shorts, polo shirt, and sunglasses pushed into blond hair styled *just so*. I needed to check my roster to confirm his name; it was Quinton or Quenton or something equally preppy. I planned to add looking him up to my to-do list when I got back to the office.

"We've covered several theories. Tell us how the study of social learning can be applied to communication on social media." I hoped he might contribute something, *anything*, to renew my faith in the modern American college student.

Instead, Quinton or Quenton leaned back and repeated, "I don't know, Dr. Turner. Um . . . there are a lot of ways because of . . . um . . . the social connection." Pen in hand, he glanced down at his "notes"—a blank sheet of paper in front of him—as if this answer should appease me.

*That wasn't even a good nonsense answer. C'mon, man.*

I stepped back to address the auditorium, pulling at the hem of my loose cardigan.

"Turn to a partner and discuss three ways we could apply these traditional theories of learning to social media." Chairs squeaked and groaned as students shifted, and voices rose.

I knew better than to judge a student so harshly based on his appearance. A penchant for Top-Siders and sherbet-colored shirts didn't influence his intellectual ability. Quinton or Quenton would either surprise me by acing the final or he'd fail the exam spectacularly in a blaze of styling gel.

I knew this, but mostly I was still annoyed by his stupid shoes.

***

Joe, my department chair, waved to me when I stepped into the hall after class. "Naya, do you have a minute?"

We took the flight of creaking stairs to our floor, where a sign with the words "The Center for Learning" etched into an ancient and scuffed plaque greeted us. The home of my specialty—math education—shared the cramped space with faculty from English and social studies education. What was left of the elementary education department took up the half of the floor above us that wasn't unusable because of water damage.

Originally constructed in 1917, the structure could best be described as decrepit. The faded, chipped paint and worn carpet were a good metaphor for our diminishing funding as the institution increasingly focused on preparing students to go into business and engineering.

When we emerged from the dim stairwell, our department secretary's efficient voice followed us down the hall. "No, you want the campus childcare center. This is the Center for Learning . . . I'll transfer you."

I wondered how many times a week she answered that same question. Dr. Anita Kline, a senior professor, was a national leader in the study of early-childhood math development and online technology, and my research on math education for English-language learners had been called groundbreaking, but most of the campus assumed our building had a swing set tucked away somewhere. We needed to think about rebranding if we wanted the campus to take seriously the cutting-edge work we were doing with the science of learning.

I attempted to close Joe's door, pulling it hard, but to no avail.

"The wood's warped with the humidity. Don't worry about it," Joe said over his shoulder.

We had a little way to go before we got to that *cutting edge*, I thought as I sat in a chair with worn, orange vinyl. "What's going on?"

The familiar smell of coffee and old books surrounded me like a fleece blanket. All our spaces were cramped, though Joe's was the most cluttered.

"Do you have anything in the hopper this summer?"

"Sure—a couple manuscripts, and some grant proposals to submit, plus working on developing that new course for the fall." *Plus whatever else I find to keep me busy.* "Why?"

He bobbed his head and shrugged in resignation, sitting back in his chair. "This new president makes me nervous, and rumor has it that he plans to make cuts. Not sure where our department will land."

After six months, Thurmond University was still spinning on its hundred-and-twenty-year-old axis and getting used to our new leader: Archibald "Flip" Lewis. He was often described as "nontraditional," a big challenge to a campus that took to change like a toddler to nap time.

"Would they really cut education? We'll always need teachers."

He smiled wanly. "I get the sense that everything's on the table."

I'd worked my butt off for six years to publish as much as I could and tirelessly improve my teaching. This was where I was good. This job was where I had solid footing, and I was going up for tenure review in the fall. Now I struggled to wrap my head around the possibility of my department being cut.

When I got hired at TU, I'd explained the concept of tenure to my grandfather as a seven-year audition for a secure job. He'd shaken his bald head and clarified that I'd gone to college for four years and graduate school another five, to then have to prove myself for another seven before my job was safe.

He'd said, "Mija, no tiene sentido!" A quick glance in my mother's direction gave me a translation. *It doesn't make sense!* I never learned Spanish, so my mom was always helping us communicate. Every time I saw him when I was growing up, he'd ask, "Estás aprendiendo?" *Are you learning?*

"You're the first doctor in our family, and I'm so proud of you, but you tell me when you're done auditioning for this job, okay? We'll have a party."

I remembered that conversation when the hours got long, the process seemed interminable, or impostor syndrome set in. When I decided to merge my love of math with my interest in education, my grandfather actually gave me the idea of what to study. He told me teachers assumed he wasn't smart as a child because Spanish was his first language. He didn't think they ever tried very hard to teach him. I wondered how I could make an impact, to prepare teachers to help all kids love math.

He was in the throes of Alzheimer's and had been for a couple years, but I couldn't wait to visit him one day and tell him I did it, that I was done auditioning. That the work I was doing would help all kids realize they were smart. He was only comfortable speaking Spanish at this point, so I knew I'd need to figure out how to say what I needed to. Joe's worry lines and the looming uncertainty made me wonder if I'd get the chance.

"If they cut our program, what happens to us?"

"Depends. Faculty handbook allows for them to lay off people with tenure if the department is cut. They might keep some of us around to teach general education and intro classes from other departments, but I doubt there would be support for much research." If it was possible to slump more, Joe did. His expression said everything I was thinking. "Without tenure . . ."

So, even if I got to keep my job, I'd spend every day teaching the Quinton or Quentons of the world who didn't want to be there. *No, thanks.* I sat in silence with Joe for a moment, letting his words sink in. I had finally gotten near that finish line, I'd run the gauntlet, and now this crushing blow loomed on the horizon.

"Just be prepared, Nay. I'd hate to lose you, but don't be caught off guard, okay?"

"Got it, Joe." I glanced back across the desk. "Is there anything else?"

"Yeah." He scrubbed his hand over his jaw and drew his mouth to one side. "I saw Davis the other day. I think he's back on campus. Have you talked to him?"

I glanced over my shoulder instinctively, as if the man in question might be lurking in the corner. "No."

Joe looked unsure. If he'd known the extent of what happened with Davis, he wouldn't have had to ask. "I thought you'd want to know."

"Sure. I'll keep an eye out, boss."

Down the hall, I closed the door on my office with a reassuring click and leaned on my desk, taking a deep breath. My mind raced and my stomach knotted as Joe's words looped in my head.

After cracking open my laptop, I searched Davis's name to see if there were any announcements about a new hire. If I could find out where he would be and when, I could shift my plans in order to avoid him, find new routines, stay holed up in my office. I'd done it before.

My cursor hovered over one of the search results. The headline read, "TU Professor Wins Prestigious Duncan Prize," and the photo featured Davis accepting a glass statue with a broad smile on his face.

I'd attended with him in a backless black gown, beading across the low neckline. Davis had picked it for me, saying he wanted me to wear something slinky and sexy, and how much he loved knowing other men would want me, but I was his.

*"I want to show you off, sweetheart."*

It had been tighter and more revealing than I would normally wear, the dark fabric hugging every curve and the back dipping to just above my butt, and I'd spent much of the evening trying my best to cover my body. Still, it made him happy, and I was determined to do that, knowing how wonderful he could be when he was in a good mood.

Despite my discomfort, I was relieved to find Davis was full of cheer and humor. He'd held me to him and kissed my forehead throughout the gala that followed the awarding of the prizes. We'd made love that night in the hotel's king-sized bed, and he'd been tender. *"This means big things for me, Naya. Big things. I'll help you get there, too."* He'd seemed genuine, and I'd thought he meant it.

I shook away the memory and didn't click on the article. Instead, I scoured the results for any recent TU references and found none. *What the hell are you doing back here?*

I glanced around my office. I'd spent so much time alone in this room over the last six years. The keyboard under my fingers, the scatter of the light as it filtered through the blinds in the morning, and the way the old building creaked late at night were all as familiar as my childhood home. The job could be demanding, but it wasn't just that. In my little office, I could control things. I'd let those four walls become my whole world, and I didn't know who I would be without them.

# Two

The sun set over the Chicago skyline, and the smell of basil and garlic hung faintly in the air from the pasta my best friends had prepared for dinner. At Aaron and Felicia's kitchen table, I was still mulling over the potential cuts, Joe's bombshell about Davis, and those damned boat shoes.

"What's up with you tonight, Nay?" Aaron took a swig from his beer when Felicia went upstairs to put their oldest to bed.

My mind had wandered, and I jerked my gaze up from where it had landed on my old friend's chest.

"Eyes up here, pervert." He covered his torso with splayed fingers. "You haven't had any action in a while, but that's no excuse to objectify me."

"Sorry, but Felicia wouldn't mind sharing."

"I know. The only way my wife would ever agree to a threesome would be with you." He gave a full-body dramatic shudder, and I threw a balled-up napkin at him.

Aaron and I had met freshman year and shared one painfully awkward date, complete with an uninspired, fumbling lip-lock. That was before he asked out my best friend, I gave her my blessing but warned her to not expect much, and they ended up married with three kids. "You're an ass."

"You love me. But seriously, why so distracted tonight?"

I'd joked with them about Quinton or Quenton. As a high school teacher, Aaron liked exchanging student stories. "I'm still annoyed about that kid today."

Aaron's tone sobered as he ticked off his fingers for each new point. "Cocky, self-assured, dismissive, the polo shirts. Sound familiar?"

I reflexively touched my left wrist. "It's not that."

Since leaving the classroom earlier, the memory had crept alongside every other thought. A few months after we started dating, I'd been excited Davis wanted to see me teach—he was taking an interest in my work, and as a professor with more experience, he could give me pointers. I'd been lively and engaging with my students in ways I hoped impressed him. I was so naive. When class was over, he'd strolled to the front of the room, his expression impassive when I asked, "What did you think?"

He didn't answer immediately, but reached for my hand and brought it to his lips. The gesture was soft, but his tone was steely. "You were flirting with the male student in the front row."

"I wasn't. I would never." I tried to pull my hand back, but he gripped it firmly.

"I was sitting right there." He'd twisted my arm behind

my back, slamming it into the wooden podium with a fast jerk, and I yelped. To anyone walking by, it would look like he was hugging me, but pain radiated up my arm from the impact. "You practically fell into the kid's lap." His face inches from mine, he'd pecked the tip of my nose with a smirk as he twisted my wrist with more force. He dropped a kiss to my mouth after that, biting my lower lip before sucking on it.

"You're hurting me, and people are right outside."

After a moment of tense silence—the only sound the ticking clock—he'd laughed, a small caustic sound. "What? You worried they'll lose respect for you? Believe me, if you always act like you did today, they already have." He'd released my arm, letting it fall at my side, and told me he'd see me after work, walking out like nothing had happened.

I stifled the shudder of revulsion, and the memory of the flowers delivered the next day, and the lie I'd told Felicia about slipping on the ice. I shook it all away, focusing on Aaron's question. "He's a kid. I don't compare my students to men I've dated. That's . . ." I searched for the phrase that best described the rising bile in my stomach and settled on "inappropriate."

Aaron shrugged and pushed back from the table to get another beer. "I'm not saying you want to sleep with the kid. I'm just saying he might remind you of Davis."

Felicia breezed into the room, plucking the beer from her husband's hand. "What did I miss?"

"I was just saying, Nay always has strong reactions to people who are self-assured."

"Definitely. Except for me. It's a miracle we've been friends so long."

My best friend since third grade when she punched a girl who was bullying me, Felicia was my opposite in every way. Bold to my timid; dark, smooth skin to my ethnically ambiguous; brave to my fearful. Her smile was contagious, and I gave her a knowing grin. They were both wrong, though. Self-assurance didn't bother me. Davis was cocky. The way his lip curled when he was upset with me and how I had learned to cower at that expression—cocky bothered me. I shook my head, willing away the image as Aaron continued.

"You're wound too tight, Nay. Always have been." Aaron popped the top off two beers and handed me one. "I bet that kid wouldn't bother you this much if you"—he lifted his brows a few times—"found someone to help you loosen up."

"My sex life has nothing to do with that kid being prepared for my class." That was true, and my interest in sex had been nonexistent for a long time. After my last relationship, I'd felt disconnected from my body, and I didn't trust anything that felt good. Then, a few months earlier, Felicia had talked me into doing yoga with her a couple times a week, and eventually I'd become more in tune with my body. Turned out, my body missed sex even though my mind was resistant to trusting someone.

Felicia settled in the chair across from me, leaning forward on the table. "*You* might be more relaxed. Maybe you'd go with the flow more. It's been a long time, girl."

I couldn't fault my friends for encouraging me to move on. It had been three years, and as far as they knew, I was over it. I skirted the issue.

"Have you ever known me to *go with the flow*?" I raised an eyebrow at her and smirked. "Besides, I can't just *get* laid. It's not like I can just pick up a guy at the drugstore along with aspirin and gum. It's not that easy."

Felicia shared a look with her husband. "You're hot and live in a major metropolitan area; it is *definitely* that easy. I'd do you myself if I wasn't so in love with my husband and his impressive—"

I held my arms up, palms out. "Do not finish that sentence, I beg you."

Felicia shrugged and smiled sweetly.

Aaron took a swig from his beer. "Don't let this go to your head, Nay, but if I was a stranger and saw you on the street, I'd think you were pretty hot. If you want to get laid, you can get laid."

I cringed at his assessment and turned to Felicia. "You're okay with him thinking that?"

Felicia looked me up and down. "You have the ass of a nineteen-year-old . . . Let's be honest, he's not wrong." She held up her hand for a high five from her husband.

I narrowed my eyes and stared at Aaron.

He shot me a rueful glance and ignored my expression. "I'm married, not dead. I stand by my assessment. Why not test the waters if you're ready?"

"I don't want to have sex with a random guy I meet in a bar or because he swiped right. I want a connection." I wasn't sure I'd ever been in love with someone I'd slept with, not real love. I had no idea how different it might be to be with someone where it was real. *Hell, it's been long enough. Do I even remember how to do it?* Somewhere in the middle of this conversation, I'd forgotten I was against the entire premise.

"I offered to set you up with my trainer. Wes is cute," Felicia chimed in.

"Isn't he dating someone?" Aaron asked.

"Details," she said with a dismissive wave. "Nay, I'm adding sex with a stranger to your list."

"What list?"

"The list of things you will do on the way to getting a life."

Aaron grabbed a notepad and pen off the counter with a laugh.

"Having sex is not the same as getting a life. And when did you start this list?" I asked.

"About three seconds ago. And you could try for both things at the same time." Felicia told Aaron to take notes, and he wrote *Nay's To-Do:* and *1. Sex with a stranger* at the top of a blank page.

"I know you. You're a list-maker. What else?" She looked up at me, eyes bright.

I made a grab for the paper, but Aaron snatched it back. "My life is fine. I don't need a list." *Except that all I do is work and I might be about to lose my job.*

The two of them shared another glance. "Nay, we're the only people you hang out with. Humor us." Aaron scratched out his notes. "You'll need to work up to sex, though. I'll move it lower on the list."

I rolled my eyes, deciding to play along. "Okay, I could stand to get out of my rut. How about 'try new things'?" *Maybe that Cuban place around the corner or joining a book club.*

He jotted it down. "Flirt. Let a guy buy you a drink."

"This sounds like an instruction manual from the fifties on how to land a man."

"You don't need to land a man, just to board one," Felicia

said, eyeing my sweater set. "And I think you might consider dressing more your age."

"What's wrong with my clothes?" I glanced down at the plum-colored, loose-fitting top and khaki pants.

"Nothing's wrong with them, but you never look comfortable wearing them, and there's no way those are your size."

I shied away from revealing or tight-fitting clothes. Wear shapeless sweaters and pants a size or two too big, and colleagues don't accuse you of being a slut. *Unless your ex already told them you were.*

Aaron read through the notes in his jagged script. "This is good. Stop dressing like you're on your way to bingo. I'm also adding 'get drunk in public and do something embarrassing.'"

"Why?" I never knew if a student or colleague might be nearby, or what they might think, so I rarely drank in public.

"Mostly because I want to hear the story of you doing something dumb." Aaron cast a playful, brotherly look across the table. "And you're fun after you've had a few."

*I kind of miss being fun.*

Aaron held up the list triumphantly. "You're agreeing to do everything that's on it by accepting this."

"Yeah, right," I said, stretching to grab it from him. "These are all about hooking up with a guy. I want more from my life than that." *Also, I would need to google how to flirt before even attempting it.*

Felicia batted my hand away. "Keep adding to it. And we're mostly kidding—you don't need to run out and get down with some random person."

I read through the items and wondered if it might work. As I went down the list, I mentally added:

*Stand up for myself*
*Take risks*
*Let someone else get me to orgasm*
*Trust a man again*

"Okay, whatever. I'll see what I can do." I laughed, snapping a picture of the list with my phone. "Work is intense right now with this new president shaking things up. I need to focus. I'm not going to put time into searching for some dude to sleep with or *getting a life*."

"Work and men don't have to be mutually exclusive." Aaron rapped the tabletop with his knuckles, a sly grin spreading across his face as he exchanged another look with his wife. "What are you doing tomorrow night?"

"Nothing. Why?"

"Throw some condoms in your purse. We're getting a babysitter and taking you out to a bar." Aaron rose and grabbed the empty bottles from the table.

"You're ridiculous. I'm not actually doing any of this. Besides, who goes out on a Tuesday?"

"Old married couples and social recluses, apparently," Felicia said. "Plus it will be less crowded, so you can ease into it with a little breathing room."

Aaron set the bottles on the counter and returned to lean against the table. "Nay, you were different after you broke up with Davis. Still you, but with the volume turned down." He patted my shoulder. "We'd love to see the volume go back up."

I *had* turned my volume down so he could be the one whose voice was loudest—that's how he'd liked things—and I'd even pulled back from Felicia and Aaron, knowing they'd figure out what was happening. I'd questioned myself for a long time after we broke up, wondering if he was right about me speaking up.

*Who am I kidding? I'm still questioning myself.* I glanced back at the list, rereading the items and wondering. *What if?*

Aaron spoke over his shoulder. "We'll have a few drinks—don't worry, nothing wild."

*Maybe drinking on a weeknight will be good practice for when I no longer have a job to wake up for in the mornings.*

Felicia flashed me a sly grin. "But you never know when that stranger might show up."

# Three

I pushed through the crowds at Spur, surprised Aaron had picked a spot in the Loop with so many tourists. The trendy place was packed with bodies even on a Tuesday night, but I managed to grab the lone open seat at the bar while I waited for my friends.

"What can I get you?" The young bartender's gaze darted from me to the perky blonde on my left who cried, "Woo-hoo!" several times along with her friends, arms waving in the air and breasts spilling out of her top.

Compared to her, I looked like Mary Poppins, or a more conservatively dressed version of Mary Poppins. I unbuttoned the cardigan sweater to reveal the neckline of the dress I'd pulled from the back of my closet. I considered the challenge to wear better-fitting clothes and glanced at the bartender. He was kind of cute, in a scruffy twentysomething I-have-a-decade-of-bad-decisions-ahead-of-me way. *Couldn't hurt to try . . .*

As he approached with the drink, I leaned forward, pushing my breasts together with my arms, and smiled as the articles I'd read on flirting suggested. I gave myself a pep talk. *You're going to check this off the list.*

When Twentysomething took my credit card and set down my gin and tonic, he spilled a third of the contents on the bar without looking at me or apologizing. A smile was plastered on my face like an idiot as he eyed the woo-hoo girls.

*Fail.*

I exhaled and relaxed my arms. Felicia would have demanded another drink, but I wiped up the spilled liquor with a napkin and took a sip from my glass. It wasn't worth drawing attention to myself, especially after he completely ignored me, and I wasn't quite pathetic enough to pull up the how-to articles again while sitting there. I re-buttoned my cardigan, admitting my unsuccessful attempt, and looked around for Felicia and Aaron. *This was such a bad idea.*

The woman who'd been in the seat next to me had slipped out while I focused on my mortification. A man took that stool, and catching sight of him in my peripheral vision, I coughed, choking on the drink. The straight posture, the athletic build, the polo shirt. My pulse raced, and my muscles tensed. I searched out the exits, making sure I had a clear path away from the bar.

*It's not him. It's not him.*

I returned my gaze to the bar, but not before a memory left me momentarily frozen. One night after we'd been dating a couple months, out with Davis's friends in a bar like this, I'd corrected a mistake he'd made in relaying a story from the *New*

*Yorker.* He'd joked about it in the moment, but on the drive home, he was silent, his lips pressed into a firm line. When we got into my apartment, he'd gripped my upper arms hard and ignored my cry of pain.

"Don't do that again." His voice had remained steady, even, and quiet as his fingers continued digging into my flesh despite my protests. "It won't make people think you're smart or interesting. It just makes them think you don't respect me."

I'd stared, wide-eyed, as he dropped his hands and strode into my bedroom as if nothing had happened. Later that night, he'd kissed me and apologized, telling me he was just stressed. In retrospect, I knew it wasn't normal for men to get violent, but I reasoned that he hadn't hit me, and I'd embarrassed him. He was just more sensitive than I'd thought. From then on, though, I questioned myself before speaking up, increasingly attuned to his reactions during our two-year relationship.

I shook away the memory, rubbing my upper arm absently where the small, round bruises had taken two weeks to fade.

*I have to stop looking for him.*

I knew that logically, but the message didn't always reach my brain. I glanced toward the door for Felicia and Aaron again, anxious for the distraction they always provided. I could usually get out of my head when they were around.

I drew a slow breath before downing a large gulp to settle my nerves. I tried to signal the bartender for another. He looked at me with a bored expression that left me feeling frumpy, like I annoyed him by pulling his attention from the hot girls who had moved to the other end of the bar. Out of the corner of my eye, I noticed the stranger also studying the woman and her friends.

*Of course he is.*

My phone vibrated with an incoming call from Aaron. The ambient sounds of the speakerphone came through the line.

"You guys stuck in traffic?"

"Hey. My mom was admitted to the hospital—I'm driving home."

"Oh my God. What happened? Is she going to be okay?" Aaron's mom was the healthiest woman I knew. Well into her sixties, she ran marathons and led spin classes.

*I should start working out more. Adding that to the list.*

"She got hurt while . . . exercising."

"Fell while running or something?"

"Um, no."

He was being oddly cagey. I asked him again what happened while indicating to the bartender I wanted another.

Aaron sighed. "They want to keep her overnight for observation, and my sister is worried. Apparently, she fell and hit her head pretty hard and injured her leg during a new class."

"Spin class?"

"No."

"What, then?"

He grumbled, "A pole dancing class."

"Your mom is hospitalized with a pole dancing injury?" The man next to me cocked his head and glanced my way, but I tried to focus on Aaron. I didn't want to laugh—the woman was in the hospital, for goodness' sake—but I couldn't shake the image of Mrs. Daniels's long gray hair flying as she twirled around a pole.

"I'm sorry, Aar. Send her my love."

"Thanks. I'm worried she's going to want to tell me about the class."

I let a grin crack across my face. "Have singles ready, then."

"I hate you."

"Is Felicia still coming?"

"As far as I know. She should be there soon."

We hung up and I opened the picture of the list. I couldn't do these things. Look how badly my pathetic attempt at flirting with the bartender had gone. The guy hadn't just ignored me, he'd ignored me while spilling my overpriced drink. I couldn't imagine going from that awkward encounter to sex with a stranger. Hell, sex with anyone. I toyed with the top button of my cardigan again, remembering Aaron's words. *Still you, but with the volume turned down.* I bit the corner of my lip and glanced again at the stranger next to me. Like the bartender, he wasn't paying me any attention. That was usually a relief. If men didn't see me, they couldn't hurt me. Still, after admiring him again, a little part of me wanted the man next to me with the broad chest and strong jaw to notice me, want me, and touch me. It had been way too long, and a forgotten belly flutter made me glance over a second time.

He drank from his glass, and I was in the middle of an internal debate about whether to attempt a flirtatious greeting when he unexpectedly met my eyes. On closer inspection, his posture was different from Davis's, not so stiff, and his hair was closer to a chestnut brown than dirty blond. As we made eye contact, a swirl of energy curled between my thighs, and a loud cheer from the woo-hoo girls rang out.

"Now, what's the point of that?" He motioned to the blonde and her friends.

"I have no idea." I returned his smile before looking away, searching out the bartender, then glancing at my phone. The image of the list remained on the screen.

"It's interesting," he mused.

"Why?" I sipped my drink and unbuttoned my cardigan again. *I'll do it. I'll try one more time.*

He dipped his head and adopted a questionable Australian accent. "Observe the whooping female in her natural habitat."

His impression was bad, really bad, but I laughed.

"See how the loud, ritualistic mating call signals to the rest of the herd to mimic their leader." He added, breaking from the accent, "Could be a good documentary, don't you think?"

"Um . . . Crikey!"

He seemed impressed at my equally sorry attempt at an accent.

"I'm Jake." He glanced at me again before adding, "And I can call you . . . ?"

I reached to shake his hand. *No ring. No telltale tan line.* I considered giving him my real name, but "Naya" wasn't common, so I shared my middle name instead. *Err on the side of safety.*

"Michelle."

I glanced toward the entrance, checking for Felicia again.

"Michelle," he repeated. His voice was low without being gravelly. "What brings you here?" Jake kept his body angled toward mine, leaning in to be heard as the woo-hoo girls' volume increased.

"Um, work." I wasn't sure why I lied, but him thinking I was a tourist made me feel safer. "I'm meeting a friend who is running late, though. I'm sure she'll fly in any moment."

He grinned. "Her arms will be tired."

I scrunched my nose and shook my head. "That was awful."

He chuckled again, scrubbing a hand over his jaw. "Bad jokes are my thing." He paused, taking in my reaction before asking, "Not even a pity laugh?"

"I couldn't in good conscience." I smiled, swallowing the last of my drink and slipping the sweater off my shoulders. I'd consumed the second gin and tonic quickly, and my smile emerged without me thinking. "What about you? Here for business or pleasure?"

"Pleasure, I suppose."

My cheeks heated, but I was confident he wouldn't notice in the bar's low light. I blamed my empty stomach and the gin for the image that ran, unbidden, through my head. After only a brief conversation with this guy, my mind was conjuring something worthy of Cinemax late night. *I do need to break this dry spell.*

The rich tone of his voice wasn't helping. "I'm here for a friend's wedding. Might get a little work in, too. You know, two birds, one flight."

My phone vibrated.

FELICIA: UR gonna kill me! Miles and Ari both got sick—
    Vomit-palooza hit me on my way out the door.

"Sorry, it's my friend," I said before tapping out a reply.

NAYA: Vomit or illness hit you?

FELICIA: Both. It's like the girl from the Exorcist ate gas station
    sushi. I can't leave the babysitter with this and Aaron had to
    go be with his mom.

Jake looked over at me. "Everything okay?"

"My friend's twin boys are sick and she's telling me about

it in graphic detail," I said, meeting his eye. "I guess she's not coming."

"That's too bad." He took a sip from his glass and looked at the TV screen above the bar.

FELICIA: I'm so sorry, Turner.

NAYA: Do you need me to help?

FELICIA: Stay away. I would hate to get sick on your shoes.

Though, I've seen your shoes. Might be an improvement.

NAYA: They're new. But let me know if you need anything.

I glanced back at Jake staring at the baseball game and tipped my glass to take a cube of ice into my mouth. I paused, crunching. Part of me hoped that Felicia would hold me to sticking to the list. "I guess that's my cue to go."

His knee bumped mine as he turned to face me. His glance flicked down to the bare skin above my breasts and then back up. I should have been offended, but I liked that he saw me. "You could always stay and keep a lonely guy company."

My body stirred, heat spreading. Two drinks that fast on an empty stomach was probably a mistake, and he was asking me to keep him company. *Is that code?*

Jake winced in response to my awkward silence. "Too cheesy? I'm sorry."

"No. I mean . . . yeah, it was cheesy," I said, resettling on my seat. "But that's not a bad thing."

He signaled for the bartender, then tilted his head toward me. "Another?"

"Why not?"

"Another for the lady," he added, to the distracted bartender.

The corners of Jake's lips curled, revealing tiny dimples

and laugh lines at the edge of his mouth. He leaned close, making it easier for me to hear him over the bar noise, and when the bartender set down my drink, just a little splashed over the side this time.

*Let someone buy me a drink.*

"Check," I said under my breath.

"Check?" He cocked his head. "Oh, my treat. Unless . . . do you have to go?"

"No, sorry. It's silly."

"I like silly."

"It's *really* silly," I insisted, taking a sip.

"I like really silly," he said, his light-colored eyes dancing. "C'mon. I gave you my best bad joke. It's only fair."

"My friends thought I needed coaching on *how to get a life.* They made me a to-do list." *God, why am I telling him this?*

"And you checked something off the list?"

"Yes," I admitted, taking another sip from my drink to avoid eye contact.

"What was it?"

"Let someone buy me a drink."

"Glad to be of service." His lips turned up. "What else is on this list?"

"I'm usually a homebody. All the items lead to me acting a bit irresponsible." *Like giving all this information to a complete stranger who could be a serial killer.*

The royal blue fabric of his shirt stretched across well-developed pecs and a flat stomach I kind of wanted to reach out and touch. He toyed with a coaster on the bar and eyed the horde of women over my shoulder. A Tuesday seemed a strange night for a bachelorette party, but our initial subject, the blonde, had donned a veil and a tiara made of tiny pink plastic penises dotted with rhinestones that glowed and sparkled as someone snapped a photo using the flash. *I wonder how buying that impacted her recommendations on Amazon.*

"I could help you check other things off."

*Want to join me in a dark corner?* I smiled at the bold voice in my head, and my knee shook under the bar.

"I shouldn't monopolize your night." I checked my phone, and I groaned internally. Barely eight o'clock. Normally, I'd be in my pajamas.

"It's a selfish request. I've been stuck helping with wedding things since I arrived this morning, and my friend's future wife is acting a lot like her." He gestured toward the blonde. "I could use a break and to spend time with a grown-up."

"How do you know I'm not actually one of them?"

"Good point. I guess I don't." The knee of Jake's jeans again grazed my bare leg below the hem of my dress. The nudge felt sinful, and another wave of heat spread through my body. He dipped his head close to mine. "How many erotic tiaras do you own?"

I counted off my fingers. "Technically, four, but I lent one out for the royal wedding and haven't gotten it back yet."

"I might be willing to take my chances." He raised his glass. "What do you say?"

*C'mon, girl. Volume up.*

I clinked my glass to his bottle. "I have just one condition."

"Name it."

"Can we promise to stay away from real-life details like

work and last names?" I sounded like an unhinged person, but I couldn't abandon years of protecting myself, and I knew a stranger having your personal information could go bad quickly.

His full lips stretched into an amused smile. It was hard to tell the exact color of his eyes in this light. They were pale, maybe blue or green, but completely mesmerizing. "Sure . . . just Jake and Michelle. Like Sonny and Cher."

His next question caught me off guard. "What is your favorite snack?"

"Like, to eat?" I took another sip and realized I was beyond tipsy.

His eyes narrowed. "What would 'snack' be slang for?" He held up his palm before continuing. "Wait, don't answer. Nothing appropriate comes to mind."

The drinks left me a little out of my head, and I thought back to the list. *Flirt.* "Sometimes appropriate is overrated." I averted my gaze, but a quick glance back at him showed a surprised expression on his face.

"Good to know," he said into his bottle with a smile before tipping it to his lips.

"I like ice cream," I said quickly, to hide my embarrassment.

"I like ice cream, too." Jake signaled toward the bartender to close out his tab. "We could stay here or track down some ice cream?" He pulled his phone out and tapped a search for a nearby location. "There's a shop not far from here."

I weighed out the safety of going with a stranger, but the area was well lit and packed with people. *I have pepper spray if I need it.* I'd been considering joining Felicia for her kickboxing class. I always felt vulnerable when I was out alone, and I didn't like that feeling.

Jake tucked his wallet into his back pocket, and I imagined being wrapped in his arms, feeling protected by his embrace. The thought was equal parts wonderful and scary.

"Let's go." The hem of my dress shifted across my thighs as I slid off the stool, and his eyes darted over my bare legs. I didn't know why his gaze felt so intense, but it did.

One of the woo-hoo girls approached him and motioned to the bride-to-be, who was now across the room with lollipops taped to her shirt. "It's my best friend's bachelorette vacation— five days to go wild!" The woman squealed and flashed a toothy grin. She dressed like many of my students, skintight jeans and a cotton candy pink top that dipped so low, it revealed everything except her nipples. "Suck for a buck?" she asked in a sugary voice.

Jake frowned as she grabbed at his arm, pushing her breasts against him. I guessed she was easily fifteen years his junior, and he avoided staring down her low-cut shirt.

She motioned to her friend again. "Please? She's shy, that's why she's not asking herself, but you're so cute!"

He inched closer to me, creating distance between himself and the woo-hoo girl, and I took pity on him and stepped forward, edging her back. "Honey," I said, lacing my fingers through his. They were surprisingly warm and curled with mine immediately, sending an unexpected rush through me. "We need to get going. You've got that appointment in the morning."

The young woman seemed to notice me for the first time but didn't release her grip.

*Damn, that was bold.*

"With the proctologist," I added, hoping to prompt her to walk away.

She was like a puppy hearing an unfamiliar command.

"About your chronic hemorrhoids."

The woman giggled. "Um, never mind!"

Jake stared at me, his expression hovering between shock and amusement. Finally, he laughed, leading me toward the exit as the pink envoy scurried back to her coven of bachelorettes. "You couldn't have said it was an appointment to have my Ferrari detailed or something?" He was still holding my hand as we walked through the door, and the giggles dissipated as we shifted into the warm night air.

"I'm not sure she knew what 'proctologist' meant."

Storefronts and restaurants lined the streets, and white twinkle lights were strung along wrought iron gates surrounding a patio.

"But, hemorrhoids?" He shook his head. "I don't know what to make of a beautiful woman talking about the state of my . . . backside."

*Beautiful?*

"Do you want me to run back in and set the record straight?" I turned to the bar, our hands falling apart.

"No!" He wrapped his long fingers loosely around my wrist, the lightest pressure there before his hand fell away.

I flinched, just for a moment. He didn't seem to notice, and after a slow breath, I kind of wanted him to touch me again.

*What would his hands feel like elsewhere on my body?*

I raised a three-finger salute as we continued down the street, where people shuffled along crowded sidewalks and milled in small groups. "On my honor, I promise to not mention your colon or any related topics for the rest of the night."

*Not even a six-volume anthology on flirting could save me at this point.*

"Thank you."

"But it must be a little ego boost, being hit on like that."

"They were way too young and too . . . loud." He nodded to the ice cream shop, and we walked that way.

"I've had my fill of young and loud with my friend's fiancée and her entourage. Besides, you agreed to get ice cream with me, so my ego is plenty boosted."

"Are they young, your friends?"

"Thomas is a few years older than me, close to forty. Madison . . . graduates from college next spring."

"How old is she?"

"Twenty-one." He shook his head. "Like I said, that woman back there? No, thanks."

My gin-fueled buzz was some kind of magical cloak, leaving me light and silly, but not drunk or sloppy. I had enough courage to break the silence. "So then, you're telling me you like women who are old and, what, quiet? Like white-haired librarians in sexy cardigan sweaters and support hose?" I cringed, tossing my own cardigan over my purse.

"Do you know any?" He flashed his brilliant smile. "When they shush you, it's mind-blowing."

A group of teenagers nearby eyed us as I laughed harder, picturing Mrs. Haley, the stooped, ninety-year-old volunteer librarian from my hometown, in a leather corset with a riding crop.

"And the glasses on a chain?" He fanned himself.

I snorted as we approached a small storefront with a neon

ice cream cone in the window. Music wafted from the crowded corner where a young man in a flannel shirt strummed his guitar next to an open case.

Jake held the door as the sweet, nutty smell and telltale chill of the ice cream shop surrounded me. Inside, the space was retro by design, with kitschy linoleum tables edged with shiny aluminum molding and a jukebox in the corner. There was a line, and we both inspected the display cases. "Know what you want?" he asked.

I always chose vanilla, but in that moment, it sounded so plain, so boring, so, well, vanilla. I read some options. Pumpkin *stracciatella*. Peanut butter bacon. Lemon pomegranate granita.

"Not sure . . ." I reviewed the options and tried to ignore how much I enjoyed the heat radiating from his body.

He stared into the display as we moved forward in line. "I think I should get kiwi-strawberry mocha, you know, owing to my Australian filmmaker roots."

"That sounds disgusting," I whispered, hoping the employees couldn't hear me, as it was listed as a signature flavor. "And isn't kiwi fruit more of a New Zealand thing?"

I stilled. I'd corrected him without thinking about it.

"I'll have to look it up the next time I'm at the library." He smiled and took it in stride.

*Okay, not the reaction I expected.*

"You're taking chances tonight, right? Let's pick flavors for each other. Close your eyes," he coaxed.

I cast him a nervous glance before closing them.

"Pick a number between one and four and then a letter between A and . . . F," he instructed, all business.

"Two and . . . D."

"Okay, open your eyes." He touched my elbow, the brief brush of his fingertips eliciting a sweet sensation of tingles. "There are four cases, and I assigned a letter to each flavor in the case. Now I know what you're ordering."

"So, what's my flavor?"

"It's a surprise. Do me." He closed his eyes without waiting for me to respond.

*Freudian slip?*

I let my eyes wander unabashedly while his were shut. He was tan like he spent time outside. His fingers were long, and his nails were neat without being overly manicured. My stomach fluttered thinking about how those fingers could slide inside me. *Good Lord, I am drunk and horny.*

"Did you abandon me?" he asked nervously.

I snapped my head back up. "One through four, and then a color. I'm assigning the cases each a color."

"Okay, four and . . . blue." He opened his eyes.

We moved to the front of the line, and Jake ordered for me first, a large scoop of dulce de leche.

It sounded amazing. I stepped closer and ordered for him, asking for a scoop of kiwi-strawberry mocha, tickled he'd picked blue.

We left through the shop's back door and looked for a table on their patio, where white twinkle lights strung above us made the space feel magical. I attempted to scan the crowd, making sure Davis wasn't there. I always checked.

"I mean this in the nicest way, Jake, but you're kind of a nerd, huh?"

"How did you guess?" He eyed the neon green scoop with flecks of chocolate in his bowl.

"The whole numbers and letters thing; you were excited about that." I licked a spot of ice cream threatening to drip down the side of my bowl and moaned while we walked. I could have fallen to the sidewalk and melted into a puddle.

His grin widened. "That good, huh? To your question, it depends. Do you like nerds?"

We sat at a bistro table in the corner. "I definitely like nerds," I said, pushing imaginary glasses up on my nose. "But more importantly, do you like your ice cream?"

Jake eyed his bowl skeptically, then shot his gaze to me.

"You picked blue! I had to follow your rules."

Taking a tiny portion on his spoon, his whole face collapsed as he tasted it. "First hemorrhoids and now this. You don't like me very much, do you?" He pushed it toward me. "Do you want to try?"

I took another bite of my new favorite flavor. "No way, but you can share mine. Be warned, though: It's like a sweet little orgasm for your mouth, only cold." I froze, my cheeks heating. I clapped my hand over my mouth. *I just referenced orgasms . . . in his mouth . . . in public.*

*Forget the anthology. I'm hopeless.*

He blinked, his jaw slack for a moment. "Never had a cold one," he said slowly before taking a small bite from my bowl. "But, wow, you're right, that is good." He shifted his eyes left to right. "Did you cheat my system? Are you some kind of ice cream hustler?"

I offered my bowl to him again, urging him to take another bite. "No, just luck of the draw. But this is the best thing I've ever tasted."

His gaze skimmed over my face, pausing momentarily on my lips.

*I wonder how he tastes.*

I stifled the urge to hide my mouth behind a napkin. "Do you want the last bite?"

"No, thanks."

"You sure? I feel bad ordering that flavor for you."

He leaned forward, elbows on the table. "I'd much rather watch you enjoy it."

"Oh?" I slipped the spoon to my mouth, tracing my tongue along the underside to stop its contents from dripping down my chin, then taking it between my lips.

He followed my movements intently, and a pulse thrummed low in my body when his tongue peeked out over his lower lip. "Definitely." His gaze returned to my eyes.

I fumbled with my spoon, unsteady at his attention. All that sexual charisma I channeled with the spoon in my mouth disappeared. "Do you want to do something else to me?"

His eyes widened, and I stammered a correction.

"I mean, with me! Rather, go somewhere else?" *Good save.*

"Sure. Unless ice cream was on your list, you've still got work to do, right?" He gathered our bowls, and I admired the lines of his arms. "Where do you want to go?"

The angel and the devil on my shoulder bickered.

*Somewhere public! Get to know him and stay safe.*

*Somewhere private! Take off his pants!*

"We could find a club or something?" I hoped my voice

sounded surer than I felt. The thumping bass and wall-to-wall people were not my scene at all, but I didn't want to sound prudish.

"If you want." He rubbed his hand over the back of his neck. "I'm not much of a club guy, though."

"Thank God." I smiled, relief filling me.

# Four

The city below sparkled from the ninety-fourth floor of the 360-degree observation deck of the Hancock Building, and Lake Michigan provided a dark contrast to the city lights. I looked around at the thinning crowds—it was nearing closing time, and we were almost to the front of the line. We'd seen a sign advertising TILT on the way in.

"I can't believe I let you talk me into this," I said.

"Believe me, I didn't talk you into anything." Jake's hand brushed mine. "*You* suggested this after the last round of drinks."

"That doesn't sound like me." *Am I slurring my words?*

We stepped forward in line. "You said you needed to try something new and marched right over to buy tickets. I tried to pay, and you wouldn't let me. You were a little bossy about it," he said, playfully.

Standing in a glass cubicle as it tilted forward over the Magnificent Mile fit the bill for taking a risk. Doing it next to my handsome stranger made the risk that much more appealing.

"Insisting on paying sounds like me." I giggled, then paused, remembering the flirting articles. "Is that a turnoff, when a woman wants to pay?"

His hand fell to my lower back. "I don't think anything about you is a turnoff. I'm going with you, aren't I?"

My back straightened at his touch, the tingle extending lower. "And I didn't even have to twist your arm."

"No, I came willingly." Jake dipped his face close to me, and his mouth was near my ear.

He smelled like the scotch he'd ordered after we arrived. The strong scent was not something I normally enjoyed, but it made me feel warm and tingly.

My cheeks flamed, and a swirl of excitement twisted low in my body. He'd found small ways to touch me since we'd left the ice cream shop. Brushing his arm against mine as we wandered the observatory, or his fingers lingering near mine when he handed me a drink. The pressure of Jake's hand on my back was intoxicating in a different way. His wide palm swept up my spine, and I imagined it traversing my hips.

"And bossy doesn't bother you, huh?"

"I have four sisters. I spent a lot of years being told what to do."

"Well, I am usually quiet like a little mouse," I mused, taking a step forward to the first position in line with Jake, his hand sliding down my back.

"Really?" He quirked an eyebrow. "That's hard to believe—you seem pretty outgoing."

"It's an act," I said in a quiet voice. "Squeak!"

His laugh was low and hearty, and his big hand slipped further to rest on my waist before pulling me against his side.

I allowed my eyes to close and focused on his palm stroking between my waist and hip and not on how many drinks I'd had throughout the night. My thoughts were fuzzy and my limbs loose. *Six?* Smiling at my joke, I let my head fall against his shoulder. "Do you have a wedge of cheddar?"

"That was cheesy."

I groaned, opening my eyes and looking up. "Your joke was worse than mine."

His cheeks were a little red—he'd been drinking strong beer before switching to scotch. "You don't think I'm funny?"

"I think it's a good thing you're cute," I volleyed back, and his grip on my waist tightened, his fingers stretching toward my stomach and his thumb rubbing small circles on my lower back.

"So, you think I'm cute?"

He opened his mouth to say something else, but the staff motioned us forward to take our places in the cubicle, guiding us to the last two spots. I shot Jake a wide-eyed stare as we settled in front of the floor-to-ceiling windows. The city stretched out in front of us, the lights from thousands of other people's nights twinkling.

"You ready?" he asked as the staff prepared us for the apparatus to shift.

"Ready or not," I responded as the structure tilted forward, the hydraulic mechanism loud in my ears. The view shifted, and we were no longer looking out across the city; we were looking down on it. I felt like I was flying above the streets, above the people, above everything that normally kept me quiet. My head spun as the angle increased, and I gripped the handrail. Below us, cars flew by in streams of white and red, and the shadowed rooftops of nearby buildings came into view.

"Oh, shit. We're really up here," Jake said, his gaze sweeping around us. "This is . . . wow." He stretched his arm and settled his palm on my handrail, his thumb grazing the back of my hand, and the sensation thrummed with more force than the ride's mechanics.

Feeling suspended, a thousand feet in the air, I couldn't hold in a squeal or a nervous laugh as we tipped forward again.

Jake's gaze was intent from his position two feet away, but he wasn't taking in the view; he was looking at me. *Holy hell.*

When we tilted back to normal, two or three minutes later, he reached for my hand as we stepped back away from the glass. My head spun from the alcohol and the shift in perspective.

"We should commemorate," he said, pulling his phone from his pocket. I tucked my face in by his chest as he pulled me to him and snapped a selfie. "Another thing off your list, right?" He lingered next to my ear after that, the heat from his mouth and his warm breath tickling me, sending a zing through my body.

*I can do this. He's nice; he's attractive and into me. I can hook up with him.*

"Two things," I responded, letting my head loll just a little closer to his ear, but stumbling as I lost my balance. "Do something new and flirt."

"With danger?"

Something about knowing he was looking at me, taking

in my skin and curves, lit me up inside. I tried to pull myself back into the moment, motioning to his phone. "No, silly. With you." I punched him on the arm, letting my hand linger on his biceps to take in its size and to steady myself. "This is me flirting. You might not have known because I'm not good at it."

His hands dropped to my waist. "I don't think you're giving yourself enough credit. And, what a coincidence," he said, taking a small step closer. "This is me flirting, too."

Feeling bold, I grazed my fingers up his neck.

He gave a quick inhale when I reached his hairline. It was exciting to know my touch affected him.

"Let's get out of here," I said.

His eyebrows raised in surprise, but he responded quickly with an eager nod. "Okay."

I walked with heavy, intentional steps as we weaved through the crowd toward the high-speed elevator that would take us to street level. *Drunk. I am drunk.* I was being irresponsible and kind of reckless and I felt uncharacteristically comfortable. I loved it.

"Will you send me that photo?"

"Of course," he said, navigating through the app with his thumb. "Is that a sneaky way to get my phone number?" Jake handed me the phone with the contact screen open for me to enter my number.

"Seems you're getting mine, too."

I was breaking my own rules, but what could a phone number hurt?

"You," he laughed, the sound light and playful near my ear, "are dangerous."

"Me?" I feigned incredulity, pressing closer to him when the car filled with a few more people as the attraction neared closing time. "No one in my life has ever called me dangerous."

"You got me in a glass box a thousand feet in the air." His smile broadened, and he flattened both hands against his chest for effect. "I don't do heights." His consonants were a little mushy from the alcohol as we spilled from the elevator into the lobby and walked toward the street.

"Why agree to come up here?"

"The plan was to stay a few feet away from the glass."

"I feel bad. I didn't know."

He took my hand as we pushed through the doors. "It was only mildly terrifying."

"You should have said something." The cool breeze washed over me as we stepped out onto the street. "We could have done something else."

"And tell the sexy-as-sin woman I'm trying to impress I'm scared of heights? No way."

"You're trying to impress me?"

He surprised me by turning to wrap both his arms around my waist, bringing us together. "Is it working?"

"Yes." I marveled again that him touching me, pulling me, felt good. The familiar tension wasn't there. It might have been the alcohol, but something told me that wasn't everything. Somewhere between wanting the list to be the key and this guy's smile, I was relaxed.

He tipped his chin down, and his voice softened. "Is there anything on that list about being kissed on a street corner?"

*Maybe Felicia was right about this being easy.*

"There is now."

His hand slid from my waist slowly up my back, the other cupping my neck. Our lips came together tentatively, slowly. He tasted like scotch and sugar as his tongue brushed across my lips before gliding over my tongue. My pulse quickened as his hold tightened. I was breathless and thoughtless; the only thing in the world I craved was more of him.

When we broke apart, the sounds of the city swirled around us—cars honking, music playing from some street performer, and a distant siren wailing. I pulled in a ragged breath.

"Check," he said in a low voice that overtook the din as we stood, wrapped in each other's arms.

My heart thumped, and a coiling need urged me forward. An unexpected fountain of confidence bubbled up. "Do you want to go back to your hotel?"

Jake's gaze was intent, flashing to my mouth. "More than you can imagine."

A bolt of desire surged through my body when he looked at my lips that way, eyelids hooded. A breeze picked up again, and a shiver ran up my spine, but not from the chill. This was the boldest thing I'd done in years, and I was exposed. "Let's go."

He nodded, blew out a slow breath, and laced his fingers with mine.

———

In the back of the Uber, he traced circles over my hand and stroked my knee, inching up my thigh. The driver was two feet away, but when Jake leaned down to brush his lips to mine,

I kissed him back, sweeping my tongue across his bottom lip. I hadn't been touched in that slow, erotic way in so long. I wanted more.

Despite the hour, the hotel lobby was busy, and several other people climbed onto the elevator with us. They pressed me up against Jake, and he wrapped an arm behind me, his palm resting on my hip. "Are you sure?"

I leaned back on his hard chest. "Yes."

His body tensed against mine. The sparks of electricity that had been coursing through me since he'd first grazed my skin now popped and flashed. Three people stepped off the elevator on floor sixteen, and we no longer needed to be so close, but we didn't move until the ding of the elevator signaled his floor.

*I'm really going to do this.*

We stepped into the hall, and I held on to his arm as panic settled low in my body. I was following him to his room the night I'd met him, after drinking. Did he expect me to take charge or . . . what did he expect? I wanted him to move the action forward, so I didn't have to. *Feminist card: Revoked.*

"I'm so glad I went into that bar tonight," he said, his voice hoarse. He glanced down, a slow, admiring sweep of my body, and the heat of his gaze left me tingling.

"Me, too."

He inserted the card twice to unlock the door, fumbling with the plastic. I smiled at his nervous movements, hoping it belied my own anxiety.

*Does he have protection?*

*Will he care that my bra and panties don't match?*

*Do you cuddle after a one-night stand?*

*Thank God I shaved my legs this morning.*

*Wait, did I?*

The green light finally flashed, and he opened the door, something fluttering in my chest as we stepped inside and he flicked on the light.

*What now?*

Looking at my feet and tugging at my dress as we stood awkwardly inside his room, I wobbled, head light with alcohol. My breath quickened as Jake reached for me. His hand drifted over my shoulder, and his fingers wove into the strands of hair at the base of my neck.

"Hi," I murmured, looking up at his face and inhaling his clean scent. My mind, normally racing with worst-case scenarios, was focused solely on the touch of his lips.

Our kisses grew hungrier, more demanding, and his fingers tangled in my hair, with just enough force to make me want to kiss him harder. I met his intensity, heat radiating between us, and I clung to him.

His fingers slipped from the back of my head down the side of my neck, and I shivered with the wave of pleasure that brief, gentle movement aroused in me. He planted three lingering kisses at my throat. The pace was so slow, I worried he was regretting the decisions and maybe thinking of a way out.

My heart thumped as the words fell from my mouth. "Do you still want . . . ?"

His wordless reaction to my question was immediate. He slanted his lips against mine, and the wet tip of his tongue swept over me with a slow, controlled pace, seeking entry. And his erection—*Goddamn, his erection*—imposing and wedged against my hip, twitched.

I was breathless by the time we pulled apart, his mouth pressing to the delicate skin by my ear, and I changed my mind about the slow kisses. Every time he shifted to a new spot, my body lit up.

"Yes, I still definitely want to. I'm just a little drunk," he said into my neck. The vibrations of his voice rumbled against my skin.

"I'm a lottle drunk," I said on an exhale, then giggled, stumbling as we crossed the room entwined. "Wait, lottle's not a word."

*Get drunk in public. Definitely checked that one off.*

He flashed a grin. "I like your made-up word. I like it a lottle." His lips returned to mine hungrily as his hands slid up my body, his thumbs grazing the sides of my breasts through the thin fabric of my dress. His palms were wide, and when his long fingers rolled over my hard nipples in teasing, measured strokes, I moaned in his mouth, reeling at the pressure on my sensitive skin.

"Your body is amazing," he rasped between kisses, and I dragged my mouth to his neck, the bristle of his stubble against my tongue oddly appealing. He groaned and pulled me to him, the rigid bulge pressing into my stomach.

*Yes.*

My insides flipped with the excitement of his touch, and my head spun in anticipation.

*Yes.*

A flush ran across my chest.

*No, wait, this is something else.*

This was not my stomach flipping; this was more of a churning sensation.

*No, no, no.*

I pushed backward from Jake as a familiar rising feeling left me lurching for the bathroom door behind me. Falling to my knees, I hunched over the toilet bowl and retched. My body reminded me of each gin and tonic.

*Touché, Universe.*

After a few moments, Jake swept my hair back and began rubbing circles on my back. "Are you okay?"

I buried my face in the crook of my elbow over the toilet, my stomach slowing its revolt. I was mortified. "I'm throwing up in your bathroom."

He chuckled behind me. "Yeah, I kind of pieced that together."

"I wanted a one-night stand, and I did it wrong," I groaned, keeping my forehead pressed to my arms to avoid him seeing my face and to stop the pristine white room from spinning.

He laughed, quietly, still rubbing slow circles over my back. "Do you want a glass of water?"

I shook my head without looking up, shame prodding at every part of my body. "Can you give me a minute?"

He stepped back and closed the door, leaving me alone.

*I can't believe this is happening.*

I flushed the toilet and wiped my mouth before standing on unsteady legs. The reflection in the mirror made me cringe— my cheeks were red and splotchy, and my watering eyes had smeared my mascara.

*Pathetic.*

I tore open the mouthwash provided by the hotel and swished while doing my best to fix the black streaks around my eyes. My hair was disheveled from his hands running through it in passion and then in pity. My toes curled in shame as I washed my hands.

When I stumbled from the bathroom, Jake was seated at the end of the hotel bed, forearms resting on his thighs, concern etched in his features, and my face heated again.

"I'm gonna go," I muttered, frantically searching the floor for the purse I'd dropped when we came in the door.

The bed creaked, and he stood, handing me my bag. "Are you okay? Do you need anything? To lie down?"

"No. I'm fine. Going home to die of embarrassment."

He touched a finger to my shoulder, though it lacked the heat of his earlier caresses. This was a utilitarian touch. He might have just been worried I'd fall over. "Don't die," he said in a sweet, low voice that just amplified my embarrassment. "It would be a real shame if you didn't finish your list."

"You're too nice," I almost whispered, tears welling in my eyes now. I couldn't help it—his comment had been playful and even sweet, but he didn't know the half of it. I'd looked at that list as important, like a genuine step-by-step way to get my life back before my job disappeared, and I'd failed right out of the gate.

"It was nice to meet you, Michelle." He met my eyes.

"That's not even my real name." Tears fell down my cheeks, and I sobbed, no, more blubbered. "You're so nice, and I gave you a fake name."

I reached behind me to pull down on the door handle. "I'm sorry. I'm gonna go." Avoiding his gaze, I spilled out into the hallway and hurriedly stumbled toward the elevator.

As the cab pulled away from the hotel and I sank into the seat, wiping my face, my phone buzzed with two incoming text messages.

JAKE: I had fun tonight (pre-vomit).

JAKE: I hope you feel better.

I cradled my face in my palms, metaphorically punching myself in the stomach for drinking so much. Here was this sexy guy who wanted me, who was funny and polite and ready to go, and I spoiled our night by throwing up. Shaking my head, I tried to quiet old memories.

*Why did I think I could do this?*

A third text came through. I didn't want to look. I knew it would be pity or a request to never contact him again. Instead, I tucked the phone into my bag before stepping out at my building.

Later, I steeled myself to open the message with timid fingers.

JAKE: BTW, what's your real name?

# Five

The next morning, I stretched under the sheets while texting Felicia.

NAYA: Status update? Are you still alive?

I squeezed my eyes shut and tried to block out the headache and memories of the night before. A torrent of embarrassment hit me at the thought of being so drunk I'd had to throw up in the middle of making out with a guy. A hot guy. *To do: Delete Felicia and Aaron's list.*

FELICIA: Barely.

NAYA: What do you need?

FELICIA: This might be Ebola. Stay away. Is it wrong to ask the CDC to quarantine my kids?

I tapped out a message reminding her to let me know if she needed anything later and toggled to the messages from Jake. The photo he'd sent from the observation deck popped up. Despite my mortification about how the night ended, the picture stirred me unexpectedly. My face showed a playful expression, and I zoomed in, almost not recognizing the woman smiling back at me.

I'd left his last message unanswered, and a mixture of guilt and misgiving crept through my mind. He seemed like a nice guy, and I felt bad giving him a fake name and not responding to his messages, but there was no way I could face him. There was a decent chance I wouldn't attempt flirting ever again.

Climbing out of bed, my stomach roiled. I needed a hot shower and Tylenol. As I clambered toward my bathroom, I paused and grabbed my phone, shooting off a quick text because *why not embarrass myself further?*

NAYA: I had fun, too, and I'm sorry I bolted. Good luck with the wedding.

The hot water cleared my head as I let it run over me. I had to give an exam that morning, but otherwise I had an entire day to focus on writing. I trailed a soapy hand over my belly and up my chest. Or maybe to allow myself to think about Jake, whose kisses had made me forget what time zone I was in. *This has to stop.* I squeezed my eyes shut, willing the vivid memories away. *I'm never going to see this guy again. Focus.*

When I emerged from the shower and wrapped myself in a towel, I felt relatively more human, but a dull ache remained behind my eyes. I glanced at my phone, but there were no new messages. Acrid disappointment settled in my chest more than I wanted to admit, but when my phone buzzed a moment later, I hurried across the room and clicked on the notification without looking.

Reminder: *ED 205 Final Exam; 2 hours.*

I tossed the phone on my bed and began pulling clothes from my closet, once again chastising myself for my behavior, and for my continued glances at my notificationless device. *Giving a final exam while hungover and sexually frustrated. What a perfect metaphor for my life right now.*

---

"Ten more minutes," I announced. The room was almost empty as the last few students hurriedly scribbled out their answers. I glanced up from my perch at the front of the room.

Quinton or Quenton looked like a deer in headlights. Color had drained from his face, and his foot tapped incessantly on the tiled floor as he appeared to read and reread the questions.

*Called that one.*

I glanced at the clock and fiddled with my phone as more students finished and filed past, dropping their exams on my desk. Words with Friends and scrolling through social media didn't stop me from looking for a text reply continuously, though.

*What do I even want him to say?*

FELICIA: Can we discuss how my mother-in-law was taking a
   pole dancing class?

FELICIA: Also, I didn't ask earlier. How was your night?

I took a large gulp from my water bottle, still trying to re-hydrate.

NAYA: Unexpected.

FELICIA: What does that mean?

FELICIA: Crap, I gotta go. Kid emergency. Call me later!

With a few minutes left, Quinton or Quenton—*His last*

*name is Sterling*—was the only one left, and I decided to be kind. "Do you need an extra ten minutes?"

He nodded, a harried and flustered expression crossing his normally smooth face as he scribbled in the exam book.

I started organizing the completed tests, mentally creating a to-do list for all the end-of-term things that needed to happen after I finished grading exams. *Lists.* My head still ached with a dull throb. I toggled to the photo of Aaron and Felicia's list, my thumb hovering over the delete button when the notification indicator flashed.

JAKE: A night of drinking was easier 10 years ago, wasn't it?

I stared at the screen, unsure how to respond and trying to silence that negative voice in my head and the embarrassed voice in my heart. The voice crying out from my neglected lady parts won, though.

NAYA: Feeling a little green?

JAKE: A little of every color. Are you feeling better?

NAYA: Only slightly colorful.

JAKE: Hue are lucky.

NAYA: Aww . . . you are in-tint on making me laugh.

JAKE: I'd like to try. Will you go out with me tonight?

My thumbs stilled as I reread his question. A giddy anticipation and a sinking feeling pulled at me with equal force.

JAKE: I can buy you dinner, you can demand I confront a phobia, we'll make out in the back of a cab . . . normal date stuff.

JAKE: You said you were looking for a one-night stand, but since that didn't work out . . .

I told him that? *Farewell, gin. It's been real.*

NAYA: I was so drunk last night. I shouldn't.

JAKE: You left your sweater in my room. I could give it back to you.

The squeak of boat shoes on the tile pulled me from my phone as Quinton or Quenton slumped toward me, handing me his exam with a sullen expression.

"Is there, like, any extra credit?" he asked without making eye contact.

"This is the last day of class," I said, my eyes doing a quick skim of the slashes and scratch marks across the first page. I added, adopting the kindest tone I could, "Sorry, but there aren't any opportunities for extra credit at this point. Maybe you did better than you think."

"I doubt it," he mumbled, turning to saunter out of the classroom. "See ya, Dr. Turner," he called over his shoulder with a two-finger wave. His swagger only faltered for a moment, then he adjusted the sunglasses on his head and strode out into the world. *Maybe I could learn a thing or two from Quinton or Quenton.*

JAKE: I could sweeten the deal with a joke.

JAKE: Who tells the best egg jokes?

JAKE: Comedi-hens.

I shook my head and gathered the exams in a pile to walk the short distance back to my office. As I stood, I felt a little taller and, just a little bit, like things might be okay.

NAYA: I'm convinced.

As I stepped into the hall, my phone rang. "Hey, Joe. What's up? How's the conference?"

"Naya! Thank God. Are you free tomorrow evening?" He

sounded flustered. A cacophony of chatter raged in the background.

"Everything okay?"

"I'm supposed to attend an event hosted by President Lewis tomorrow night. All the department chairs are required to be there, but I'm stuck in Miami. I doubt I'll get out in time. Can you attend in my place?"

"What kind of event?" I stepped inside my office. I wanted nothing to do with a stuffy gathering of department chairs.

"He's keeping it hush-hush, but every department needs to be represented, and it's at the Barth." Joe sounded frustrated, his words clipped, and he said something away from the phone. Barth House was the president's mansion. An opulent, columned monstrosity that I tried my best to avoid. The university was a little bit like my high school cafeteria. I learned quickly where I belonged and rarely ventured into the orbit of the popular crowd.

"I don't know. Shouldn't someone more senior go?"

"Normally, I'd say yes, but no one is in town. I'm begging you, Naya."

Maybe being seen at the event would show others on campus I was trusted and important. It couldn't hurt to mingle with the people who might have a say in my promotion, especially not knowing what was coming. "Okay, boss."

*To do: Figure out what to wear to this thing.*

# Six

"Wait, he asked you out *after* you threw up on him?" Felicia's voice rang out through my phone. "Is this a fetish or something?"

I pulled the device away from my ear while trying to keep my towel from slipping. My anxiety at full throttle after arriving home late, I pushed the clothes hanging in my closet aside as I grew frustrated with my lack of date-appropriate apparel. "I didn't throw up on him. Just . . . near him."

"Oh, Nay." Felicia adopted her *you're hopeless* tone. "Where do I start?"

"I don't have time for the lecture, Fel. We're meeting in, like, an hour, and I'm freaking out."

"Okay, okay," Felicia laughed. "What has you so riled?"

"What if he expects sex?"

"Isn't that why you're going out with him?"

"No!" I paused in my comparison of two sweater sets. "I mean, maybe? That's all I wanted the other night, but then he was sweet." *And he's funny and has kind eyes and I felt safe with him.*

"Candy is sweet, but dick is better."

I laughed, despite my rising panic. "God, Fel. Who says that? Please, be serious. I'm minutes away from losing it."

"Calm down. If the guy wants it and you don't, he can go home alone and get acquainted with his right hand."

"That's not what has me worried." I sighed, hanging both sweater sets back in my closet. *Shapeless cardigans for a date? C'mon.* "I don't know. You guys talked me into that list, and now I kind of want to try."

Felicia was silent for a beat, and I imagined her biting her lip, brows knit on the other end of the line as she weighed out how to best advise me. "Here's what you do. Take a few deep breaths when you start to get worked up. You said he's here just for the weekend, right? You'll be careful, so best-case scenario, you have some consequence-free fun. Worst-case scenario, you have an awkward, sexless date. Either way, he leaves town in a few days and life goes on."

"You're right," I huffed, pulling a mint green tank top from the back of my closet. It was a relic from a shopping trip with Felicia, and I'd never even taken the tags off. Stroking the thin knit fabric of the back and letting the sheer, wispy overlay slip between my fingers, I nodded my head. "You're right. I'm overthinking this."

"It's what you do best. Where are you going, anyway? Somewhere public in case he ends up being a sociopath?"

"Who's a sosopath, Mommy?" Felicia's daughter Emily's voice came through the phone.

"Aunt Naya's boyfriend, sweetie. Don't worry about it."

"Aunt Naya's going to kiss a sosopath!" Emily's shout faded as she probably ran down the hall to tell her brothers.

"Thank you for that," I muttered, opening my top left drawer. The stores of fancy underwear were on the left—lace and satin arranged by color. The everyday cotton in white and earth tones were on the right. My hands hovered before I reached for a pair of mint-colored satin panties and searched for the matching bra. *Can't hurt to be prepared.*

"So, where are you going?"

"I suggested Navy Pier. I figured it would be crowded with tourists." I clipped the tags from the shirt and pulled it over my head. The cotton hugged my body, but the sheer overlay cascaded gently over my curves to my waist.

"Well, that's definitely public."

I pulled a flowy black skirt over my hips and slipped my feet into a pair of strappy gold sandals. "Okay, I feel better. You're right. I should finish getting ready. Talk to you later?"

"Sure. And it should go without saying, but try not to throw up on him. It's been a long time since you dated, but just for the record, that's too casual."

# Seven

The sun hung low in the sky, and the crowded pier was awash in a warm, golden light. My heart raced, and I closed my eyes, taking a moment to psych myself up. *Breathe. Breathe.* The driver eyed me suspiciously, so I hurried out the door with a quick thanks and scanned the crowd for Jake.

"Hey." His broad smile greeted me as soon as I turned. *The dimples. Those lips.* "I was a little worried you'd change your mind." He looked relieved, and I didn't know why that made butterflies flutter in my stomach.

"I couldn't let you keep my favorite sweater."

He had the arms of the pink fabric draped over his shoulders and loosely knotted over the top of his blue-and-white button-down shirt. "What do you think? Pulling it off?" He stepped back so I could admire the accessory.

My smile broke into a laugh, and I shook my head.

"No?"

"Not even a little."

"Damn." He gently pulled it from his shoulders, his finger-tips brushing mine as he handed it over. "That's okay. It looks better on you anyway."

I caught the faint whiff of him on the fabric—the scent of sandalwood mixed with the hotel's soap. As we strolled down the walkway, I added, "Carnation pink just might not be your color."

"You're probably right, but it made you smile, so worth it either way."

I dipped my head and bit my lower lip.

"Sorry, I seem to get extra cheesy around you."

When I glanced up, the idea he was a little unsure made me feel more at ease. I didn't want cocky. I'd been down that road before.

"Nah, you're Gouda."

His stare was blank for a beat, and I worried I'd said something stupid, maybe letting my quirkiness out of the bag a little too soon, then the edges of his eyes crinkled to accompany his low and sexy rumbling laugh.

"A cheese pun. You might be the coolest woman I've ever met."

I knew a blush was rising on my cheeks, so I looked out toward the water of Lake Michigan glistening under the sinking sun. "I don't give those puns to just anyone, so feel honored."

"I do. Any other secrets up your sleeve? Perhaps your real name?"

I laced my fingers together, twirling the small gold ring I wore on my right middle finger. There really wasn't any danger in him knowing my first name.

"It's Naya. Like a papaya."

He smiled at the device I'd used since I was a kid. "Nice to meet you, Naya like a papaya. Have you been here before?"

Since I'd never told him I actually lived here before insisting we not share details, I stumbled for a moment on the question. On one hand, I was still kind of anonymous with him not knowing where I lived. On the other hand, I was lying to him.

"I haven't been here in a long time." *Not exactly a lie.* I avoided crowded places.

He laced his fingers through mine, an intimate gesture that made me feel strangely girlish. "Let's explore, then."

His hand was so much bigger than mine, and a strange sense of contentment pooled around me. That was ridiculous, but still, his fingers wrapped around mine in this solid manner kept my doubts at bay as we wandered the pier. Walking in the warm night air, I was comfortable, and our conversation fell into an easy give-and-take. I pointed to the Ferris wheel and told him my favorite thing as a kid was when the carnival came to town and I could ride one. I always loved being on top of the world like that. He told me about his big family as we ate tacos from a food truck, and I made him laugh, telling him about my cousins trying to teach me, the lone girl, to pee against a tree when I was a kid.

"I never quite got the hang of it."

"I have no words." As we neared the water, the breeze picked up, whipping my hair onto my face, and he leaned over to tuck the strands back for me. It was the kind of romantic gesture I'd convinced myself I didn't want, three years ago when I'd decided that men weren't worth the risk. But with his fingertip lingering along my ear, a flurry of sensation ran up my spine, taking me back to the taste of his kisses.

"Thank you." My voice came out softer than normal.

"No problem." His smile faltered, and his eyes sparkled with an emotion I couldn't place.

*Did he feel that, too?*

We stayed like that for a few moments, the rush of the water below us mixed with the sounds of laughter and people moving behind us. Over the normal noises of the pier, a Latin beat floated around us. There was a concert and a gathering crowd not far from us.

Jake craned his neck. "It looks like people are dancing over there. Want to try?"

I never danced in public. My dad teased me that whatever musical skills I should have gained from being of both African and Mexican descent seemed to have been obliterated by my rural Iowa upbringing—I had no rhythm. I shook my head slowly. "I have a hard rule about dancing in front of people."

He raised an eyebrow. "C'mon, I'm sure if they're public lessons, it's just the basics."

I bit my lip again, looking over his shoulder at the gathering crowd. A tinge of worry skittered through me, unsure about interrupting this odd sensation of confidence I felt standing and talking with him. I was getting used to our back-and-forth, gaining certainty he was into me. "I am a terrible dancer. It will be embarrassing."

His grin was easy, and he wasn't what I'd expected when we met—I'd been so sure his polo shirt and developed muscles were cues he'd be cocky and demanding. Jake was a nerd—a hot nerd—and seemed completely comfortable with himself.

"Are you worried that knowing you're a bad dancer will make me like you less? Give me some ammunition to use later?"

I winced and willed my body to not recoil. *Ammunition is exactly what I'm worried about.* "I don't know," I said, glancing at the growing crowds, then back to my date.

"What if I told you something I'm bad at? Then we'd be even, right?"

"Maybe . . ."

"Imagine the shortest, least-coordinated person you knew in high school, the one who wore suspenders to gym class and corrected everyone's grammar. The grown version of that guy gets picked for basketball teams before me," he said with a straight face. "I am horrible. People think because I'm tall, I might have skills, but I can't make a free throw to save my life."

"No one ever taught you?"

"No," he hedged, squinting one eye and twisting his face. "I was taught. Repeatedly. My dad's a high school basketball coach, and my twin sister played in college. I just never could get the hang of it. My buddy Eric asked me to consider just keeping stats for our rec league instead of actually playing."

My lips turned up at his story, and I had to hide my amusement. Something about the image of my tall, broad companion missing shot after shot from the free-throw line eased my mind. More than the image making me smile, his ability to admit it, to just put his shortcomings out into the world to make me feel better . . . that was unexpected.

"Did I convince you to dance with me?"

I raised my arms over my head, positioning my hands the way my dad had taught me in my childhood driveway, and mimicked shooting a basket. "Nothing but net."

*Do something embarrassing. Here goes nothing.*

He reached for my hand, lacing his fingers with mine, and we walked together toward the crowd, where the music blared from large speakers, the percussion and horns building a palpable energy around us. Jake gripped my hand tighter as we ducked through the throng of bodies.

Onstage, a man with a microphone instructed the crowd. Near us, a middle-aged couple in matching blue T-shirts and jean shorts held each other, and two women in their seventies juggling brightly colored cocktails and pretzels ignored the instructions and made up their own steps.

The voice boomed from the stage. "Okay! Let's get going, now that we've learned the basic steps."

"We missed the beginning already," I said into Jake's ear.

He shrugged. "We'll catch up."

"Jake!" I hissed again, a touch of panic rising in me, not knowing what would come next. I looked at the couples near us to see their movements, trying to memorize how they moved to the loud beat.

"We'll be fine," Jake encouraged as he slid his arm around me, his palm resting against a shoulder blade. "Follow my lead. I'll step forward and you step back, and then the other way." His lips grazed the top of my ear, and I willed him to trail down to my neck again to that spot that had made me shudder in anticipation the night before.

From the stage, the voice boomed through the microphone. "And one, two, three." Around us, the crowd undulated like a wave.

Jake pushed toward me gently, stepping forward with one foot, but I was focused on what the woman next to me was doing and I didn't move in time, so his body collided with mine. He chuckled and spread his fingers across my back, which felt amazing, and I got distracted and stepped with the wrong foot the next time, bumping into his chest again. My gracelessness knew no bounds.

*How does everyone else already know how to do this?*

I growled at myself, huffing out a heavy breath and pausing my movements to catch back up to the beat. All I had to do was step forward and back, right? *I have a flippin' PhD. I can figure this out.*

"You're doing great," he encouraged, squeezing my hand.

"You're a bad liar," I returned over the music, taking a successful step forward but then second-guessing myself on the next beat and stepping on Jake's foot. *It's literally counting to three and knowing left from right.*

"Here," Jake said, pulling me flush against him, our thighs touching, chests against each other. Sandalwood and soap filled my nostrils, and my frustration about dancing ebbed into more memories from the night before. "I'll push my leg against yours, and we'll step together, okay?" He nudged my left leg with his right on the beat, and our hips twisted in unison, then back, and I followed his movements, relishing the roll of his body against mine as we moved with the music. The crowd fell away. There was only the beat and him. I stopped worrying about the steps and followed his lead. A minute passed, the music swirling around us, our bodies still flush.

"Don't overthink it." Jake spoke near my ear, his hot breath stroking my skin, and I stifled a sigh, a tingle zipping through me. "Trust me, okay?"

*He has no idea what he's asking.* I'd never been a good dancer, but I *had* been an eager dancer for most of my life. Not know-ing the steps and being hopelessly without rhythm had never stopped me from getting on the dance floor until Davis told me I was embarrassing him. By the time he stopped telling me and started showing his disappointment or anger, I'd long since stopped dancing.

"One, two, three," the man onstage counted, and he and his partner demonstrated some kind of complicated spin as we rocked back and forth. He said something about the left foot—or was it the right? Crap, I'd missed a few key details. I was com-fortable with the step we'd been doing—that was my dancing sweet spot, and I worried if I broke the rhythm it would never come back.

"Five, six, seven." The instructor counted the beats from the stage. *Did he say step forward on four or five?*

Jake squeezed my hand and raised his arm with a reassuring grin, nudging me to spin. The slick soles of my sandals helped my movement, and I twirled, clutching his hand, the breeze and motion catching the light fabric of my top. I spun once, then twice, the crowd and the lights from the stage a blur. I wasn't graceful, and the spin stopped when I tripped into Jake, steady-ing myself against him.

I laughed into his chest. "I told you I was no good."

"I'm having fun." He guided me back to the beat, and we moved together. "Plus, it gives me an excuse to touch you."

I glanced up to meet his eyes. "Were you looking for one?"

His hips rolled with mine, and a heavy breath escaped my lips as he cupped the back of my neck. "Hoping for one." The pressure and rhythm of our bodies in the middle of this crowd, the music blasting all around us—it was too much. We'd been laughing and teasing, but that all seemed to fade into the heat of the moment as our steps slowed. His gaze was intent on mine like he was seeing something rare and cataloging it in every detail.

*No one has ever looked at me like this.*

He lowered his chin, and I closed my eyes in anticipation of his soft but unyielding kisses. I opened my eyes suddenly when the music changed and the surrounding crowd surged at the popular tune, jostling us. New people moved closer to the stage, and the already crowded dance floor was instantly packed. I glanced left and right, panicked at the sudden influx.

Jake must have read my expression, because he took my hand. "C'mon. I've got an idea. You'll like this better."

# Eight

Jake squeezed my hand, casting his gaze toward the massive gears of the Ferris wheel as we jostled forward and began our ascent into the sky.

"You okay?" I asked.

He looked a little pale, his body rigid. "I must really like you. I can't believe I suggested riding this thing."

As we rotated higher into the night, I touched the plexiglass surrounding us and then looked back to Jake. It was late, and we'd managed to snag a car all to ourselves. I'd told him we didn't have to ride it, even though I'd admitted to loving Ferris wheels earlier in the evening. He'd insisted, and we, once again, found ourselves suspended in the air.

"Tell me more things about you. It distracts me."

"Um . . . let's see. My favorite food isn't ice cream. I told a little white lie last night." *Well, I told more than one, but let's keep this light.*

"What is it?"

"It's cake, but that sounds so gluttonous."

"Maybe if your favorite food is an *entire* sheet cake," he joked. "What else?"

"I kissed my best friend's husband back in college, before they were together."

"Awkward?"

"You'd think, but no. They are, like, the perfect couple and we joke about it now. I'm not sure what else to tell you. I don't have that many interesting things to share. What about you? What Jake trivia should I know?"

"People seem to think it's strange that I've never seen *Star Wars.*"

"How is that even possible?"

"You look shocked—do you like the movie?"

"*Movies*—there are many, but yes, the original trilogy is at the top of my best-films-of-all-time list." I elbowed him playfully in the side. "I'm not sure we can still hang out . . . This is a big revelation."

"Well, since you can't ditch me at the moment, it's your turn." He nudged his closed hand against the outside of my thigh.

The pressure of his touch against my leg sent all kinds of sensations pinging through me. It short-circuited my thoughts, and I said the first thing that came to mind. "I own an embarrassing amount of fancy lingerie I never wear."

A curious expression crossed his features, and his gaze fell to my chest, his eyes darkening.

My nipples pebbled, and I gasped, realizing what I'd implied and what he might be imagining. "Oh! No! I always wear underwear! I mean, of course, not always, like not in the shower. I–I just meant I buy fancy, expensive stuff I never wear." *Open mouth. Insert entire leg.*

He laughed, his tone husky, and rested our linked fingers on my knee. The same spark from earlier flashed up my thighs. Shaking his head as if resetting, the edges of his mouth tipped up. "My turn?"

I nodded, eager to move past my gaffe.

"What are the odds? I also own a staggering number of lacy underthings I never wear."

I released his fingers and slid my hand up his arm to push his shoulder, feeling silly and buoyant and miles away from ordinary. He was making fun of me, but it didn't feel cruel. "C'mon, a real one!"

"Okay, okay." He glanced over my shoulder at the view, then focused on my face again. "Hm." He ran a hand through his hair. He tilted his head. "Did we agree these needed to be embarrassing?"

"I think it's safe to say I've set a precedent."

"Fair enough. Okay . . . I was a virgin until I was twenty-three." His voice lifted at the end of his statement as he considered the number.

"Really?"

"I was a chubby, shy kid through college." He rocked forward in his seat, folding his fingers over the edge. "If I'm honest, women kind of scared me back then, so I was a late bloomer well into working on my MBA."

"Seems like you've figured out how to talk to women since then."

"It might just be you." He flashed a boyish, playful smile. "That one must earn me something juicy, right?"

I stretched to stroke my fingernails over his shoulders, then let my hand fall to scratch lightly up and down his spine. I was about to pull my hand away, embarrassed at the intimacy of the gesture and unsure why I'd done it, when his voice rumbled with a low groan.

"That feels really good."

My heart thudded in response to his words, the low timbre of his voice, and the way his body curled at my touch, and he inhaled sharply when I increased the pressure. "That's not getting you out of your turn, but I can't remember the last time someone scratched my back."

The fluttering low in my belly diverted energy from my brain, and I blurted out the first thing that came to mind again. "I haven't had sex in over three years."

"Wow," he mouthed, slowly.

It didn't seem that shocking until I said it out loud. *Three years.* It was even longer since I'd enjoyed it, and I'd never gotten to the big finale, not with anyone else. The sex with Davis had never been good, but eventually, I dreaded it. On the rare occasions he was interested in me enjoying myself, he'd lose patience quickly, asking *aren't you done yet?*

Jake's voice dipped low. "Why so long?"

"That's the last time I dated anyone, and work got busy. It kind of just happened." I let my hand fall from his back and gazed out at the twinkling city and the lights reflecting off Lake Michigan, sensing his stare but avoiding his face, afraid I would find pity there. It *was* pitiful.

His head bobbed out of the corner of my eye.

"What about you?"

His elbow brushed against mine. "No one's made my heart skip and my toes curl in quite a while."

"I'm not sure I've ever been with someone who made me feel that." *But you kind of do.*

We sat in companionable silence for a minute before he spoke. "I have to go back to the no-sex admission. Three years? Are you ready to explode all the time?"

"Sometimes," I admitted with a shrug. It wasn't until the last few months that I'd felt antsy, missing sex. I didn't plan on saying more, but something about the heat from his body made me keep talking. "But I have ten fingers, an expensive vibrator, and a stash of AA batteries. I get by."

Jake's mouth dropped a little as his gaze wandered to my fingers.

With a chuckle, I wiggled them in a quick flourish before changing the subject. "So, are you always like this?"

He paused before shaking his head, looking at me with surprise, eyelids a bit hooded as his gaze fell on my fingers again. "Sorry, I'm going to need a minute after that."

He scrubbed his hand over his jaw. "Am I always like this . . . spilling my guts and praying I don't plummet to my death on a weeknight?"

I bumped my shoulder against his and grinned. "You know what I mean."

"No, it's definitely not normal to spend a night like this, but I'm not usually spending nights with sexy, funny, interesting, sexy women. What about you?"

"Not normal for me, either." This night was shaping up to

be the furthest I'd been from normal in years. "And you said sexy twice."

"It was intentional." He curled his fingers with mine again as he'd done all night, his thumb tracing over my palm. "I'm glad I'm not just another in a string of men you've taken to fake proctology appointments."

"I promise, you were my first."

He pulled my hand to his lips. My breath hitched as he dropped a kiss on my knuckles. "I'm honored to hold that distinction."

Jake squeezed my hand again, eyes still locked on mine.

"Are you staring at me to avoid seeing how high up we are?"

His gaze warmed me from inside out and made me nervous at the same time.

"Yes." He trailed the pad of his thumb over my lower lip, then against my cheekbone. "That and . . ." He lowered his lips to mine, slowly, his fingers curling around my neck. The view, the night sky, and the people below became background noise.

In the back of my mind, I counted the moments like the dance steps. *One, two, three.* But when his soft tongue nudged at my lips, I stopped counting. The force of the kiss took my breath, but I didn't want it back. When we pulled apart, he stared at me, a heat in his gaze that made me feel powerful.

"Damn," he said quietly, still holding my head.

"Damn," I repeated. I wanted to be kissed like that again, like I was something special, something wanted, like I was . . . someone.

# Nine

My hands shook at my sides, and I tried to control my nerves, but my pulse quickened as I once again watched Jake open the door to his room. This time he didn't fumble with the key card, and once the door closed, our eyes met for a moment, a taut undercurrent of want passing between us.

I opened my mouth to say something, to make a joke, but gasped instead as he wrapped his arms around my waist and pulled me to him.

His mouth closed over mine, unyielding, as he held my face to his. Fingers dug into my hair, and a moan fell from my mouth as he pressed his lips to the side of my chin and down the column of my throat. The nice guy, my quirky nerd, had been replaced with this dominant, hungry man, and I liked it.

Placing my palm on his hard chest, I felt his heart racing. *Glad I'm not the only one.*

My hands explored downward over his flat stomach. The

ridges of his abs were like magnets for my fingers through the smooth fabric of his shirt, and I traced the muscles down to his belt, letting my fingers grip the leather.

Jake sat on the edge of the mattress and pulled me onto his lap, dotting kisses along my cheek and down my jawline, gently cupping my neck in his broad hand. "Your skin is so soft," he murmured into my shoulder, lightly nipping, then kissing.

We stayed like that, oscillating between frenzied tongues and sweet kisses, soft strokes and firm grips. I fell into that moment, and there was just his mouth and his hands and our bodies. The night before had been hot, but the memory was blurry, the edges soft from the alcohol. Sitting with him on the bed, I was aware of every touch.

His fingers trailed up my spine, and he twisted, dipping me toward the bed, giggling as I fell backward. His tongue peeked out from between his lips, and he dragged a fingertip from my knee with painfully slow deliberation toward my hip bone.

My giggle faded, and we lay on the bed, wrapped in each other. "Hi," I murmured.

"Hi." He moved one palm to my hip, and our eyes locked. "No cheesy lines now?"

He shook his head and cupped my ass, massaging and stroking. "I can't think of anything besides touching you." His fingers fluttered closer to where I wanted him, to where I hadn't welcomed anyone in so long.

"Good. You cheddar not stop," I murmured on a fluttery exhale.

He smiled against my neck as his fingers brushed over the

wet panel of my panties. I inched my thighs apart, and my breath caught in my throat as he traced along my seam through the fabric.

"You want this?" he asked, voice husky. He continued to trace long lines back and forth. Electricity arced through me as I rocked my pelvis toward his fingers.

"Yes," I croaked, my breaths coming in sharp, short bursts. No man had ever asked me if I wanted *this*, and I liked it. "It's been a long time, but yes."

"The Ferris wheel was worth it." He ran his palm over my stomach and down my hips, then back up my skirt, his warm palm trailing over my thighs. "To kiss you," he rasped. He slid into my panties, his long fingers stroking and his thumb teasing me with the lightest pressure. "To feel you."

I arched, back bowing off the bed at his touch. *I want this. I want this. I want this.*

"So perfect," he breathed out again, pressing his lips along my collarbone, then to my breast, sucking gently on a hard nipple through my thin shirt. His fingers continued to tease, and his lips left me frazzled with pent-up anticipation. I pulled my tank top over my head, anxious to remove the barrier. Jake didn't miss a beat, immediately pushing the cups of my bra down and taking me into his mouth. Watching his lips on me was mesmerizing.

I inhaled sharply. The sensation floored me. Part of me needed everything, every touch all at once, before he pulled away. I reached to push down my underwear, but he caught my hand, then dragged the lacy fabric down my legs himself, his movements slow and deliberate. I couldn't take my eyes off his hand traveling down my leg.

After tossing the fabric aside, he dotted kisses on each of my breasts, sweet little pecks before he returned his hand to between my legs. His finger inched inside me, moving in and out slowly before pressing deeper, searching. He crooked his finger, and I cried out, tipping my head back as he stroked against the sensitive spot.

"I couldn't stop thinking about all the ways I could make you smile. God, you have a great smile." He thrust his fingers faster, treating and tormenting the spot deep inside me.

I held my breath. Lost in sensation, I clutched Jake's shoulder. *Don't stop.*

"Jake, please," I whimpered before kissing him hard, our lips and tongues clashing, willing him to keep going. In seconds, I cried out, an orgasm rushing through my body like a wave crashing to shore after building to a lofty crest. I floundered to clutch the sheets as I thrashed and then trembled.

His fingers slowed, his palm gently pressing against me, and my body convulsed as I felt his smile against my neck.

*Let someone else bring me to orgasm. Check. Check. Check.*

My breath was shaky, the tremors of pleasure still echoing.

His eyes met mine, and the look that passed between us reinforced for me how different this was than any other experience, and the feeling left my head spinning. It hadn't been just sexual; he'd released some valve on human connection I'd long felt was rusted shut.

"You're shaking," he said, sliding the back of his other hand over the side of my face, brushing strands of hair away. "Are you okay?"

Something in the gentle way he touched me combined with the overwhelming desire I had to be closer to him—to have every inch of our bodies connected—made tears well in my eyes, one falling down my cheek.

"Did I . . . hurt you?" he asked, concern coloring his face, and he brushed the tear away with his thumb.

I shook my head, embarrassment heating my skin. "No. God, no!" This was so many miles away from hurting, but another tear fell. *What is wrong with me?* "I just wasn't ready for it to be that . . . good. That intense. I don't know why I'm crying."

His gaze wandered over my face, his thumbs sweeping away more tears.

"I'm sorry. How embarrassing," I said, trying to cover my eyes.

"Don't apologize," he said, voice dipping in volume. "You said it's been a long time. We'll only do what you want, what you're ready for."

Though his arousal was imposing between us, he dragged my hand, not to his pants, but to his lips, planting tiny kisses down the side of my thumb at the sensitive skin on the underside of my wrist, stopping me from hiding my face.

---

An hour later, we lay facing each other on the bed, our breathing steady and even. A blanket of contentment settled over me after coming undone in his arms a second time and bringing him to an eruptive climax with my hands. Without taking things *all the way*, the connection between us was undeniable. He seemed to intuit that I needed time to jump in, more than I had realized, but I hadn't felt rushed or self-conscious. My tinges of self-doubt, that he must be bored or think me childish, were always met with more sweet kisses, electrifying touches, or achingly slow caresses.

Jake trailed his finger over the shell of my ear, pushing a strand of hair off my face. I loved his touch against my skin, grazing so gently one moment and erotically the next. I'd never felt so drawn to someone.

"Tell me something about yourself," I whispered.

"Are you collecting all my secrets?" he asked, sleepily. I nodded, and he stretched one arm up above his head, his eyes raised to the ceiling as he thought about a response. As he stretched, I admired how his stomach tapered into a V.

"Doesn't have to be a secret." I searched his face, taking in the lines and shadows. This was incredible, but I had to remind myself that this was not my real life.

"I've been successful in my career, made a lot of money, and I love what I do. I was able to strike out and start my own business recently. It's scary and exciting, but sometimes, it all feels a little . . . empty."

"Don't think I didn't notice how you worked in that you make a lot of money. You already got into my pants." I slid a hand down his arm.

Our clothes had come off slowly. My bra and skirt were somewhere across the room near his pants, and I had no idea where he'd tossed my underwear. We lay together naked.

"You weren't wearing any." He swatted my bare bottom lightly. "Anyway, I don't think you're the kind of woman who would be interested in men because of money. You're too . . . good."

"I don't think anything we just did is in the good girl's handbook."

"Agree to disagree," he chuckled, stroking my hip.

"Anyway, you said it feels empty. How do you mean?"

"I work long hours and come home to an empty place. I don't even have a cat. I worry I've missed a step along the way."

"Yeah?"

"It gets lonely, is all. I always pictured my life with some-one, really with them, you know? Like having a real partner, a family, all of that."

I bit my tongue. Even after everything we'd just done, this conversation felt too intimate.

In that moment, I also wanted to confess everything. How I was lonely, too, and why I'd been closed off for so long. I wanted to tell him about being scared I was broken, because no one's touch had ever done the things that his had. That I knew exactly what he meant when he talked about feeling empty, and how scared I was of not having my job as a refuge. I opened my mouth, but I held back. *He's not a stranger anymore, but he might as well be.*

"I'm not sure why I'm telling you all this. I guess you're just easy to talk to," he said after I'd been silent for a moment. "Tell *me* a secret. Why did you want a one-night stand? That seems out of character."

A tingle swept across the back of my neck, and I winced, remembering the last time I'd been in this room. "It is unlike me." I buried my face in his chest, the warmth of his arm at my back.

The urge to share everything bubbled up inside me again, but I pressed my eyelids together, commanded my head to take back control from my heart, and told him the part of the truth that didn't make me look so helpless. "I wanted to get out of my rule-following life and do something a little wild."

"I'm not complaining."

I pulled back so I could look up into his face, and in that moment realized I didn't know the answer to the question that suddenly overtook me. "Do you think, or . . . um? *Is* this a one-night stand?"

"I hope not," he said in a low voice, brushing hair off my face again, a gesture I was quickly coming to adore. "This is night number two, so it's a mathematical impossibility." His mouth twitched as if he was about to say something else, but he nodded instead, and we lay in silence once more. The unspoken addition to his sentence was that whatever this was had an expiration after a few more days when he flew home. That's what I'd wanted, but a sudden wave of loss settled over me.

"Why did you talk to me in the bar?"

"I was intrigued by the pole dancing conversation. Is that woman okay?"

"Seems to be on the mend. I guess I should thank her."

"Me, too." He laughed before his index finger tipped up my chin. "That was part of it, but look at you. You're gorgeous, and when I heard you on the phone and knew you were funny, too . . ." He paused his sentence with a kiss dropped on my lips. "I had to say something."

We lay together in silence. His breathing slowed, and I wondered if he'd fallen asleep by the time he finally spoke. "Tell me something else, Naya like a papaya."

"I'm scared of butterflies." I shuddered at the thought.

He chuckled. "Butterflies?" His breath caressed my ear.

"All bugs, but butterflies are the worst."

He walked his fingertips up my ribs like a spider, and I smacked his hand. His low rumble of a laugh reverberated against my back. When his hand crawled over my hip, I scurried to a sitting position.

"Hey!" I squealed.

I couldn't get enough of his body heat, and that drowsy, surrounded feeling of being next to him. The wheels in my head wanted to turn, to analyze the situation and look for exit strategies—old habits died hard. But he wrapped his palm around my ankle, stroking upward over my calf, and the wheels stilled. I didn't want to escape. I didn't want to move an inch.

"Do you mind that we haven't . . ." I let my voice trail off into the air. I'd arrived at the hotel planning to take a leap, to have sex with my handsome stranger. His fingers inside me had been so intense, I'd nearly doubled over with the physical pleasure, but also with the weight of the connection coursing between us. I wasn't sure how he knew it was hitting me so hard, but he hadn't pushed or prodded or made me feel guilty. I wasn't used to someone waiting for me. Still, I worried I'd let him down.

He planted a few pecks on my knee. "No, I don't mind," he murmured against my skin, moving his hand up and down my thigh, fingers grazing the skin a little higher with each pass. He looked to me, eyebrows raised as if for permission, and I nodded. "Don't get me wrong, I definitely want more, but when, or if, you want me inside you, I don't want you to have any doubts. I'm happy to keep making you feel good."

My pulse quickened, and I settled back, sinking deeper against the pillows and headboard. Previous lovers had tried to get me to climax like this. There was never a big finale. I began to just fake it, so the guy didn't feel bad.

"Okay?" he asked, and I nodded again. "Good." His tone was distracted as he planted sweet kisses higher on my thigh, his tongue wet on my skin for brief moments.

"Jake." I purred his name, my head bobbing backward.

"Mm?" He spread my legs wider, arms wrapping around my thighs as he kissed only a few inches from my center. He stilled, his eyes meeting mine. "Do you want me to stop?"

My knees slowly fell apart as he settled between them. My words were punctuated with stuttered breaths, anticipation taking hold. "No. I, uh. Don't stop." My hips gyrated as he shifted higher, and I swayed between desperately wanting his mouth on me and cringing at the shame I'd feel if I couldn't get there. "I might take a while to finish, though."

He smiled up at me, that cute crooked grin, then looked down at where my legs met, his gaze intense. I was open to him, bare in so many ways, and he settled his hands on my thighs as he continued to kiss higher. "I'm in no hurry. Tell me what feels good, okay?"

As his mouth met its destination and his tongue began a slow trail, my head fell back against the pillows. *I had no idea this was what I was missing.* I moaned as he glided over my slick, sensitive folds, expertly flicking, circling, and stroking, leading me to the edge until I reeled.

# Ten

JAKE: I can't wait to see you again.

JAKE: When are you free? I should be good after 9:00.

I wrapped a fluffy towel around my chest and leaned against the sink in my bathroom. I'd left Jake's hotel room around two in the morning and taken an Uber home after a searing kiss in the hotel lobby. He'd invited me to stay, but that felt too big, so I told him I had an early meeting. After only five hours of sleep, I should have been a wreck, but I was buzzing with energy. *Multiple orgasms: more effective than coffee. Who knew?*

NAYA: I have to do a favor for my boss tonight so 9 will be good.

JAKE: I can't wait to see you again.

NAYA: You already said that ☺

JAKE: I know. I have no chill.

JAKE: Also, I can't wait to see you again.

Positioning the camera in selfie mode and finding that perfect angle that thinned my face, I snapped a photo. My shoulders were dappled with water drops, the towel hugged my breasts, and the sunlight from my bathroom window cast my skin in a great light.

Though the thrill of being a little naughty and turning him on made my temperature rise, I debated whether I should send it. Davis had taken photos of me when we dated, and I always feared he'd share them.

*But Jake's not Davis.*

Once again, I imagined the sweet smile from the ice cream shop and the heated gaze after we kissed. "They're different," I said to the empty room, and hit send.

NAYA: And now you don't have to wait to see me.

The three dots bounced, indicating he was composing a reply before the buzz came a minute later.

JAKE: Wow.

JAKE: I will have this image at my fingertips all day—you are so cruel.

I walked casually across the quad between meetings, enjoying the fresh air and open sidewalks. Students had started their mass exodus from campus, and everything was peaceful. I'd wanted to work at TU because of the chance to collaborate with top scholars, but the campus grounds still took my breath away after all these years. Daylilies peeked up toward the sky, dotting the manicured lawn with yellow and red touches that made the sunshine just a bit brighter. Nearby, the splash of water from a stone fountain mixed with the sounds of music blasting from a group of students gathered around a laptop.

This looked like the cover of an instructional manual on how to have the perfect day. I briefly considered twirling in the breeze.

*What the hell is going on with me?*

What was going on with me was definitely my handsome stranger who didn't seem like much of a stranger anymore. I continued down the path to my office, a smile plastered on my face.

"You look like you're in a good mood." The familiar voice of a colleague interrupted my thoughts as she slowed her speed going in the other direction. "End of the year, right?"

I chuckled and nodded. "Exactly." Jill was a few years my junior and taught in the business school. We'd served on a few committees and project groups together, and she was always kind and pleasant. *The perfect person to chat with when I feel this good.* "Do you have plans for the summer?"

"Hopefully not looking for another job. Do you know much about the rumors of departments getting cut?"

"Not much," I conceded, though I couldn't imagine her area—accounting—going anywhere. *Mine, on the other hand . . .*

"A mentor of mine at State used to work here." She looked left and right and leaned in to speak in a low voice, as if having a mentor at one of the area's elite universities was classified information. "He gave me the inside scoop, and I guess the president is bringing in some people and pulling together committees or something."

Her face twisted into a grimace, and I didn't blame her. Every time I tried to think through what it would mean to lose this job, I wanted to cower. In that moment, though, I still felt like I was floating a few inches in the air. Even talking about the rumor of cuts wasn't quite pulling me back to Earth.

"It will be an interesting summer," she said, shaking her head. "Davis said—"

"What?" I heard my own voice become strained, my mood plummeting to the ground. I intentionally slowed my speech. "I mean, sorry, did you say Davis?"

She may not have noticed the shift. "Davis Garner. Did you know him? I don't think he's ever mentioned you."

My feet were now firmly planted, though my stomach lurched. My clothes suddenly felt too constricting and the sun's rays too bright. I counted to three in my head, trying to dull the panic her words had inspired. She was looking at me expectantly, and I stammered out, "I knew him, yes."

"Well, anyway, if I hear anything else, I'll keep you posted. Talk to you later, Naya." She flashed a bright grin before turning to head in the other direction.

"Same here, Jill." My response was markedly less enthusiastic, but I returned her smile and waved. I hated how his name still sent me into this physical state where I wanted to jump out of my own skin and curl up in an out-of-the-way corner.

In my pocket, my phone buzzed.

JAKE: What should we do tonight?

JAKE: BASE jumping? Skydiving? You seem to have a thing for heights.

I tapped my fingers against the side of the phone, glancing from the screen to the direction Jill had walked. I'd allowed myself to feel excited and take risks in the last few days. It was a shift I liked, and I didn't want to waste the opportunity.

With another deep breath, I took a step forward.

# Eleven

At the reception, I silently cursed Joe, Miami, and Hurricane Beatrice. Everyone in the room outranked me by two or three pay grades. Though I'd chosen an unadorned, high-necked black dress and simple black heels, I felt like a child playing dress-up at an adult party.

The university's upper administration huddled in small groups, sipping wine and talking in low, nervous murmurs. Two people I recognized from another campus department walked in. I didn't particularly like Bea or Gregory, because they were consummate gossips, but I smiled as I walked toward them across the shiny hardwood floor. *Play nice. Make friends.*

They welcomed me into their small circle, and I learned that no one knew the reason for the impromptu event. Anxiety was plentiful as the volume in the room grew. I glanced at my watch. The thought of being near Jake again sent a pleasurable jolt through my belly, and I bit my lip to stop from grinning like I'd been doing all day. I tried to focus on the tail end of the conversation.

Bea chimed in with her nasally voice. "I should reach out to Davis Garner—he's still so well-connected here."

I tensed at his name, and Gregory coughed, darting his eyes in my direction. *Subtle.* "That's not a bad idea," I interjected before he started trying to talk in code, hoping that my change in mood didn't show. Gregory's shoulders seemed to relax, and Bea continued talking, apparently unaware of the entire exchange. Davis had worked for another university for years, but a sinking feeling made me scan the room so I could be prepared for his sneer, his cutting words, or worse. The number of times his name had come up in the last few days made the hairs on the back of my neck stand up.

President Lewis stepped to the microphone at the front of the room. Voices hushed as the tall, slender man looked over the group of senior faculty and staff. Flip Lewis carried himself with a squareness to his shoulders that bespoke a youthful arrogance turned to aged confidence. In his seventies, with white hair, his eyes always struck me as kind, and he smiled a lot.

"Thank you." He cleared his throat. "Thank you all for joining me this evening. I have an announcement, and it is important you hear it directly and all at the same time." His voice was pleasant, but expressions, and probably sphincters, tightened around the room as he spoke. An introduction like that was never going to mean good news.

"Thurmond University is a fine institution, and since my arrival last year I have been listening and learning everything

I can about your departments, research, our students, and the alumni."

I stood in the area farthest from the president, my back to a wall filled with portraits of previous presidents, and I slipped my phone from my purse to glance at the screen. I remembered Quinton or Quentin texting during my class, and the irony wasn't lost on me.

JAKE: I am ready to get my hands on you again.

JAKE: Sexy or creepy?

I smiled, my chest fluttering as I flicked my gaze to President Lewis gesturing to his wife. "When Rebecca and I moved here . . ." I was comfortable that whatever story was beginning would take a minute or two to wind down.

NAYA: Mostly creepy. 70/30?

JAKE: Only 30? You're hard to please. Though . . . it's fun
to try.

"And that's how I concluded that it's time for Thurmond to move in a new direction and make a shift from being an excellent institution to being the top university in the country. This summer, we are going to embark on a journey toward reaching that goal."

JAKE: Have to go but I'll see if I can earn a few more points
later. I'll msg you when I'm done.

"I will invite Carlton Brohm to join me." A stocky man in an expensive-looking, tailored navy suit smiled and moved to stand next to President Lewis. "Carlton runs a management consulting firm, Brohm, Shaw and Associates, that will help us chart our course."

A collective inhalation spread around the room. Management consultants plus "a new direction" meant cuts and significant changes—none of which were going to be popular. I nervously tapped my fingers against my thigh.

"Thank you for inviting us," the shorter man said in a booming voice that ricocheted off the walls in the small space. "BSA is a new company, and we bring unique analytic, strategic, and innovation-centered skills to our work. We look forward to helping you capitalize on your strengths."

I nodded, as did those around me, well aware that "capitalizing on your strengths" usually meant eliminating your weaknesses. We were about to be measured.

"More details will be forthcoming, but I want to introduce someone else you'll get to know well."

Carlton's partner joined him on the platform, and my breath caught in my throat.

# Twelve

My eyes widened, and a voice in my head screeched to a halt.

The president assured the collected group this was ultimately going to be a good experience even though change was anxiety inducing. I stopped listening, and my eyes followed Jake as he stepped offstage, whispering with his colleague as the president finished speaking and invited guests to stay and enjoy a drink.

Everyone paused, the room still, before they all began talking at once. My pulse raced, and panic inched up my body. I excused myself from the conversation to move into the less congested hallway.

*Breathe. Breathe.*

I couldn't appear like I would faint in the middle of a crowd of senior colleagues and notorious gossips who already had a low opinion of me. Instead, I looked down at my phone.

JAKE: Just about done.

JAKE: Any thoughts to how I can even out that creepy/sexy ratio?

JAKE: I have more cheese puns just in queso emergency.

I stared at the message, and the laugh froze in my throat. *What if someone finds out I'm sleeping with him? They'll assume I'm trying to sway him.* Women had been professionally blackballed for less.

I considered fleeing the mansion. Ahead of me, Jake stood at the other end of the hallway with a group of men in suits, his back to me as he looked down at his phone, then back up to finish a conversation with Carlton.

They laughed, and Jake clapped the other man on the shoulder. A fleeting thought had me worried he was laughing at me, and every available insecurity crept into my consciousness. My hand trembled, and I typed out a reply.

NAYA: I'm standing behind you.

JAKE: See, that's more creepy than sexy.

"Jake," I said as his partner stepped away.

Jake turned, confusion clear on his face until we made eye contact. His eyes were wide, and his lips tipped to the side, a cautious half smile spreading across his face under furrowed brows as he walked to me. "What are you . . . doing here?"

"I work here," I said unsteadily, and took a small step backward as a stream of administrators left the large room where we'd gathered. Apparently, an open bar wasn't enough of a draw to stay after the bombshell that had been dropped.

He cocked his head. "I thought you were in town on business," he reasoned, more to himself than to me.

"You never said you did consulting, especially not with colleges."

"You didn't want to reveal anything work related, remember?" His expression was even, his posture relaxed. In the midst of the crushing fear of losing my job, I imagined his fingertips and lips on me, all the while holding the pink slip. Of all the men in all the bars in the city, I picked this one to flex my flirtation skills on.

A raspy, almost desperate-sounding laugh escaped my lips. "This is so bad," I whispered, taking in the familiar aroma of sandalwood.

"It's not *so* bad," he reassured, tracing a fingertip over my shoulder as he brushed my hair away. The intimacy of the gesture rocked me unexpectedly, both in how much I enjoyed it and how terrified I was of others observing us. I stepped back again, and recognition crossed his face as he dropped his hand. "Okay, it's not great, but it could be worse."

"How?"

"Let's talk somewhere with a little more privacy, okay? This thing is winding down." He waved to the shorter man, Carlton, who tipped his chin toward us before walking back into the gathering. "Is your office close by?"

I shook my head, still glancing around. "If anyone saw us, it would raise questions. You'd have no reason to be there." Nervous energy coursed through me. Logically, I knew no one had probably even noticed us, but I was still fighting the urge to look over my shoulder for Davis.

His voice dropped to a barely audible whisper. "Your place, then? It feels a little illicit to hand you my hotel room key here."

"Okay," I said in a small voice.

"We'll talk it through. It will be okay. I promise." His arm twitched, and my eyes widened, hoping he wouldn't touch me again here. His eyes were curious, and a crease appeared between his eyebrows.

*This guy must think I am nuts.*

"I'm sorry, I just . . ." I didn't know how to finish the sentence once I started it, still conscious of eyes on me. The back of my neck tingled, and a thousand thoughts tripped over one another. "I'll text you my address."

He nodded slowly, and I turned and exited the mansion alongside the stream of people. I didn't look back at him or at the others as we walked into the warm evening, a light breeze shifting the air around us. I paused on the sidewalk, and my hands shook as I opened the Uber app. Luckily, I'd only have to wait a few minutes before I could step away from what was increasingly feeling like a stage.

I looked from left to right again to make sure no one I knew had been watching me. I needed to tell Joe about the announcement, but I didn't plan to tell him I had slept with one of the consultants. Bea and Gregory waved as both walked hurriedly past me, and my phone buzzed in my hand, making me jump.

JAKE: Don't freak out, okay? It will be okay.

I couldn't do anything other than stare at the message. It wouldn't be okay—there was no way we could keep going with whatever we were doing. I cursed myself for not wanting to talk about work. I could have avoided all this the night we met. *But then he would never have kissed me. And I wouldn't know how his hands curve to the back of my neck or how it feels when his eyes lock with mine, looking at me like I am the only person in the city.*

The car pulled up, and I climbed into the back seat, tucking my phone back into my purse.

*What am I going to do?*

# Thirteen

After answering the buzzer, I paced my living room, waiting for Jake.

*I need to calmly and quickly tell him we have to stop. That it's no one's fault, but it's the smart thing to do. Ethical thing to do? No, I'll go with smart. That's it. No funny business, just a quick split.*

A knock pulled me from my thoughts, and I rolled my shoulders. *I can do this.*

"Hey," Jake said when I opened the door. He'd loosened his tie, his jacket was in his hands, and his shirt was rolled up his forearms. His hair was a little tousled, like he might have run his hands through it a few times.

"Hey." *Do I hug him before I end things? I really want to hug him.* I motioned for him to come in, ultimately keeping my hands to myself.

"So," we said in unison. We let out barely audible, awkward laughs, and Jake deferred to me.

"I can't believe I was so stupid as to not talk about work." I wrung my hands. "And to lie about living here."

"It wasn't stupid." He set his jacket on the nearby counter and brushed his fingertips along my arms. "We had no reason to assume this would happen. It's a big city."

He followed me to the living room couch, settling next to me, our thighs millimeters apart. "You said you were here for a wedding."

*And if he lied about that . . .* Suddenly, I questioned the memories of how his touches made me feel.

"I am. The high-maintenance bride, the whooping girl entourage, it's all true. The timing just happened to work out to come into town early and get started with Thurmond. It's one of our first big accounts, and I didn't want to waste the opportunity." He nudged my knee with his. "Talk to me, Naya like a papaya. Why does this have you so anxious?"

*The department where I work with other PhDs is mistaken for the campus day care center at least three times a day, and it's your job to find that out. Oh, and everyone I work with already thinks I sleep around.*

I let out a small, choked laugh. "Besides the fact you're in charge of me keeping my job?"

"Yeah, I guess, besides that." His expression a little sheepish, he laced his fingers with mine. The response would have sounded flippant from anyone else, but something in his tone made it softer. "What's your role at TU?"

At first I hesitated, but he was right. There was no point withholding any details now. "I'm a professor in education, and I don't want it to seem like this"—I motioned between us—"is me trying to gain an advantage or something. Even in education, women are judged harshly. People talk, they like to talk a lot, and that could be terrible for me if anyone found out we were . . ." *What are we doing?*

"I understand."

"So, it's better if we . . ." I looked down at our laced fingers and inched mine back. "If we don't see each other again. I mean, you're only here a few more days, anyway."

Jake lowered his face to catch my gaze. "You're right," he said, his voice low. "That's the smart thing to do, to cut ties." He held my gaze, his eyes boring into mine, and I shifted my gaze, unable to handle the weight, the examination.

"I know," I said into my lap.

"And it's the responsible thing, probably the ethical thing, too." He stroked my palm with a slow, deliberate glide I didn't want to end.

My urge to pull our fingers apart stalled, and our fingertips still mingled.

He had this way of grazing over my skin that relaxed and electrified my nerve endings, leaving me with a confusing need to both climb the walls and sink into him. "But I'm having a hard time thinking about ethics because I've been aching to kiss your perfect mouth since I walked in the door."

My body betrayed my resolve, and flickers of arousal pinged at his words.

*Don't remind me how much I want this.*

"I leave in a few days, but I was hoping to spend as much of that time with you as possible. You're intriguing, and funny, and so damn sexy."

His intense stare pinned me in my place.

*This is wrong. It's unprofessional. It's irresponsible.*

"Naya, do you—"

*But I want it. I want him.*

I slipped my hand to the back of his neck and pulled his face to mine roughly. I'd never taken control of a kiss like that, and adrenaline surged through me.

Jake was still for a beat before kissing me back, pulling me onto his lap. Our mouths met frantically, tongues dancing, like the kiss was oxygen.

I hadn't wanted to kiss him; I'd needed to. The way his lips played over mine had sent me into a place where I was all instinct. I shifted to straddle him, and he groaned, pulling me closer and gripping my backside as my dress inched up my thighs.

"Naya." He panted before meeting my lips again. My center slid along his hard length, and he hissed, pressing his lips to the column of my throat and sucking gently.

Every touch of his mouth was pushing me forward, a little unsteady, a little elated.

"A few days, right?" I tugged at his shirt, pulling it from his pants and slipping my fingers underneath to stroke his abs before working at the buttons.

"A few days," he murmured into my neck, the words vibrating into my skin as he ground his hips up to meet me.

I tried to think through the situation, but with each bump and rub of Jake's body against mine, my mind reset. *No one has to find out. God, his hands.*

When I sat back and pressed both palms to his neck, Jake's eyes were wide, pupils dilated, and his breath was coming fast and heavy. "A few days," I repeated, losing my words as his hands drifted up my ribs, his thumbs caressing the sides of my breasts through my dress.

Jake nodded.

*A few days of this, a few days of him, and then back to real life.*

"Take me to my bedroom."

*Do something reckless. Check.*

# Fourteen

Jake's gaze swept over my exposed skin after my black dress fell to the bedroom floor and I stood before him in bra and panties. The way his eyes roamed the length of my body was like he was memorizing me.

"So, this is me." I tucked my hair behind my ears and glanced away as his eyes reached my face.

"I like you," Jake murmured while walking me backward toward the bed. "I can't decide where to start." One hand slid down my back, stroking the sensitive skin above my hip.

Splaying my hands over his chest, I pushed his shirt off his shoulders. The pressure of his thighs against mine reminded me of dancing with him on the pier. *One, two, three.* I reached back and unhooked my bra, letting my breasts tumble free as the lacy fabric fell. His appreciative stare made me want to giggle, but then his hands were cupping and squeezing my breasts, and circling my hard nipples with his thumb. A low groan escaped my mouth.

"I want you." His lips trailed down my neck with soft, wet kisses punctuating his words. "I've wanted you since I first touched you."

"Me, too." I didn't recognize my voice; it was throaty and bold. "Get on the bed."

Jake tossed a condom on the duvet and pushed down his pants and boxer briefs, and then my handsome stranger lay in front of me naked and ready, his erection thick and rigid, his gaze intent on me. I hooked my thumbs into my black satin panties, pushed them down my hips, and climbed onto the bed.

He slid deft fingers between my legs, stroking and teasing, but I wanted more.

I placed my hand over his and met his eyes. "I want you inside me."

He nodded, and the sound of the foil tearing was like music, and Jake rolled a condom down his length.

It was anticipation and not fear or anxiety that pulsed through me. I was going to be on top, in control, and he was okay with it. *This is actually happening.*

"You're incredible," he said, his eyes traveling over my body as he gripped my hips. He met my eyes again. "We don't have to if you're not ready, though."

Him asking, making sure I was on board for everything happening, was beyond sexy. It made me feel safe, and I rested my palms on his chest. "I'm ready. I want this."

He pressed against my entrance, and then he was filling and stretching me.

As I sank down, I panted his name repeatedly and ground against him. My body lit up as he bucked, reaching deeper and hitting the perfect spots. Seeing his expression, feeling the way his muscles flexed under me and the growing friction—I was overwhelmed, truly, for the first time in my life.

"You feel so damn good," he panted, drawing me down to suck on one of my nipples, teasing it with his tongue. Flickers of pleasure moved across my chest and out to my fingertips, the tension pooling in my spine.

We slid against each other, building to a steady and maddening rhythm. My climax blossomed deep within my body.

I pressed my hands to his chest for balance and rocked against him, seeking my orgasm. With him, like this, our bodies glistening with sweat, I wasn't thinking; I was pure sensation.

His thumb made a slow circle over my clit, and I let out a cry, further excited by his blue eyes on me, his neck muscles straining.

My nerves all sparked as my back arched and an incomprehensible string of words left my mouth.

His expression changed to intense concentration, and his breath grew labored. With a loud groan, his body jerked under me with the power of his own release.

We both lay damp with sweat, naked, as the air-conditioning blew over us. Heat radiated between our limp bodies as we sank against each other. I tried desperately to catalog the moment, but brief tremors of pleasure still rolled through me as I caught my breath, and my thoughts went fuzzy. Minutes passed in silence—for me, it was the silence of satisfaction and disbelief.

"I'll be right back," he finally said, easing off the bed to dispose of the condom in my bathroom. I lolled to my side and admired Jake as he returned. His hair was matted with sweat, and I followed the lines of his neck muscles down over his shoulders.

"Were you checking me out?" he asked with a crooked smile as he climbed back into bed.

"You're not bad to look at."

He wrapped his arms around me, our faces inches apart.

"I hope that's not too forward," I joked.

"I think under the circumstances, it's acceptable." He planted a sweet, slow kiss on my waiting lips. Jake stroked my hair behind my ear and slowly combed his fingers through the strands. "Naya like a papaya . . ." He said it wistfully, stretching out the vowels. "I love your name. Where does it come from?"

"It's Arabic. Means 'new.'"

"Is your family from the Middle East?"

A chord of realization thrummed somewhere in my body. It had taken him three days to ask about my ethnicity. *Three days!* "What are you?" was almost a standard greeting after "nice to meet you." I hated that before people knew anything about me, they needed to know how to classify my ethnicity.

"No," I said with a small laugh. "My dad read it in a book or something. He's Black, and my mom is Irish and Mexican." Growing up multiracial, I sometimes didn't know where I fit. I remembered Felicia's sister telling me I had "good hair," which I thought was a compliment until I realized that meant my best friend's hair, thicker and kinkier than mine, wasn't good. My high school boyfriend told me his mom was fine with us dating because I wasn't like other Black people. My life had been filled with those moments, reminding me I was different. Jake didn't seem thrown, though.

Jake traced a lazy pattern over my shoulder. "Must have been something to grow up with multiple cultures."

It could have been a swirl of traditions, but my parents wanted us to blend into our small town, so I grew up with no real cultural traditions at all. I didn't speak Spanish, I was fair skinned, and I "sounded white" according to my Black cousins. Davis told me once I was lucky to be so racially ambiguous that no one had to know I wasn't white. He'd even encouraged me to publish under my middle name, which sounded "less urban." I'd hated myself for letting him say that without challenging him. I wanted to do something to reclaim the parts of myself I'd allowed him and so many others to make me think were unfavorable. I wanted to be able to talk to my grandfather in his native language before it was too late. *To do: Learn Spanish.*

I shrugged. "Sometimes, when I was a kid, I wished they had named me Jessica or Heather."

"I think Naya suits you better." Jake looked down, catching my eye as his palm skimmed my lower back.

"Just once, I want to find my name on a novelty pencil."

"Huh, I guess I never thought about that."

"Any story behind your name?"

"My grandfather is named Jacob. That's why I've always gone by Jake." He traced his fingers over my shoulders, lightly kneading the muscles between my back and neck.

"Were you close?"

"When I was little, I wanted to be just like him. He taught

me how to fish and that women were trouble, but the good kind. He still tells me that, actually. He's pretty busy these days as the Casanova of his assisted-living facility."

"So, you come by your charm genetically, huh?"

Jake laughed softly.

"My dad always told me boys were trouble, but he didn't mean the good kind."

"You think I'm the bad kind of trouble?"

"You're not so bad," I said, settling against him.

Our chuckles subsided, and we lay in another perfect, loose-limbed silence for several minutes.

My palm resting on his abs, I took in his face. "You look like you're thinking. Want to share?"

He trailed his hand up my arm. "I wish we had a little more time."

*I can't let myself think about having more time.* "I was thinking I can't move after that." I smiled, expecting him to have a joke ready, but he continued to look into my eyes the way he did when I tried to change the subject. His penetrating gaze made me wonder if he could tell I was avoiding something.

"You know, you're so beautiful when you get there," he said. "I could watch your face in those moments for hours. It's like you give up control and your features relax, even as the rest of your body is tensing." His voice was quiet and gravelly, and he grazed his thumb over my lips as he spoke. "Then, at the moment right before you come, your mouth opens, just a little, and you bite the corner of your lip. It's perfect. It might be my new favorite image."

"You're the only one who's ever seen it," I said, resting my cheek into his palm.

"What?"

*Oh crap, why did I admit that? I'm pretty sure that's on the list of things not to say after sex or, you know, ever.* "It's embarrassing."

"What did you mean?"

"I've never, you know . . . with someone else."

"Ever?"

*Kill me now.* "I just never . . . got there, and the guys never seemed to . . . um, I don't know, notice or care, I guess."

Gently, he pulled my hands from my face. "You've been with selfish men."

*Understatement.*

He kissed the corner of my mouth. "Am I a bad guy if I'm kind of proud to be the first?"

"Not in my book."

"I like the bossy side of you. And you'll tell me if you want something different, right? Harder, slower, to the left." He grinned, swiping his thumbs in slow circles at the nape of my neck. "Or just . . . keep going."

I laughed. "I promise to be as bossy as possible." Though, so far, he seemed to know exactly what I wanted.

I tucked against him and he rolled so we could slide under the sheet and comforter, creating a cocoon around our bodies. "Stay with me tonight?"

"I was really hoping you wouldn't kick me out." Jake pressed in behind me, his arm wrapping around my waist.

*A few days. A few days. A few days.* Enveloped in his warmth, I had to remind myself what this was, because he felt like safety, like home, like more.

# Fifteen

A streak of sunshine traversed my small room, leaving my face in a warm smattering of light. The blissful, bold euphoria of the night before, that magical state of sexual release, floated around me until that moment and then hurtled to the ground. I looked at the closed door to my bathroom, where the sound of running water emanated. *What was I thinking, putting my career at risk for sex?* Admittedly, it was really good, did–I–dream–that sex, but still.

I had to find some clothing. I needed to think clearly, and being naked wasn't helping. Jake's shirt on the floor was closer than my dresser, and I snatched it up, pulling the buttons closed and rolling up the sleeves. I paced by the window, biting the side of my thumbnail.

*I could tell him I changed my mind. Maybe I'll just ghost him after he leaves.*

The door opened, and Jake emerged, all tan muscles and piercing eyes. His black boxer briefs rode low on his hips, revealing his flat stomach, and he flashed me a sweet, playful grin.

"Good morning, Bossy. I like how you look in my shirt." His eyes skated up my body.

*Well, my career might not mean that much to me, after all.*

"I'm not sure I love that nickname. Do you really think I'm bossy?"

He sat on the edge of the bed and pulled me into his warm embrace for a soft kiss.

"I like that you say what you want, but I can pick another name." He rubbed his chin and let out a thoughtful "hm."

"I have to weigh my options," he said, sliding a hand down my back. "I could call you Fear Factor, if you prefer? I'm assuming you'll be digging into my psyche to figure out any other phobias and how else to test my mettle."

I rested my hands on his shoulders. "Hmm, what *are* your other fears? Clowns? Snakes?"

"No way I'm telling you. Who knows what you'd have me doing before I flew back to North Carolina."

*Subtle reminder: He is leaving.* "Wow. North Carolina. That's so far away. There's so much I don't know about you." I gazed around the room, playing with the ring on my right hand.

"I'll tell you anything you want to know, Naya like a papaya. Are you nervous?" His hands settled at my waist. I hadn't realized I'd been shifting from one foot to the other. "Work?"

"How did you know?"

He shrugged. "Just a guess. It is a *little* dicey, ethically, but I'll talk to our HR person."

I inhaled slowly and willed my hands to stop fidgeting. "Do you want to change the plan?"

He shook his head, and a mixture of relief and more questions flooded my chest.

"Isn't it a conflict of interest for you? Besides, what would you tell HR? 'I screwed the brains out of one of the faculty members at the school, but it won't impair my judgment'?"

Jake chuckled in response, and I cracked a smile, despite my anxiety—his humor was contagious. "Our HR director is my mother's age and kind of reminds me of my fourth-grade teacher, so I won't say *I screwed your brains out* . . ." His grin widened. "Unless you prefer I give her the full play-by-play?" He slid his fingers under the shirt to tickle my ribs, and goose bumps prickled as his palms skirted up my bare skin.

I rolled my eyes, but my body responded to him without my permission. "Seriously. What do you actually do, Jake? How bad could this be?" *To do: Google management consulting.*

"We determine which areas of the university are contributing and which are draining, financially or otherwise, and then we offer recommendations. It's a lot more complex than that, but essentially, that covers it." He fixed me with a pointed gaze, his hands sliding to rest at my waist again, thumbs making small circles on my hips. "Carlton is the front man on this, anyway."

"I don't think this is right," I insisted.

"I'll bring it up when I get back to the office. I promise."

"All right," I murmured, imagining the worst but resigned that I couldn't do anything that morning. Still, his thumbs made wider and wider circles, inching closer to where I wanted to feel him again.

"I'll give Muriel a hypothetical—"

I cut him off with a smirk and a raised eyebrow. "Muriel? Not Gladys?"

Jake's face cracked into a grin, and he pulled me closer, dropping a kiss on the tip of my nose. "You're beautiful."

"When I'm giving you shit?"

"Yes." His voice softened. "But the rest of the time, too."

I didn't know what to say to that, but my heart thumped wildly.

"Now," he added, his breath against my neck and his palms wandering, "will you come back to bed so I have more juicy things to confess to HR?"

# Sixteen

I filed the last email into the proper folder.

*Is there anything as satisfying as an empty inbox?*

I clenched my thighs as I had been doing all day. The slight ache there reminded me of the night before and that morning. *Maybe a few things are better.*

Campus was quiet enough that I could savor the feeling of having made it through the year. A definite upside of my job was having control over my summers—I didn't have to be in the office and could spend my days writing. That's what I did ordinarily. Maybe this summer, I'd try a few other things.

My phone buzzed, and I smiled before I flipped it over.

JAKE: How did work go today after Flip's announcement last night?

The warmth that spread through my chest had nothing to do with the sun beating through the windows from the cloudless sky or even the memory of multiple orgasms. I reread the message. He was thinking about me, and he thought to ask

about my work. I reminded myself this was a fling. I told myself that, but I grinned as I typed a reply.

>NAYA: Good. Boss is freaking out like everyone else, but I am
>celebrating the end of the year.

>JAKE: How are you celebrating?

I snapped a photo of my empty inbox, making sure my
email address and last name didn't show on the screen.

>JAKE: You don't know this, but that image is equivalent to
>pornography for me. So sexy.

>NAYA: How are the wedding preparations?

>JAKE: We're on hour three of decorating the reception hall.
>Apparently, we should be done with things by five . . . with
>an hour to spare before the rehearsal dinner.

>NAYA: That's brutal.

>JAKE: I don't know if I'll get to see you tonight until late.

>NAYA: I'm sure we'll figure it out.

My phone pinged with a photo message from him. It was
a selfie, his skeptical expression in the foreground and behind
him, a petite woman in a white T-shirt with *Bride* spelled out
in glittery pink script. She was surrounded by women in neon
pink T-shirts that read *Bridesmaid* in a matching font. They
were in one of the hotel ballrooms, and the bride appeared to
be scolding the leftmost woman.

>NAYA: Yikes. Intimidating . . . Don't screw up.

>NAYA: Wait, everyone in the background is in pink T-shirts . . .

The dots appeared, and a photo came through, another selfie,
but in this one, I could see his broad chest in a pink T-shirt,
his muscles defined under glittery script reading *Groomsman*.
My smile spread.

>JAKE: Offering you a glimpse into my own personal hell.

NAYA: You look good in pink. Will you model it for me in person?

JAKE: I would, if I didn't plan to burn it.

NAYA: You're no fun.

JAKE: That's not what you said this morning.

———

I finished a few last tasks and locked up my office to head home, fingering the screen of my phone on the walk to my car. I opened the app to type a new message but paused, realizing I had nothing to say. *Isn't mindless texting something you do in a relationship?* I slipped my phone back into my bag, because I was asking for trouble.

*I'm asking for trouble either way, right?* I pulled my phone back out when I thought back to his earlier texts that were cute and sweet. When I glanced up, I froze, nearly dropping my device.

Ahead of me, Davis was chatting with a tall brunette I didn't recognize. His gait and the way he held his head at an angle, chin tipped up all the time, sent blood rushing through my ears. He looked over in my direction, and our eyes met. A look of surprise crossed his face, and he paused his stride, then smirked. A chill wound up my spine as he raised his eyebrow, tipped his head slightly, then returned his gaze to his companion.

Terror stole my breath, and I took a few steps back, lingering in the doorway of a nearby building. My cheeks burned, and my heart thudded at that familiar, derisive expression.

*He's not supposed to be here.*

The panic that coursed through my body was worse than

it had been in years, and I struggled to keep myself from shaking as adrenaline flooded my system.

He and his companion laughed as they turned a corner and disappeared from my sight, but I worried he'd come back or wait for me. The image of him lingering by the car with no one around left my hands trembling, and I clasped them together. *I never got around to taking that self-defense class.*

Still, I didn't move. Each time I'd run into him after we split, I'd cowered and tried to make myself invisible. *That doesn't belong in past tense. I've been trying to make myself invisible ever since.*

I took a deep breath and tentatively stepped out of the doorway, glancing around and listening for voices from the parking lot. When I heard none, I grasped my phone and sprinted toward my car.

*I wish Jake was here.*

The thought ricocheted in my head. *Jake thinks I'm strong and know what I want.* I straightened my spine to tamp down the nervous energy threatening to overtake my body. When I reached my car, the lot was nearly empty, and Davis was nowhere in sight. Still, I slammed the car door and locked it within seconds. I didn't take a full breath until I was out of the parking lot. Even then, the hairs on the back of my neck stood on end, as if he was watching me through the car windows, waiting and scheming.

———

My unease hadn't settled by the time I stepped into the restaurant near Felicia's where I was picking up food. Across the room, an older couple read a newspaper together and a young mother tried to wrangle a squirming toddler into a high chair. My heart clenched, and I exhaled a breath I hadn't realized I'd been holding.

I'd built my career by staying late, doing more, working longer hours than others, and leveraging everything I could. I didn't regret it—I did, however, wonder who would read the paper with me when I was old and if I'd missed my window to have my own wriggling toddler.

*Thirty-three's not so old, is it?*

I watched a group of teenagers giggling as a handsome waiter exited the kitchen carrying a tray of sizzling fajitas. A man in a suit behind them rolled his eyes and looked at his watch, a bit more dramatically than was necessary.

My phone buzzed in my pocket, and an unknown number with an out-of-town area code flashed on the screen with a text.

UNKNOWN: It was nice to see you today.

UNKNOWN: Jill Jameson said she and you were
discussing me.

UNKNOWN: Good to know you're still thinking of me,
pretty girl.

I shivered and looked around the diner, but I knew he wasn't hiding there somewhere. He didn't have to. With those messages, I felt like he was standing next to me regardless.

# Seventeen

Felicia's kids had fled to the playroom after dinner, and we stretched out in her toy-strewn living room. A shock of hair from a doll's head precariously dangled out the side hatch of a toy helicopter on the end table next to me. The chaos of their house was always calming.

I'd sat in the restaurant parking lot with my eyes tightly closed and my phone shoved in my bag, as if the darkness of my purse could swallow up the texts. I willed myself to calm down and put it out of my head. Felicia would know something was up in an instant if I didn't lock away everything I was feeling, and I hated her worrying about me. *Put on a happy face.*

"Turner, you have no idea how bad I felt that both of us had to bail on you Tuesday."

After playing with the kids and joking with Felicia, my body had relaxed. Even if my life was in tatters, their house was safe. "It's okay. I understand. Aaron had to be with his mom, and I didn't want to catch your stomach flu, that's for sure."

She groaned. "I don't want to think about it. I even had to miss my workout with Wes the sexy trainer, and you know how bad it had to be for *that* to happen."

Felicia never exercised when we were kids or through college. She was one of those annoying people who didn't work out, gorged on whatever she wanted, and maintained a great figure. After the twins, though, she'd struggled to feel good about her body and started working out with a personal trainer. I was a little jealous—she looked great, of course, but she'd tell me about all the new things Wes was getting her to do: kickboxing, weight lifting, and even Pilates. I kind of wanted that, too.

"So, tell me about your date!"

I leaned back further into the comfortable couch and took a sip of coffee. I needed the caffeine after the late nights and the exhausting day. Despite everything else, a smile crossed my lips at the thought of Jake. My mind drifted to how his hips felt pressed to me during the dance lesson and the way his eyes kind of danced when he laughed. "I had a nice night."

"Did you sleep with him?" She eyed me. "You have no poker face. You slept with him. How was it? What happened?"

"It was . . . nice."

Her lips quirked up. "Bitch, you know that level of detail is insufficient. I can tell from your dopey expression that you're underselling." She pushed her hair off her shoulder and sat up straight.

She listened intently as I described everything from him

showing up with my sweater to kisses on the Ferris wheel and the night in his hotel room.

"Wow," she responded. "That's intense, Nay. And he's good with his hands?" Felicia waggled her perfectly shaped eyebrows. "Like, on a scale from Aiden to your wildest, porniest dreams, where would he fall?"

I laughed, remembering clumsy, fumbling Aiden Howard, my date to the senior prom who had finished in his pants without warning after I barely touched his zipper. At least we'd already taken photos. *That tux never stood a chance.*

"He's—" I searched for the right word, remembering how Jake's voice dipped low and got kind of gravelly and how he'd rubbed my back when I got sick in his hotel room that first night. "He's a class unto himself."

I paused again, taking a drink of my coffee. "And then last night . . ."

Felicia's jaw hit the floor when I explained the president's announcement and finding out Jake owned the consulting company.

"Are you allowed to hook up with him?"

"Probably not." The anxiety that had been lingering at the base of my neck all morning returned. "He came over after the event. We talked about it." I glanced at my mug to avoid her scrutiny.

"You talked?" Felicia asked before her eyes opened wide and her face lit up. "You were right and properly serviced last night, weren't you?"

I nodded, pressing my lips together to pull in my smile, and holding up three fingers. "And then again this morning."

"Shit, Turner. When you step out of your box, you really step out."

"I know, but . . ."

She gave me a knowing look. "It was that good, huh?"

"It was so far beyond good." Flashes of memory danced in my mind. "But it could be so bad for me if anyone found out."

Felicia sat back in her chair. "It doesn't sound like you'll be doing much besides tangling the sheets. You can keep it quiet."

"I hope so."

"Girl, this is big. You've been so closed off, especially with men. And I get it after what you went through, but . . ."

I nodded, doing my best to push that thought from my head again. Instead, I pulled up the photo of Jake and me from that first night and handed her my phone. "I've never reacted to someone like I do to him, and he's . . . generous."

"Shit." She exhaled slowly with a grin. "Does he have a brother?"

"You're married."

"I've been married a long time." Felicia laughed. "Gonna see him again?"

"I hope so. He's here through the end of the weekend, but he's in a wedding tomorrow."

She took another sip of her coffee and shook her head. "I'm glad he's good in bed. You deserve some quality action after your re-virginizing dry spell. Not that guys before that were anything to write home about."

That made me wince, remembering the guy I'd been with in graduate school and how he'd spend two minutes groping my breasts with kind of a honking motion before moving on to the main event. *Foreplay? Schmorplay.* It left me not only un-satisfied, but frustrated and embarrassed, like there was some-thing wrong with me.

I set my cup down. "It's weird. I feel . . . good with him. Not at all self-conscious. It's like I can get out of my head."

Felicia's boys flew into the living room and simultaneously screamed for her attention. While she played referee, I warily pulled my buzzing phone from my pocket. If it kept buzz-ing without me answering, Felicia would know something was wrong.

JAKE: Thomas wants to celebrate his last night of freedom by drinking all the whiskey in Chicago.

JAKE: Am I a bad groomsman if I ditch this fool to be with you?

NAYA: You must stay with your groom, for better or worse.

NAYA: Isn't there a bros before hoes clause in the man code?

JAKE: The loophole to that clause is a gorgeous woman who thinks I'm cute.

I closed the text window and looked up to see Felicia's self-satisfied smile.

"Who's that?" She sipped from her cup, giving me a know-ing look over the rim.

"Shut up."

# Eighteen

I set my glass on the counter and tied my robe. The scent of the lavender-infused candle filled my small bathroom and wafted into the bedroom. My muscles had relaxed after dinner with Felicia and the kids and two glasses of wine, but I was still a little jittery from seeing Davis and getting his texts. Outside my window, the streetlights cast circles of golden light over the uneven sidewalks below.

My phone chirped, and I spun to retrieve it from my nightstand, hoping it was Jake. It was, though on the screen was a photo of four scantily clad women doing shots with a guy who looked to be around forty.

JAKE: Remember the woo-hoo girls from the night we met? Their clones are here.

NAYA: Are you mixing and mingling?

JAKE: I am texting you.

NAYA: Let me guess . . . you'd prefer an intimate, dignified

gathering of gentlemen, sipping scotch in high-backed
chairs while smoking cigars? Discussing policy and finance?

JAKE: Because I'm a railroad tycoon from the 20s?

I carried my phone to the bed and lay back against the pillows, a grin on my face as my thumbs moved across my screen.

NAYA: Or a modern-day railroad tycoon.

JAKE: Do not pass go. Do not collect $200.

NAYA: Ba-dum-dum. What would you prefer to be doing?

JAKE: Anything involving you.

I read and reread the last text, goose bumps rising on my skin and my thighs clenching.

NAYA: Skydiving? Bungee jumping? Basketball?

JAKE: You're funny.

My fingers danced over my collarbone, and I remembered the taste of dulce de leche and scotch. My thumbs hovered over the screen in a temporary text paralysis. Arousal unfurled from low in my belly and spread out to my fingertips, which rested over my racing heart. I slid my thumb over the screen, unsure where this boldness was coming from all of a sudden. The ache between my legs definitely had something to do with it, but it was more knowing somehow that Jake would not judge me, that he'd go with me down the rabbit hole.

NAYA: Something naughtier?

NAYA: What's on the table?

JAKE: My jaw. Are you sexting me?

His last messages sent a jolt through me, and my center pulsed. I didn't exactly know what sexting entailed, but something told me Jake would be good at it, and I wanted to find out.

NAYA: Which emoji am I supposed to use?

JAKE: I'm no expert, but . . .

I watched the three dots disappear, and then the cake emoji popped up on the screen. I laughed, the sound filling my bedroom, and an oddly gleeful feeling mixed with my arousal.

NAYA: How did you know that would get me so hot?

JAKE: Lucky guess. I like getting you hot.

JAKE: Makes me imagine all the different ways I could . . .
     warm you up.

My nipples tightened to hard buds under my robe at the memory of his big hands pulling my body against him, the firm way he'd held me to him, and his dimples, deep divots that appeared when he smiled. All of it pushed me on.

NAYA: Between that and the cake, you're really succeeding.

JAKE: Was it mostly the cake?

NAYA: How do you know me so well?

NAYA: I'm just about to get in the bath and am all alone
     imagining you warming me up . . .

JAKE: Whatever will you do?

I snapped a photo of my fingers on the tied belt of my robe, and hit send along with the message Ten fingers, remember?

Being bold was natural with him. Of course, being behind a screen made it easier, but I had this sense he wouldn't think badly of me, that I could be this person with him without any real consequences.

JAKE: You're killing me.

JAKE: Are you touching yourself?

I grazed my free hand between my breasts, the tip of my middle finger over one pert nipple. Him asking felt so intimate, like he could see me. The thought of his eyes on me was more exciting than I would have predicted.

NAYA: 😊

JAKE: I want to continue this conversation, but I'm in public. The thing you're tempting me to do would get me arrested.

NAYA: I don't want to be responsible for yet ANOTHER man landing in jail for public indecency.

JAKE: So, you have a pattern. A dirty pattern.

NAYA: Hence the bath.

JAKE: There's a nice tub in my hotel room if you wanted to use it. I could meet you there in an hour.

JAKE: I'll have the desk give you a key.

NAYA: Are you asking me to keep my fingers at bay?

JAKE: Not at all. Not even a little. Just asking you to bring them closer to me. I just need to get the groom home safe.

JAKE: I'd love to see you tonight. Will you consider it while I corral him?

NAYA: Ok. Think of railroad tycoons and baseball in the interim.

JAKE: There is a 0% chance of me thinking of anything besides you and your ten talented fingers.

# Nineteen

I'd been lying on the luxurious hotel bed for ten minutes, dressed only in the pink groomsman T-shirt I'd found tossed over a chair. The fabric smelled faintly of Jake's cologne and his natural scent. A quick rap on the door and the beep of the lock drew my attention forward.

I'd envisioned doing a sexy slink to the end of the bed on my hands and knees and saying something breathy and alluring when he opened the door. What I actually did fell a little short of that, but Jake didn't seem to notice. "Hi," I said with a small, awkward wave. *Smooth.*

The surprise on his face made me wonder if he hadn't expected me to take him up on his offer. "You're in my bed . . . in my shirt."

I lifted my chin and shifted, as if to climb off the mattress. "Maybe I have the wrong room. I was supposed to meet an old-timey railroad tycoon."

He stood at the foot of the bed, mouth slightly agape, before crawling toward me. He looked up, heat in his eyes, and his fingers grazed reverently over my hip. "I'd have a joke for you, but thinking about your fingers has consumed all my brain power."

My skin tingled under his touch, and my core was increasingly wet with every caress. My anxiety began to calm, which was happening more and more often with his hands on my body.

"I should leave if I'm distracting you. I don't want to be responsible for a dearth of bad jokes."

"No, look at you . . . My God. Stay."

I laughed. "Well, I guess I could give you a minute or two."

"I don't know if I should be more offended that you believe I'd only last that long"—he returned to my neck and then back to my lips—"or that you'd be okay with leaving."

I slid my fingertips over the warm, taut skin along his abs and beneath the waistband of his jeans. The tension in the room heightened, our banter forgotten. His zipper slid down smoothly, and I reached inside to stroke his rigid length. He inhaled with a hiss, his mouth at my throat and his hands trailing down my spine.

"I'm not leaving," I whispered. I'd never taken control like this, and his sharp intake of breath pushed me forward. "Just in case you were wondering."

"Thank God," he murmured into my neck, before I slid down his body to take him in my mouth.

Jake's excitement, his obvious pleasure, sent a bolt of arousal through me. The way his groans rumbled from him in a frantic burst drove me so wild, I didn't want to stop. This wasn't the first time I'd done this, but it was the first time I'd enjoyed it. When I finished, his heavy breathing filled the room, and I slowly pulled away, embarrassed by how much that had turned me on. Something in the combination of his reaction and knowing that I was giving him that feeling, that I had the power to drive him to a place where he lost control, filled me with an odd burst of confidence. The sensible woman in my head reminded me I had given a blow job and not discovered the secret to world peace, but I ignored her. This felt great.

Jake opened his arms and pulled me to lay next to him, his hooded gaze scanning my face, sweeping his long fingers along my neck. "You're amazing."

"I might have read a few how-to articles in magazines," I joked.

He chuckled. "*That* was amazing, yes, but more than that . . . tonight . . . you being here . . . greeting me like this . . . all of it."

"Yeah?" I moved to my side as well, facing him, our bodies aligned, chests pressed together.

"You're so . . . unexpected." His index finger traced the top of my ear and down my jawline, and his expression was intense, like he was fighting with himself.

I glanced away from his stare, examining the stubble on his chin. His eyes bored into me, and I couldn't always handle it.

"It's not something I do. I need you to know that," he added.

I smiled, one eyebrow cocked. "You seemed to enjoy your first time."

He chuckled, his intense stare relenting. "No, there've been lots of women for that . . . Gladys, Mabel, Gertrude, Estelle . . ." He wrapped his arm around me, splaying his fingers across my back as I feigned offense.

"How do I rank?"

"Second only to Gladys," he returned, laughing at my indignant expression. "She didn't have any teeth!" We both let our giggles fade into smiles, staring into each other's eyes again.

"I'm serious, though. I don't know if you believe me. That sounds like something all guys say, but it's true." With a brush of his fingertips down my cheek, he added, "I think you're special. So even though this is just—"

"A few days." I finished his phrase.

"A few days," he repeated, "I don't want you to think you're a notch in my bedpost or something."

"I believe you." *Despite all my experience telling me not to.*

He kissed me, unhurried, and arousal pooled in my belly. "How was the bath?"

"I knew the jets could do a number on me, but I took a chance and waited for you." I stroked the nape of his neck, drawing circles on his skin.

"Mm, waited for me to take a bath *with you* or to do a number *on you*?"

"Both?" I rested my head against his chest.

His hand slipped down the back of my hair, combing through my tresses. "Whatever you want."

"Honestly, this is nice, right here." I had no intention of telling him why I longed for this sense of protection and being surrounded. Jake was everything I needed in a distraction. "How was the groom's last night as a bachelor?"

"Revealing," he said. "Thomas told us all about why he loves her, the rich tapestry that is Madison, more and more after each drink."

"That's not so shocking, is it?"

"I guess it shouldn't be. Thomas usually keeps his cards to his chest, but he was just . . . out there, open. Drunk off his ass, but still, madly in love with his twenty-one-year-old bride."

"That's sweet," I murmured.

"Made me wonder if I'll ever feel that way about someone." Jake's voice turned a little sad, and I bit my lip to stop myself from pressing further. His voice had a tinge of something different, something between bitterness and sadness.

I deflected, trying to put his change in tone out of my mind. "What time do you have to do wedding stuff tomorrow?"

"Meeting at nine to get a straight-razor shave at a barbershop, then we start up at ten thirty with three hours of photos."

"Wait, three hours? That's ridiculous, like diagnosably unhinged bridezilla behavior."

"Tell me about it. Then a ceremony at the church and the reception in a ballroom downstairs. The rehearsal tonight was chaos, so we'll see."

"Sounds like you'll have a busy day."

"I'm honestly more interested in my busy night." Jake's palms slid down my body, then inched back up my ribs, pushing the shirt over my head.

"Plans?" My words caught in my throat as he pressed his lips to one of my nipples, rolling his tongue in languid circles.

"Big plans," he murmured against my breastbone, the vibrations leaving my next breath a shaky inhale.

"I like plans." I sighed, my head falling back against the pillow as his hands caressed and stroked, telling me all the things he wanted to do.

Hours later, his body heat enveloped me. I didn't move a muscle, and I wasn't sure I could. "Hey, Jake?" I wanted to tell him I wasn't ready for our few days together to end, that the last week was unlike anything I'd experienced in my life, and I was afraid I'd never be this content again. But that also meant risking my career and everything I'd worked so hard to reclaim. *It means risking more than that.*

"Mm?" His sleep-heavy warm breaths puffed over the top of my ear.

I wanted to tell him we could screw the rules and see where this led, but that would mean trusting him and giving him the power to hurt me, or to control me, and I'd sworn I'd never do that again. I was already putting myself in a precarious situation if anyone from work found out.

*But he's not Davis.*

*And no one has to know.*

"Nothing."

He kissed my neck, his body relaxing against me, and my eyes drooped. I fell asleep with his hard, warm chest against my back.

---

I had every intention of slipping out of bed and taking an Uber home after a quick pleasure-induced catnap. But when I woke again, the room was filled with a dim light, and I was alone in the bed. My eyes snapped open as I tried to get my bearings in an unfamiliar environment.

The bathroom door swung open, and Jake emerged, scrubbing at his hair with a towel. "Did I wake you?"

"You didn't." I rubbed at my eyes and sat up against the

headboard, pulling the sheet up to cover my breasts. "What time is it? I'm sorry. I didn't mean to stay over."

"About eight forty-five—I have to meet Thomas and get to the barbershop soon." Jake grabbed a pair of jeans from his nearby suitcase and pulled them up and over his thighs. When he settled on the bed next to me, his hair was in all different directions, and there were a few drops of water on his shoulders I wanted to kiss away. "Good morning," he said with a smile, leaning in to plant a soft peck on my lips. "I'm glad you stayed. I wish we had more time for a proper good morning, but you looked so peaceful sleeping, I didn't want to wake you."

I swept a hand over his tousled locks. Jake closed his eyes briefly as my fingernails grazed his scalp. A barely audible sigh slipped from his mouth, and my lips turned up as I took in his long eyelashes and the firm set of his jaw. I imagined waking up like this every morning with those soft, sexy moments together. I'd slept like a rock without the usual middle-of-the-night startles or bouts of insomnia.

*Stop it. It's a few days.*

"I'll get out of here so you can go," I said after a moment, letting my hands fall and breaking the kiss. "It will only take me a few minutes to get ready."

"Stay," Jake said, not pulling back. His blue eyes were still focused on my mouth.

"I shouldn't." I made a move to stand, but I was still covered in only the sheet.

"Up to you, but you could sleep longer or take that bath we never got around to. No need for you to rush on my account. We didn't exactly get a lot of rest last night." Jake grinned before glancing over my shoulder at the bedside clock. "Shit, I have to go." He reluctantly rose, pulled a T-shirt from his suitcase, and grabbed his watch and wallet from the dresser.

I followed the lines of his back and shoulders as he pulled on shoes and glanced at the clock again. "I have wedding stuff all day. But I'll talk to you later?"

I nodded, and he pressed his mouth to mine again, his tongue sweeping my bottom lip. He tasted like toothpaste, which I found oddly comforting and familiar.

"It will be pretty amazing knowing you're here, naked in my room," he said with a wink before he stepped into the hallway.

It *was* kind of amazing. Every time I woke up with him, I couldn't help but wonder if I was waking up to myself a little more. I leaned my head back against the headboard with a sigh and held in my smile, trying to rein in my reactions to this man who seemed a little more irresistible with every interaction. *It's just sex. It's just sex. It's just—* Before the door clicked shut, I heard a husky alto voice call out from nearby. "Good morning, Jacob."

My head snapped back up at the use of his full name. I pulled the sheet around me and tiptoed closer to the door. I felt utterly ridiculous spying on the conversation, but I listened anyway.

The woman's voice came through the door, so they must have been standing close. "Quite the coincidence that we're neighbors," she said. This time it sounded like a purr. Something a lot like jealousy rose in me.

"You know I prefer Jake, and I'm sure it isn't. Good morning, Gretchen." Jake's voice, even muffled through the door, sounded formal and stiff. I'd never heard his words so clipped or his consonants so tightly articulated.

My muscles tensed, and goose bumps formed on my arms. *Who is Gretchen?*

"I've always called you Jacob. You know I detest nick-names."

"Well, I no longer have to care what you detest."

There was a pause before she spoke again. "Have fun with your overnight guest?"

"That's not really your business, Gretch."

"Well, I am your wife, so I'd say it's my business."

# Twenty

*I let someone in for the first time in three years and he's cheating on his wife?* A flush rose up my neck, and shame settled as a heavy lump in my belly. I hadn't realized I'd taken a couple steps away from the door, my arms crossed over my stomach. *No, no, no.* I looked around the room as if someone would materialize to absolve my guilt or justify my rage. *How did I read this so wrong?*

The woman's voice continued. "The walls are thin, and whoever you picked up was quite . . . vocal, so it's not like you need to tell me."

I cringed, trying to recall the number of times I'd cried out, unable to control my voice or my body. *How mortifying for me. How agonizing for her. Oh, God.*

"Do you already have someone on the side?"

Jake's voice rumbled. "We're separated, so if I *am* seeing someone, she's not *on the side*, she'd be at the center." He continued, his voice lower. "*On the side* is what you and Charlie did."

"You're going to throw that in my face here? At least *Charles* made time for me. Does your girlfriend know you'd rather pore over spreadsheets than get between the sheets? That nothing comes ahead of work?"

"Please, keep your voice down."

I pictured him running a hand through his hair the way I'd seen him do the night of the party at Flip's house. I also wondered if him continuing to dismiss the work conflict between us was him putting me ahead of work. Though, maybe being with a workaholic would take the pressure off me to balance everything. *Who cares? He's married!*

"Did you come out here just to yell at me? Is there something you want, Gretchen?"

Another beat of silence passed before she spoke again. Her voice had softened. "No, Jacob, wait. I'm sorry. That was out of line. You know how I get when I'm stressed. I can't stand Thomas's barely legal bride, and I'm worried he's making a huge mistake."

"She's not that young, and he loves her."

"Love isn't always enough." Her voice further softened, and I wondered if they'd walked down the hall.

The edge faded from Jake's tone by a fraction. "Maybe with the right person, it is."

I imagined her wincing at his words. When she spoke again, her voice had returned to a louder, more clipped tone.

"You promised you'd keep up appearances around my family. Please do."

"I already promised I would. I need to go, Gretch. Your brother and the guys are waiting." Jake's voice faded as the sentence continued, and I realized he must have been walking away.

Gretchen's voice was still clear and loud. "Try not to sleep with anyone else on the way to the lobby, will you? My parents are staying in this hotel, too."

I held my breath, an unrealistic fear taking over my body that she would rush the door and confront me in person, but she remained silent, and then I heard the beep from the room next door.

Walking back across the room and looking for my phone, I released the breath. *What the hell?* What was I doing standing naked in a room where the scent of sex still hung in the air twenty feet from his wife? I needed advice and dialed Felicia's number.

Felicia picked up after three rings. "You never call me this early in the morning. What's going on?"

Remembering Gretchen's comments about the thin walls, I lowered my voice and slipped into the bathroom. "I need your help."

"Sure . . . kids are in a Netflix trance. I have a few minutes. Why are you whispering? Are you okay?"

"His *wife* is in the room next door. She heard us, and now I need to get out of here."

"Slow down. Back up . . . He's married?" I pictured Felicia's knit brow as she tried to make sense of my hurried, hissed speech.

"I just overheard . . . I think he's separated, but he never said anything about it, and she's right next door. She heard us. What if she sees me?"

"Just walk out. Unless . . ." She paused, and I heard the smile in her voice. "You're not, like, tied to a bed or something, are you?"

"No, of course not!"

"Just checking—don't act like you haven't been doing a lot of things outside the norm lately!"

"Fel, this is serious. What do I do?"

I leaned against the bathroom counter and caught my reflection. I looked properly sexed up—hair in tangles and my eyes sleepy from the late-night exertions. My late-night exertions with someone else's husband.

Felicia continued. "I don't know. What exactly did you hear?"

I recounted the parts I could remember, prickles of embarrassment winding up my body. "It was so bitter."

"Certainly sounds like two people in a bad marriage."

I nodded, trying to come up with a plan.

"You'll be fine, Nay. Take a shower, get dressed, and just walk out."

Felicia's reassurance set my nerves slightly at ease. Though, I still pictured this faceless woman cornering me in the lobby and yelling at me for sleeping with her husband while hundreds of strangers looked on.

"Please tell me the sex was at least good, though? If he ends up being a cheating jackass, I want you to have gotten a few good orgasms out of it. I spent the last hour watching a cartoon pig solve mysteries by learning to spell . . . I need adult details."

I glanced at my reflection again. My chin was a little red from his stubble. I flexed my hand—the outer part of my palm hurt from when I'd smacked it into the wooden bedside table when Jake had done something with his tongue that set me on fire. "I'm not giving you a play-by-play while your kids watch cartoons ten feet away. But yes, it was good." *Great. Amazing. Holy hell.*

Felicia sighed. "I like this new version of you, Turner. The confident and sex-crazed version."

I rolled my eyes, though I kind of liked this version, too. I wondered what would happen in two days when this experiment ended. It was hard to imagine starting over again and trying to flirt with another bartender. "Okay, thanks for talking me down, Fel."

"Go home and take a nap since you were up all night with Mr. Consultant-the-Wonder-Cock."

"Jesus, Fel. Aren't your kids right there?"

"You don't seem to understand what I mean when I say they're in a *Netflix trance.* The house could burn down around them and they wouldn't notice."

Following Felicia's pep talk, I took a quick shower and snuck out of the room, closing the door softly, before almost sprinting to the elevators.

*Walk of shame after sleeping with a married man. Seems a fitting addition to the list. Check.*

———

I tried napping but felt jittery all morning. I paced my small living room, trying to find one thing to focus on, but my head swirled with everything going on.

*My job's in jeopardy.*

*I'm sleeping with the married consultant hired to make that decision.*

*Oh, and Davis is back and who knows what he's planning to do.*

It was after noon when I fell onto my couch with an exasperated sigh and stared at my ceiling. I'd woken up feeling like I had things in my grasp, and after learning Jake was married, I was questioning everything again. My phone buzzed, and I glanced at it. Jake had texted a few times that morning, but I hadn't replied, and I considered not responding to any future messages. I looked at my phone again, though. Ignoring it was what old Naya would do, so I thought about the list and mentally added *Demand answers*. This time, I opened his message.

> JAKE: I wish you were here. Want to crash the bridal party photos?
>
> NAYA: How could you not tell me you're married?

The dots indicating he was typing moved and then stopped, started again and then disappeared. I waited an entire two minutes, which felt like an eternity, watching the dots bounce and disappear.

> JAKE: I'm sorry. Will you let me explain?
>
> NAYA: Why should I?
>
> JAKE: You probably shouldn't, but will you give me a chance anyway?

I'd risen to my feet, pacing as I thought of a response. I didn't want to let him explain. I'd made promises to myself about not putting up with liars, about cutting manipulators out of my life. I hadn't expected Jake to fall into either of those categories, but it looked like he might fall into both.

> JAKE: You don't have to forgive me. I just want to apologize in person for hurting you.

I bit my lower lip, resolve chipping away.

# Twenty-one

I opened the door to Jake in his tux. His jaw was smooth, though his expression was frantic.

"I'm sorry." The words spilled out and brought my attention back to the moment. "I'm married. But only legally. We've been separated for over a year, I swear."

I avoided eye contact with him, glancing at my feet instead. It wasn't fine. I stepped aside to let him in—seeing him in person was probably a mistake, because my body still reacted to him as if nothing had changed. "I overheard you talking in the hall this morning."

"Shit." He reached for my hand, his fingers grazing my wrist, and I recoiled. His shoulders slumped a little, his eyes wide. "Ten minutes. Please, let me at least explain."

I didn't want to care about his explanation, but I couldn't shake how he'd made me feel the last few days. "Fine. Ten minutes," I said with a tilt of my head, inviting him in.

*Pushover.*

I searched for similarities to Davis, scrutinizing the cut of his jaw and the shift of his eyes as he spoke, looking for tells that he was lying, looking for evidence he wasn't worth it.

"We were married for six years, and then I found out she was having an affair with our neighbor." Jake glanced away. "Her family . . . her parents are like the Cleavers and really conservative. She begged me to keep the real reason for our split from them. I didn't do it for her, but they would have been hurt by the truth, mortified, and I didn't want to do that to them. They'd become my family, too." His voice dipped low, and I thought I saw a flash of something across his face. *Bitterness? Anger? Loss?*

"So you let them think it was you? They must hate you."

He nodded with a sigh. "I'm not very popular with them, but I could never do something to drive a wedge between her and her parents." He ran his fingers through his hair, puffing out a large breath.

His words spilled out, one on top of the other. "The divorce is almost final. I was as close with her brother as with my own sisters, and even though Gretchen and I separated, he still wanted me to be in his wedding. It was probably a bad idea."

"You're in your ex-wife's brother's wedding? Sounds . . . It sounds a little hard to believe. You didn't even tell me you'd been married." My voice was small, smaller than I wanted it to be because rage and shame tangled in my chest.

He rubbed his palms to his eyes. "Ugh, yes." He shook his head. "It sounds like a lie, but it's true. I swear. I'm sorry I didn't tell you." He spoke fast, his expression pinched and his brow wrinkling. "I should have. I just . . . We met at a bar. I didn't want to be that guy, the guy with baggage. I didn't think it mattered. It was only a drink, then just one night, and now . . ."

We sat in silence for a minute or two, and I thought about baggage.

He nudged my foot with his. "Are you kicking me out?"

"Not yet." I wrapped my arms around myself. "It's not like we're . . . I mean it's just a few days."

He took my hands in his, and I dared a glance at his face. He was staring at me again. "I've been thinking about you all day."

"I thought about you all day, too. I mean, I was furious, but still . . ."

He didn't respond immediately, and we sat in silence. "Sounds fair." His long fingers stroked up my back, rubbing the nape of my neck. "Are you still furious?"

"I'm breaking so many rules with you. I *want* to be furious."

He nodded, the hint of a smile curving on his lips. "But . . . ?"

"I have no reason to believe you . . . except that I do." I wasn't sure if I was a pushover destined to be lied to or if he was special. Maybe both.

He'd said he didn't want to be the guy with baggage, and I was hiding a full set behind my walls.

"In the last few days," he said, his voice still low and solemn, "I've been more myself with you than I have with anyone in a long time. Can we still have one more night?"

I wanted to tell him not to lie to me again, but what kind of unreal hypocrisy was that? I nodded, lifting my chin to meet his eyes. "One more night."

# Twenty-two

The faint smell of sandalwood filled my nostrils, and I pressed my face into the soft surface of my pillow. Slowly, awareness knitted together around me, and I smiled before my eyes opened. Jake's face was inches from mine, and the heat from his body made me crave more contact with his skin. He gazed at me from under impossibly thick eyelashes. How long had he been watching me sleep? *God, those eyes.* The window behind him showed a flat gray sky, no trace of sunshine on our last hours together. *Fitting.*

"Good morning."

At the sound of his gravelly morning voice, heat rose on my cheeks and spread across my chest as the memories from the night before flooded back. The feel of his hands and mouth, and how he'd looked at me like a crystal clear deluge.

I rubbed my eyes, stifling a yawn. "What time is it?"

"It's after eight." His voice was raspy and just above a whisper. "I woke up maybe an hour ago."

Under the blanket, his finger touched mine. It was a tiny, soft gesture, the smallest point of contact—a sweet reconnection. "But I didn't want to leave you yet," he added.

When he spoke, images of squirming toddlers and reading the paper together in bed ran unbidden through my mind. *Pull it together, heart.*

I admired the line of his biceps cradled beneath his head and changed the subject. "Was I interesting while I slept?"

"Very." A second finger met mine under the blankets.

"Talking? Something sultry and mysterious?"

"No." He grinned. "Just snoring."

My expression must have been one of horror, because he laughed.

"Don't make that face. It was cute."

"Oh, God. Really?" I raised my hands to cover my face. "That's so embarrassing." *Maybe my next career move will be writing a book titled* How to Fail at Flirting and Still Get Laid.

"No," he reassured me, a smile in his voice. "It was sweet. A sexy snore, even." He touched my arm, trying to tug my fingers from over my face.

"I'm going to go hide in the bathroom," I moaned. I turned to climb out of bed, realizing I was naked and I would have to walk the short distance across the room. Jake must have seen my brow furrow; the mattress dipped as he shifted.

"Here," he said, handing me his white shirt. "But will you promise to come back if I rescind my snoring comment?"

After I pulled the shirt over my head, I walked across the room, feeling his gaze on me. *I could get used to pulling on his shirts in the morning.* I smiled over my shoulder, sweetly. "We'll see." As I walked, my muscles protested, sore from last night's

workout, and with each step I remembered the ways we'd contorted our bodies on the bed, in the shower, up against the wall.
I groaned and then gaped at my reflection in the mirror—my
hair was going in every direction and my lips were swollen. I
looked happy, too, a small grin pasted onto my face when I remembered the look on his face when I'd woken up. *He heard
me snoring and still didn't want to leave.* I was sick at the thought
of never kissing him again. *And that isn't going to work, girl, because he's leaving . . . and he's married . . . and he's career suicide.*

I washed my hands and tried to flatten my hair with my
palms, which was as successful as my attempt at getting my emotions back in check—both ended up just as messy for my trying.

I took a deep breath and returned to the room, gripping
the hem of the T-shirt and tugging it down.

Jake was sitting on the edge of the bed when I emerged. His
hair was mussed, and he smiled, brows lifting. "I like you in my
clothes, but you know, I've seen you naked a few times now."

"I know . . . It's different in daylight." *Stop being so awkward.*

"Do you want me to go?" The way his eyes locked with
mine, I felt exposed far beyond my body. I didn't know how
one glance could communicate that or could scare me in a way
that made my heart jump.

"No!" I walked toward him, letting go of the hem of his
shirt. "No, I don't want you to go. I'm just bad at . . . flirting
and being cute. Can we start over?"

He tilted his head, the smile returning to his lips. "Good
morning, Naya." He gripped my waist and pulled me between
his spread knees. The skin on his shoulders was smooth and
lightly freckled, the muscles solid under my palms.

"Good morning, Jake."

His smile widened when I said his name, and my anxiety tapered off.

"You seem nervous," he said, looking up at me, his thumbs rubbing small circles over my hip bones. "And, for the record, I think you're incredibly skilled at being cute."

I didn't answer and, instead, changed the subject. "How did things go yesterday with your—um—with Gretchen?" I couldn't bring myself to say *wife*, especially after hearing their conversation yesterday morning.

"As awkward as you'd expect, but it's over, and I don't have to see her for a while."

My heart squeezed at his earnest expression.

"You still believe me, right? I swear it's over. I'm not cheating. I would never."

"I believe you." I threaded my fingers into his hair, scraping my nails along his scalp the way he liked.

A low moan escaped his lips, and his thumbs stopped their circling to migrate down to my thighs.

"You get on a plane in six hours," I said, voice breathy.

His mouth was a resigned line as he stroked my backside, then pulled me against him, still kneading in a teasing and delicious way.

I couldn't help but wonder what the line of his mouth meant. *What do I want it to mean?* "I've only got two or three hours to make sure you don't forget me," I said.

I took in the look on his face, to store the details. No matter how much I wanted this to be more, I knew it couldn't.

"Naya, I'm not going to forget you. What if—"

I kissed him, a hungry, deep kiss that stopped his words but didn't quiet my thoughts. *Don't give me the option of "if."*

Jake's tongue rolling with mine, the firm grip of his hands on my body, his arousal, undeniable between us—I cataloged it all, knowing I'd want to recall every moment later when I returned to the closed comfort of my office. Somewhere between waking and climbing on top of him, I'd tried to convince myself that my work would sustain me. If I kept telling myself I didn't need silly jokes and soft touches and kisses that left me breathless if I had my research and my teaching, would I begin to believe it? I knew it was no use. No amount of hoping would change who he was or who I was, so I memorized how it felt to live this kind of life, and when we pulled apart, I cupped the side of his face. "Three hours."

A doleful expression crossed his features before he dipped his head to kiss down my neck. "I know."

# Twenty-three

G reen umbrellas shaded the coffee shop's patio, which was the ideal location to meet Aaron and work. I'd submitted an article to a top journal about the use of computer games in teaching math, especially for students whose first language was not English. I'd been hopeful, but staring at page after page of harsh critique from the reviewers, I wondered where I would even begin revising it.

"Why do you look so angry?" Aaron returned from inside the shop holding a disposable coffee cup. He was in a suit, having just come from a job interview, and I wasn't used to him looking so dignified. His first teaching job had been in one of the city's underfunded, overburdened public high schools, and after spending a few years in the lily-white, elite, suburban private school where he worked now, he wanted to go back.

"What? I'm not angry." I looked up from a particularly scathing question about the necessity of studying math development in immigrant children. I wasn't sure why I lied—I was furious at the thinly veiled racism in the comments. I'd gotten so used to hiding when I was upset that it had become second nature. "Okay, I'm a little angry, but I'm just trying to make sense of these comments on this article."

"Can you ignore them?"

I could, but the reviews were anonymous, and I had no idea what weight that person held. I wanted a few more publications under my belt before I submitted my tenure application. I had a lot, but I preferred to leave no room for doubt. I shook my head, minimizing the window. I could go back to it when I returned to my office.

I'd been cloistered there for the last two weeks since Jake went home. Those days had been back to normal—I woke early and went for a run, worked most of the day, and relaxed at home alone in the evening. The only thing that was different was me eyeing the clock. For the first time in a long time, I admitted to myself that spending every day in my tightly regimented bubble was unsatisfying. I thought I'd have my little tryst and get it out of my system, but I kept thinking about Jake. Jake's scent. Jake's hands. Jake's laugh. Jake's job and the giant, conflict-of-interest-sized hole Jake had the potential to punch through my career.

*To do: Find more writing projects to keep my mind busy.* In my head, I crossed that out. *To do: Figure out how to make money from writing if I lose my job.* Again, I made a mental adjustment. *To do: Figure out how to make money stripping when I lose my job. Side note: Ask Aaron's mom.*

I chuckled to myself in my head as Aaron drank his coffee and checked his watch.

The afternoon sun would give way to backed-up traffic soon. "Have to go?"

He shrugged. "Soon, but Felicia told me about that guy, that married one. It's like you're in the middle of a romance or a porno or something. What gives?"

"You're the ones who gave me the list!"

"I didn't think you'd check everything off in one night. I didn't think you'd use it at all."

"I guess I can still surprise you. And, for the record, he's getting divorced."

Aaron nodded. "And . . . ?"

"He was nice. I had fun. It was . . ." I struggled for the right phrase, words I was uncomfortable with already rising in my throat.

*Paradigm altering. Hands down, the best week of my life. Real. Earth-shattering.*

"It was unexpected, but it was nice."

"Gonna see him again?"

Jake's expression from that last morning stuck in my memory. It had held a flash of sadness. In that moment, I'd wondered if we should try for something more, but it was impossible, so I told him to look for me the next time he was in a woo-hoo girl wedding. Then we'd laughed, he'd kissed me again, we said goodbye, and that was it.

"No, it was just one of those things. You know my life. I don't have time for that, and, besides, it was a no-strings thing. It would be a bad idea with work, anyway."

"Have you ever *done* a no-strings thing?"

"I guess I have now. I think of it like an extended one-night stand. A one-week stand."

Aaron cocked an eyebrow. "You, my friend, did not do no-strings or any kind of stand. You ended up in a weeklong love affair." Aaron gave me a pointed look before checking his phone again and grimacing at the time. "I better get outta here. See you later?"

After he left, I sipped my iced hazelnut latte and glanced at my laptop. I could search for Jake. It wouldn't be hard to find his company's website. I had the photo of us on my phone, but my fingers itched to click around, to collect more crumbs. I shook my head and instead opened a different project, a book chapter I wanted to polish before submitting. As I read through a paragraph, wincing at my clumsy first draft, my phone buzzed with a notification.

JAKE: Hi.

My heart rate sped up, and I stared at the simple message. I'd spent more time than I was ready to admit to reading old text exchanges, refreshing the app needlessly. I would chastise myself for being pathetic and then check my phone again for new messages. I'd been the one to clarify a few days was all we had. Of course, not five minutes after reminding myself that I'd made it clear we were only for those few days, I had returned to my phone.

I typed a reply, pushing doubt out of my head.

NAYA: Hi.

I started adding a follow-up message, typing and deleting *How are you? What's going on?* and *New phone. Who dis?*

JAKE: Listen, Gladys, I met someone while I was in Chicago.

JAKE: I'm not sure she even wants to talk to me.

JAKE: But she was pretty great, and I can't get her out of my head, so I'm trying.

NAYA: So awkward, but this isn't Gladys.

JAKE: Oh my God, Myrtle . . . don't get the wrong idea.

JAKE: Kidding. I gave up the harem of senior librarians.

JAKE: Just realized this joke makes me sound like a
womanizing asshole.

JAKE: I hope you're laughing.

NAYA: I am and I'm 99% convinced the librarians aren't real ☺

NAYA: It's nice to hear from you.

I couldn't stop the grin from spreading across my face.

JAKE: So, it turns out I need to come back to Chicago next
week for work.

JAKE: Can I see you? Take you to dinner?

I paused again, my fingers hovering over the keyboard
while I bit my lower lip. I should have responded with one of
three things. Option one: No, I can't put my career at risk. Option two: No, we agreed to a few days and that's it. Option
three: You're still married, and I can't keep ignoring my moral
compass.

NAYA: When do you arrive?

JAKE: Thursday morning.

NAYA: I can make Thursday night work.

JAKE: 😄

*I have a date, a real date.* I caught myself lifting my shoulders in a little dance and glanced around to see if anyone was
watching my silly display. No one appeared to notice the grown
woman moments away from doing the cabbage patch, and I
returned to grinning at my laptop, the writing seeming just a
little better on this pass.

My phone buzzed again, and sweet anticipation of what
Jake might say next flooded my system. I expected a fun text

or something a little naughty, but *unknown* flashed on the screen. I froze, clutching the edge of the table.

UNKNOWN: Found some old photos. Remember this one?

As the image of my naked body filled the screen, my blood went cold.

*No.*

Davis had snapped the photo without warning, which he'd started doing several months into our relationship. At first, he maintained that it was fun to have sexy photos of me, like it was a game for him to take them without my permission, even though I told him to stop. By the end, he'd dropped the pretense and it was another in a long line of things he did to keep me on edge.

UNKNOWN: Not a very professional look.

UNKNOWN: Heard you're close to tenure.

UNKNOWN: It's such a subjective process, tenure review. So many outside things can influence their decision to promote you.

*No, no, no.* I put my phone down and pressed my eyes closed. It wasn't a threat exactly. *Who am I kidding? Of course it's a threat.*

The idea of anyone seeing those pictures made me shudder. It wasn't even so much people seeing my body; it was him having control of who saw it. I didn't know what to do to stop him. I couldn't imagine admitting to someone else those photos existed. How could I face Joe or my students? *Jake. He'd be horrified.* I dropped my head into my hands and inhaled a few shallow breaths, trying to talk myself down. I'd never gone to the police or human resources after we split, convinced he'd just twist everything around to make himself look good and that no one else would think it was a big deal. And now, after waiting for so long, there'd be no way they'd take this seriously.

I typed a reply before deleting the thread.

NAYA: Don't message me again.

UNKNOWN: We'll talk soon, pretty girl.

The memory of his pet name crept over my skin. I looked around at the crowd in the coffee shop—the space bustled like normal, the friendly smile of the barista and the nutty aroma of brewing coffee undisturbed by this unexpected interruption. Wrapping a shaky hand around my coffee cup, I tried to take a drink, but it did nothing to quell the rising panic.

I shouldn't have responded and given him the satisfaction of getting under my skin. Goose bumps rose on my arms.

*Jake will be here soon. Jake will be here soon.*

I realized with striking clarity the last two times I'd freaked out about Davis, I'd run to Jake, someone I barely knew. Here I was thinking he could save and protect me, but that wasn't a solution. It wasn't even in the ballpark of a solution.

I took another sip of coffee, trying to swallow the worry and panic and fear along with the milk and espresso. *I'll deal with it. I always deal with it. I'll just be careful. I can weather this.*

I packed up my things and hurried for home, longing for the safe comfort of my locked door.

# Twenty-four

By the time Thursday arrived, I'd managed to pull myself together and had even been able to sleep a little each night. When fear or worry bubbled up, I'd repeat my mantra—*I'll deal with it*—and push the anxiety aside, convincing myself if I didn't acknowledge it, it didn't exist. I met Jake in my building's lobby, and at first glance, I felt safer than I had all week.

He leaned against a pillar and smiled from ear to ear when we made eye contact. He wore a white dress shirt with faint gray vertical stripes and gray suit pants. His face held the hint of a five-o'clock shadow, and his hair was a little shorter than it had been a few weeks ago, but his lips were the same—full and very kissable. I was glad I'd suggested the lobby—if he were at my door, I would have just pulled him inside.

"Hi." I smiled tentatively, and we stared at each other for a moment. *Well, what do we do now? Something between a handshake and dry-humping in the lobby?* I reached to his shoulder and kissed his cheek, immediately questioning if I should have gone for it and brushed my mouth to his.

"Shall we?" He motioned to the door. Our arms grazed periodically as we made our way to the exit and the bustling street beyond. As we waited for the car to arrive, he spoke in my ear. "What's at the bottom of the ocean and shivers?"

I tipped up my chin, awaiting the punch line.

"A nervous wreck."

I rolled my eyes, my lips quirking. "A joke already?"

"You like my jokes." He held the door of the car for me to slide in. Once he was settled next to me, he added, "And I was nervous to see you again."

"Me, too," I admitted as I gave the driver the address of the restaurant.

"And now?" He raised his eyebrows a fraction of an inch.

"The joke helped." I downshifted into small talk and kept reminding myself it was a bad idea to reach across the seat and pull his face to mine.

The restaurant was cozy without feeling claustrophobic. We settled at a table near the back, the lighting low while soft music hummed under the muted buzz of a multitude of private conversations. My knee bounced under the table, and we ordered wine. I set a hard limit of two glasses and renewed my commitment to avoiding gin. Though, after a few beats of awkward silence, I wondered if I should up my consumption of liquid courage. *Does he want sex or something more?* Instead, I said, "I googled you. You didn't tell me you were such a big deal." That was an understatement. Hundreds of results popped up, heralding him as some kind of virtuoso who'd consulted all over the world. From what I could decode from the financial jargon, he sounded like the second coming of Alexander Hamilton.

"I assumed searching was against the rules," he said. "What if you saw something you didn't like, and I wasn't able to explain?"

"I already know about your hemorrhoids, your wife, and the librarians. What more could there be for me to learn? That said, you didn't tell me you were *the* guy."

"I'm not *the* guy. Just *a* guy. I did well at my last firm, but running our own shop is a whole new challenge. I enjoy it, but Thurmond is one of our first big accounts, and, I'll admit, we need it to go well."

*Some of it going well is recommending people get fired, right?* I pushed down the thought.

"I haven't searched for you yet," he said, shifting focus from himself and sipping his wine. "What will I find?"

"Are you worried?" There wasn't much to find about Naya Turner. I was more concerned that he'd learn how unremarkable I was.

"No, but can you give me a hint? You don't run a drug cartel on the side or have a thriving porn career to fund your research, do you? Not deal breakers. I'd just like to be prepared."

"I gave up the cartel months ago. Who has the time?" My joke earned me a chuckle, and my knee stopped shaking under the table. I loved that he appreciated my sense of humor. I could be silly with him. "I think you'll mostly find work things."

"That's okay—we haven't talked about work yet."

"Speaking of work . . ." My stomach oscillated between

knots of anxiety and flutters of excitement with every thought of Jake and my job.

"I spared Muriel the finer details of our time together." He flashed a high-watt, crooked smile. Jake must have noticed my tense expression, because his tone sobered. "She said it was a bad idea, but—"

I stiffened. "Oh. I see."

He hurried to finish his statement. "She said it's a bad idea *in general* but wasn't talking about our specific situation. She doesn't have your name, because I don't know your last name. Muriel gave me quite the ass chewing for that, by the way." His voice was calm. "She said it's not an explicit rule, not something in writing. I think as long as we're careful, we should be able to avoid complications."

"So, what does that mean?"

"Basically, it means we're being naughty." His smile was easy, even as nerves tingled up the back of my neck. "But we're not technically breaking the rules. It might also mean you should tell me your last name so Muriel stops giving me the stink eye."

My laugh was hollow as I tried to reconcile my anxiety with my desire to throw caution to the wind.

"I know it's not ideal." His voice became more serious. "But I'm working with aspects of the project unrelated to you, and Carlton will head up the team examining the departments. So, I'll have no say in that analysis, at least not initially."

"So Carlton knows?" Panic overtook me. I didn't even know the man, but my stomach clenched at the idea of him judging.

"Sure. He's my partner. The conflict would only ever be an issue if we kept it secret *and* things looked off-kilter. And they won't *be* off-kilter. I like you, but I am good at what I do, Naya. I wouldn't show you any favoritism professionally."

His expression was uncharacteristically serious, and I caught a glimpse of the management consultant who'd shown up in my google search. Cool, purposeful, and professional. His assertions eased my nerves.

"Good. I wouldn't want you to."

"If you'll take a chance with me, we'll keep it professional for work," he added. "For example, if I were calling to ask about grant applications, I wouldn't also ask you if you're wearing any of your fancy underwear."

"Does that mean you plan to keep calling me?"

"Absolutely." His brows raised as our gazes locked.

I lowered my voice and leaned my head close to his. "Are you asking about grant applications now?"

His grin widened as he slowly shook his head.

"So, I can tell you, I *am* wearing the fancy underwear." In my head, Felicia whooped and hollered, *Get it, girl!*

He set down his glass. "I'd love to get into the details of that. Is this a yes to taking a chance?"

I nodded as the waiter returned. While we ordered, I weighed what he'd said. Many things about it were appealing. Under the radar meant casual, out of the spotlight, and away from prying eyes. I took a gulp from my wine when the waiter left. I tried to push all thoughts of work from my head. "I was surprised when you texted."

"I wasn't sure I would until I hit send." He paused, his palms moving absently over the tablecloth.

My eyes fell to those big hands, and a fleeting memory of their weight on my hips made me squirm in my seat.

"I thought about it." He tapped the table before making steady eye contact with me. "Thought about you, a lot, after I left. I just wasn't sure what to say. You seemed set on saying goodbye, and no one ever shares the protocol for these situations."

I lowered my voice and leaned forward. "I mean, what *is* the etiquette after having the best sex of your life with a relative stranger?"

His gaze tripped on my lips before flicking down. "The best, huh?"

*Crap. What if he thought it was just average?* I nodded, my face warming.

"Funny. I never thought of you as a stranger."

"You don't know my last name."

"You could tell me your last name. Then I'd know with whom I had the best sex of my life."

I released a breath, a nervous, twitchy energy coursing through me. I wanted to touch him and kiss in the middle of this upscale restaurant . . . and I wanted to run away and hide, too.

His expression softened, and he twisted his mouth to one side, a dimple appearing on his cheek. "I'll go first. My full name is Jacob Carson Shaw. I'm thirty-six years old and from a town near Seattle, I run a management consulting firm, I have an MBA from Duke, I live in Raleigh, North Carolina, and my social security number is—" He stopped as I pressed my fingers to his mouth. His eyes twinkled, and he took my hand in his, pulling it away from his mouth. "And I like you," he finished, his thumb rubbing over my palm. "I want to get to know you." He raised his eyebrows. It was my turn.

"My full name is Naya Michelle Turner. I'm thirty-three years old, and I grew up in a small town in Iowa. I'm a professor specializing in math education, and I earned my PhD at the University of Illinois at Chicago." I bit my lower lip and tried to gauge his reaction. "And I like you, too."

"It's very nice to meet you, Dr. Turner." Jake laced his fingers with mine over the top of the table, and my defenses started to crumble.

Over his New York strip and my chicken piccata, he told me about a recent trip that went wrong in every way, ending with a fistfight between the CFO and a member of the board of directors. I shared how my newest project involved interviewing fourth graders and that a particularly precocious nine-year-old boy decided I should be his girlfriend and join his kickball team.

"I didn't realize I had such fierce competition."

"I'm popular with the under-ten crowd."

"Did you join the team?"

I laughed, finishing my wine. "I was wearing the wrong shoes."

"Sounds like the kid had skills, though. I should take notes."

"Are you asking me to be on your kickball team?"

Jake wiggled his eyebrows. "Maybe. What's the shoe situation?" He glanced surreptitiously under the table, and I felt his gaze on my bare legs and down to the navy stilettos I'd paired with a white sleeveless dress. It was a quick sweep, only a second or two, but I flushed knowing he was following the lines of my body. I'd spent a long time trying not to be noticed, but this was nice. It was more than nice; it was arousing. He looked back up and subtly shook his head as the waiter began to clear our plates.

I grinned, loving the playful expression on his face. When the waiter stepped away, I responded, "Verdict?"

"Not great for kickball," he said, his gaze traveling over my legs again, this time with a longer sweep. "But I can think of other games we could play."

"There's a joke in there about rounding bases," I said with a sly smile, enjoying his laugh.

"Let's get out of here and see."

We'd barely exited the restaurant when Jake pulled me to him against the brick exterior of the building. His hard chest against my breasts, I gripped his biceps as if holding on for dear life. Maybe I was. The way he searched my face, gaze heating as his hand slid to the back of my head, I was in trouble. My eyes drifted closed, and his mouth was on mine. He tasted like the mints they delivered with our check, his lips and tongue insistently ravaging my own. Vibrations buzzed through my body as the kiss deepened, hunger and passion swirling between us as our tongues danced.

We pulled apart, chests heaving. His voice was gravelly and low. "I've wanted to do that since I first saw you." He slid a hand from my neck down my spine, sending another tingle through my body.

"I guess it's a good thing we're not strangers anymore."

# Twenty-five

J ake's warm breath puffed across the back of my neck as I emerged from sleep to find his body curled around mine, the weight of the comforter surrounding us. Sunlight peeked through the clouds, and I flexed my toes. We'd been up until one in the morning, but I didn't feel groggy. I felt fresh and new and like a fuller version of my old self.

I padded to the window to admire the spider's web of quiet streets in the early-morning sunlight. Skimming my fingers over the smooth surface of the glass, I took in the expanse of the view. I'd left my small Iowa town to move to Chicago at eighteen, and it had felt like home ever since. I knew I could live somewhere else if I had to search for a new job, but where would I go? The thought of leaving this city was exhausting.

The bed creaked behind me, and I glanced over my shoulder. Jake, hair pointing in all directions, one eye half-closed, squinted into the light as he stretched and walked to me.

"Good morning," he rasped, voice thick from sleep, as he wrapped his arms around my naked body.

"Good morning," I murmured.

Jake dotted kisses over my shoulder, and I let him mold me to him. "Not worried about me seeing you naked this time, huh?"

"I couldn't find any of your shirts. Did I wake you?"

"I'm usually an early riser. I was pretty tired after last night, though."

"That's fair." My head lolled back as his lips grazed my neck. "You worked hard."

"It was enjoyable work." He nipped at my earlobe, his hand sliding down my stomach. "Did you sleep well?"

I marveled at how well we fit together, and I arched into him. "Uh-huh."

"This is a nice way to wake up."

"I was thinking the same thing." I tried to cover my mouth when his lips neared mine. "But, I haven't brushed my teeth yet."

He maneuvered in front of my hand, kissing me, taking my top lip between his. "Neither have I."

Those sweet kisses by the window intensified, and we found ourselves enmeshed in the sheets and pillows again. Unlike the night before, when we'd come together in a frenzy, this time was slow. Every caress, stroke, and thrust melted into the next until it all crescendoed.

Resting my head on his shoulder, I caught my breath. My torrent of pleasure ebbed, and we rested in a cozy huddle until he jerked away, surprising me.

"I forgot," he said, climbing off the bed while I looked on, confused. "I brought you something."

"A present?" I propped myself on my elbows.

He handed me an envelope-sized package wrapped in plain brown paper with a pink ribbon around it. "I meant to give it to you last night but got distracted."

I took the package, glancing between him and the gift. "You brought me a present just because?" I asked again, awed.

He climbed back in bed next to me, his expression gleeful. "Open it."

I dragged my nail under the paper and pulled out a package of brightly colored pencils with my name embossed on them in gold lettering. They were the kind I always hoped for as a kid. I met his grin, and my heart did somersaults. "Where did you find these?"

He shrugged. "I have a guy."

"You have a pencil guy?" I ran my fingers over the embossing, tracing my name. The gift was perfect. He'd been thinking of me; he'd listened and knew me enough to know this simple thing would make me smile. I didn't just smile, I beamed.

"Do you like them? I was a little worried you'd think it was cheesy."

"You know I like cheesy. I love them." I set the pencils aside, wrapping my arms around his neck to kiss him again. "Thank you."

"You're welcome." He stroked my neck, and we lay in loose-limbed silence for a minute or two. "So, when do I get to see you again?"

My head shot up.

"What?" he asked, seeming both startled and amused. "I'm really not a wham-bam kind of guy."

"I know, I—" I stammered. "I mean, I'm not, either, a wham-bam girl, that is. I'm not good at relationships," I blurted. "It seems like you should know that before, or even just if, this is something . . ." I trailed off. "Not that I'm saying it has to be more than fun," I stammered and pressed my eyes shut for a moment. "Forget I said that, it's a nonissue—I know this is casual and I don't expect anything from you—"

"Hey, calm down." He rolled to his side, stretching an arm over my waist. "I don't know what this is, exactly. It's new, and I don't want to rush anything. And, if it helps, I have it on excellent authority I am not good at relationships, either. I can get caught up with work, I travel a lot, I can be too closed off, I'm not romantic enough."

He scrunched his nose and closed one eye. "Have I convinced you to keep seeing me yet?"

"You bought me pencils. That's pretty romantic." I touched his biceps, enjoying how solid he was against me. "But what I'm hearing is that you did not treat those sweet, elderly librarians very well."

"It's a good thing Gladys likes bad boys." His eyes lit up. "Here's what I do know: You're fun and funny, and you make *me* feel fun and funny, and no one has done that in a long time." His hand rubbed up and down my side, creating a friction that made me want to roll into him. "And you're beautiful. I don't hit on women in bars, ever. But I couldn't not talk to you. And then, once I did . . ." He stroked his thumb up and down the side of my face. "Well, I didn't want to stop, because I think you kind of get me, and that feels like something."

He planted a light kiss on my mouth, a sweet peck. "So, I'm okay with you having some expectations while we figure out what this is."

I'd been bracing for him to let me off the hook, to agree that this was casual. Instead, I was trying to wrap my mind around what he'd said. "I'd like that."

"I fly out tonight. Can we make plans to see each other soon?"

I let his question hang between us for a moment. I wanted to see him again, and the reasons not to take the risk kept feeling less and less significant. "Okay. Assuming Muriel doesn't put the kibosh on this whole thing, but you can't just fly across the country every week."

"You grossly underestimate the number of frequent-flier miles I accrue."

I took a breath, thinking of how to respond.

He spoke again before I finished exhaling. "Plus, I consider this recruiting for my kickball team. It's a business expense."

"You're a good negotiator."

"And you're harder to pin down than the Wall Street guys I used to work with. So, I ask again, Dr. Naya Turner, when can I next see you?"

I laughed, holding my hands up in surrender, palms toward him. "How about we meet in Cincinnati?"

He barked out a deep laugh. "Not what I was expecting you to say, but okay. Why Cincinnati?"

"Well, it's halfway between Chicago and Raleigh. I've never been, have you?" *And I don't know anyone there, which makes it an appealing location to continue our not-so-clandestine affair.*

"I haven't, but I'm psyched that you researched meeting places already. I think you might kind of like me." His lips quirked, and I was busted. "What would we do in Cincinnati? I mean, besides the obvious." We both reached for our phones and began searching, finding a zoo, shopping, trendy restaurants, and sports.

"I guess we wouldn't be bored." I held up the visitors bureau website for him to examine.

"I'm never bored with you. Except in bed. You are *really* boring in bed. Maybe we should stick to karaoke and zoos."

I glowered at him. "Your jokes don't always make you more charming. You don't seem too invested in me seeing you again."

"You know I'm playing."

"Uh-huh."

"Do you want me to give you a full list of all the ways I find you utterly fascinating, in and out of bed?"

"I like lists."

"I remember. Have we checked anything new off? At least a few things from last night were on there, hopefully."

Heat rose on my cheeks, and I shifted closer to him without answering. *Dating isn't on the list.*

"I'm guessing so, because you're blushing. I find your blushing kind of hot. It's actually on the list. I'll send you the rest of it later. I promise." He yawned again. "I never get any sleep when I'm with you, but I need to get ready for a meeting. I'm holding you to Cincinnati, though."

I ran a hand down his forearm, the short hairs tickling my palm. "Scout's honor."

Later that morning, I'd begun poring over my interview data from spring with the fourth graders. Before inviting me to play kickball, one of the kids had been telling me about the math game and how he wanted to show it to his abuela because she didn't speak English, and the game would translate his game stats to Spanish. I smiled, hearing my grandfather's voice in my head. I returned to reviewing, though my mind would trip on something Jake had said, or how he'd beamed when he gave me the pencils. I wondered if maybe in some universe I could have him, keep my job, and hold on to this contented feeling. Like he knew I was thinking of him, my phone buzzed with an incoming text from Jake followed immediately by a second, third, and fourth.

> JAKE: The spot on your neck, just below your jaw. The skin is so soft, and you make a little whimpering sound when I kiss you there. That sound ends me.
>
> JAKE: This tiny, crescent-shaped scar on your left inner thigh. How did you get that?
>
> JAKE: When your whole body quivers and shakes right before you come with my mouth on you and you grip my hair.
>
> JAKE: The way you seem to let go of every inhibition when you're on top of me, all bossy-like.

Goose bumps pricked up my arms as I read, and a tension coiled low in my belly as I flicked a glance between the manuscript sitting lifeless on the screen and the bouncing dots on my phone, indicating Jake was drafting another text.

JAKE: I had a few minutes, and I promised to share a list.

JAKE: My list of things I like about you outside bed is much longer.

JAKE: Your laugh, the look you give me when I tell a bad joke, how you get all twitchy when you're nervous.

JAKE: This is all on top of your cheese puns and kickball prowess.

NAYA: You are something else.

JAKE: Something good?

NAYA: Something very good.

JAKE: Something you can't get enough of?

NAYA: Something who ends sentences with prepositions.

JAKE: Nerd.

I set my phone down, a giddy uneasiness bubbling in me, because his texts had me making my own list about him, and it was growing longer by the minute.

# Twenty-six

The board flashed as his flight changed from "delayed" to "arrived." I looked down to find a text from Jake containing only a winking emoji, and I sniffled. What had started as a small tickle in my throat when I woke up that morning had blossomed into a runny nose, body aches, and a light head as I sat in the Cincinnati/Northern Kentucky International Airport.

I'd shaved, waxed, and plucked with care and packed my favorite lingerie for a sexy weekend. After two weeks apart, my body reverberated with the same bundle of nerves I had the first night we were together. Only this time, the onset of chills and a dull ache behind my eyes clouded everything. *I'm nothing if not on-brand.*

Jake strode through the small crowd and wrapped his long arms around me. His lightweight maroon sweater was soft against my cheek, and the closeness of his body felt right. The hug lasted only seconds, but the rest of the airport receded into the background.

"Hi," he said.

I tipped my chin up, but soon my head whipped downward and bumped gracelessly against his chest. Not in a ladylike, dainty "achoo"; this was a wet, loud, humiliating honk.

"Bless you." He looked down at me, and his expression turned to one of concern. "Are you getting sick?"

I tried to smile, shaking my head. "I'm sure it's nothing," I reasoned, fighting back the urge to sniffle and cough, losing both battles. "I was fine when I got on the plane. Now . . . this." I motioned to my face.

We'd planned on a weekend full of steamy, naked activity. We'd discussed it, at length, and in a level of detail that made me pray Muriel from HR never happened upon our texting history. Jake held the back of his hand to my forehead and cheek, his skin cool against my face. "I think you might have a fever."

I closed my eyes momentarily. "No time for that—we're in Cincinnati and only for two days."

"Uh-huh, let's get to the hotel so you can rest."

My heart sank, and I blinked slowly, slumping against him.

Jake linked his fingers with mine, steering me forward. "How was your flight?" He dipped his lips to kiss the top of my head, ignoring that I'd just sneezed all over him.

———

Our room was on the fifteenth floor with a view of Cincinnati. In the sunlight, the Ohio River reflected the blue sky, and the city's skyline sparkled. I only took in the view for a moment before sinking gracelessly to the bed like a sack of potatoes. The fever seemed to have broken, but a chill coursed through me, and I wrapped my arms around my knees.

Jake touched the back of his hand to my face again, and his mouth formed a straight line.

"I'm sorry," I said quietly, my words interrupted by sniffles. "I can get my own room. I don't want you to get sick."

"That's ridiculous." He shook his head and waved dismissively. "I'm going to get a bath going for you, then find a drugstore for some medicine." He disappeared into the bathroom while speaking, and the water began running.

"I'll be fine, really," I called through the open door, rubbing my arms for warmth. My voice came out wobbly and strained. "Don't go to the trouble. It's just a cold or something." I glimpsed his forearm over the edge of the tub, checking the water temperature. No one had drawn a bath for me since I was a child, and I felt simultaneously helpless and grateful.

"It shouldn't take me long. Hopefully the steam will help," he said, grazing one of those large hands over my shoulder.

As he stepped into the hallway, I cursed my body's inability to be a team player. First, I'd thrown up while attempting a one-night stand, and then, with a whole sexy weekend available to us, I decide to host a germ party.

The bodywash provided by the hotel smelled like oranges, and I poured a little in the water until the heady scent filled the room. Sliding beneath the bubbles and resting my head against the edge of the tub, I breathed in the steam rising off the water. I rarely got sick, but when I did, it hit hard and fast, like today.

Closing my eyes, I inhaled the steam and let my mind wander. The previous two weeks had been quiet at work except for the barrage of rumors passed on with every colleague interaction in person or on social media. *Have you heard they're going to cut people before fall semester? A friend of a friend told me everything outside engineering and business is on the chopping block. Rumor has it that the consultants have been analyzing data for a while now and decisions are already made.* I knew it was wrong to ask Jake about what I'd heard, but none of the rumors ever made me feel better about the situation. I found myself constantly stewing in anxiety, taking each piece of gossip for the realistic possibility it was.

I wasn't sure how long I'd been soaking, but two small taps at the bathroom door made me turn my head. When I pulled myself up, water sloshed against the side of the tub. "You can come in." My voice was husky in a way that might have been sexy, were it not for all the phlegm.

He stepped into the room, holding up a plastic bag. "I guessed you didn't pack a lot of lounging clothes, so I picked these up for you, too." He set the bag on the counter by the sink. "When you're ready, I got all kinds of medicine."

"Thank you." I smiled, slipping back into the water, momentarily submerging all but my head. *Where did I find this guy?*

When I walked out, he flicked his eyes up from the bed where he was reading something on his phone and smiled. "Beautiful."

I'd pulled on the clothes he bought—a T-shirt that was a few sizes too large and a pair of sweatpants sporting the Cincinnati football team's logo. I'd piled my hair on top of my head, and my makeup was scrubbed away. "You're—" I paused to blow my nose with a tissue I grabbed from the nightstand. "You're clearly lying."

"Never." He flicked his gaze down to my baggy clothes. "Sorry. That's the best I could do at the drugstore."

"They're comfy. Thank you." I glanced at the desk and brought my hand to my mouth in surprise. Neatly arranged atop it was half a pharmacy.

"I didn't know what brands you preferred, so I picked up a few different cold and flu treatments, plus some cough syrup . . ." he trailed off. Rising, he slid his hands up and down my arms and then rubbed small circles on my shoulders. The pressure and warmth of him was its own kind of medicine, and his chest was solid against my back.

"This is too much, especially since I am ruining your weekend." I popped out two gel caps from a package of cold and sinus relief medicine. "And because you might end up on a watch list for meth chemists after buying all of this."

"You're not ruining my weekend." He faced me. "I planned to spend time with you, which I'm doing."

"Yes, but we planned to be naked and sweaty all weekend."

He pressed the back of his hand gently to my cheek. "True, but the naked and sweaty was secondary." His eyes were soft as he brushed my face, tucking a curl that had escaped my messy ponytail behind my ear. Jake slid the side of his thumb along my lower lip at a glacial pace.

"I don't want to get you sick."

"Nothing risked, nothing gained." The kiss was chaste before he pulled back. He held me, and my heart thundered, my body in tune with his and hyperaware of the weight of his hands and the stretch of his fingers.

"I have one more thing." He stepped back and picked up his laptop from the bed. I sank onto the duvet as he fiddled with his keyboard. I tucked my legs to my chest and shivered, after a chill raced through me.

Jake held up the screen, the browser open to a familiar movie streaming site. I cocked my head to the side and chuckled. The cover images for the original *Star Wars* trilogy filled the window.

I winced against the ache in my shoulders and the lightness in my head, but my heart swelled at the thoughtful gesture. I snuggled into the pillows as he started the first movie before kicking off his shoes and stretching out beside me on the bed.

"How do you feel?" He glanced down at me as the movie began.

My head was fuzzy, and heat rose on my cheeks. "Guilty."

He opened his mouth to say something, then closed it. Instead, pausing the movie and setting the laptop aside, he pulled his wine-colored sweater and undershirt over his head, revealing the light smattering of hair across his chest and the thin trail down his firm stomach.

He moved down the bed to tug at my oversize sweatpants, the thick fabric slipping down my legs under his grip.

"What are you doing?"

"We're getting naked so you can stop feeling guilty." Jake grinned and tossed the sweatpants on the floor next to his sweater, reaching to pull the blanket up over my bare legs.

"This would be so erotic if I wasn't struggling to breathe and keep my eyes open." My breath hitched as he tucked the blanket around my legs.

Returning to my side, Jake stretched his arm behind me, gently pulling me to him. "Now, c'mon, woman, I've waited almost thirty years to see these movies."

*I love you.*

It popped into my head out of nowhere, and I bit back the words, if not the feeling. *Where the hell did that come from?* It was the cold medicine taking effect, of course. It was his body, which I was so drawn to, even in my drugged and achy condition. It was me clinging to something when my job was unsteady, and Davis's presence was a snake slithering back into my life. It was my inexperienced heart playing tricks on my mind.

I bit my tongue and watched the screen, but my eyes drooped before the introductory text was finished scrolling across the screen, and I rested my head against his bare chest. "Why did your wife let you go?" I'd closed my eyes, breathing him in as the medicine took effect.

He didn't answer for a few moments but then said, "Lots of reasons, probably."

"You got Sudafed and *Star Wars* for me in Cincinnati," I murmured, as the heavy drowsiness took hold. "Guys don't do that."

He shrugged, the motion rocking my head gently. "I never did anything like this for her." His voice was quiet and sounded distant as I drifted off.

*Why not?*

# Twenty-seven

When I returned to Chicago Sunday afternoon, I decided to keep my promise to join Felicia for her session with a personal trainer. She'd convinced me it would be good to try something new, and the kickboxing instructor she called Wes the Sexy Trainer agreed to train us together. Ironically, I felt good for the first time all weekend when I boarded the plane home.

Felicia stretched on the grass as we waited for her trainer. "Please tell me you rallied overnight and enjoyed your sexy weekend."

"I was sick as a dog the entire time. Asleep half the time and drugged up for the rest. I never even left the room." I reached a hand behind my head and stretched my triceps. "I've never been so embarrassed in my life."

"What did he do?" Felicia raised an eyebrow as she straightened and adjusted her ponytail.

"He bought me medicine, warm pajamas, and streamed

*Star Wars.*" My smile widened. "He snuggled with me and watched fucking *Star Wars,*" I repeated, more to myself than Felicia, shaking my head.

"He took care of you the whole weekend?" Her voice lilted, the disbelief obvious.

A light breeze swirled around us, and I cast a quick glance at a couple jogging by, their strides in sync. "I kept insisting he go or at least get a different room, but he stayed."

"That's boyfriend-level shit—you know that, right?"

"We're not labeling anything."

"Well, no matter what you call him, it's about time you were with a good guy. Why don't you make it official and have that dreaded defining-the-relationship talk?" Felicia stood, brushing dirt and grass from the tight pants that showed off her curvy but toned figure. She had always been beautiful, but I'd never seen her this muscular.

"I see you looking," she said, smacking one of her butt cheeks. "Take it in, girl. I've been telling you Wes is a miracle worker."

I laughed and swatted at her myself while my mind digested her suggestion on defining things. I remembered curling against him in the warm bed the first night before the medicine kicked in, feeling safer and more content than I could remember ever feeling. His chest and abs had been hard and warm under my hands, and the weight of his touch on my shoulder reassuring. The rest of the weekend had been fine, but we hadn't shared that level of intimacy, between me being asleep and not wanting to get him sick. I'd awoken that morning, feeling better but next to an empty pillow. He left a simple note on the dresser with a glass of water and two of the gel caps I'd been taking. *Hope you feel better—didn't want to wake you!* —*J.* I didn't quite know how to interpret that—it wasn't overly sentimental or romantic. Maybe this was a natural, if unsatisfying, end to a fling.

"I'm not going to make him define anything after he had a front row seat to my one-woman show, *Phlegm, Night Sweats, and You.*"

"Are you worried he's going to peace out because of some snot?"

"Maybe," I mumbled.

"Do you remember throwing up on him the first night you met and him still calling you?"

I cringed at the memory. "Near him."

She rested a hand on my shoulder for balance, reaching back to stretch her quads. "You're a badass, hot-as-hell, fucking brilliant doctor, not some insecure high school girl. Man up!"

"Do you know how rife with toxic masculinity the phrase *man up* is?" I challenged, mirroring her pose. "It implies that to be courageous is to be a man."

"Do you know how annoying it is when you change the subject?" Her tone was smug.

"I'm just saying, we don't need to insert men into every aspect of our language."

"Okay, ovary up. Fallopian forward. Vulva with a vengeance." She sighed dramatically, moving out of the stretch, and I stifled a laugh as I was reminded why we had been friends for so long. "Nay, you like him. Don't tell me you don't, and he sounds amazing—like unbelievable, and I'm kind of worried you're delusional and making him up. So, woman up. Person up. Have the talk."

"You're right."

"I know," she answered. "Between taking care of you when you're sick and what you've told me about his tongue, it sounds like this guy could teach a master class. Can you give Aaron his number?"

She looked over my shoulder and waved at the man jogging toward us.

"I'm sure Aar would love to hear you say that."

"He'd get over it."

"Hey," the trainer said, holding out his hand to me. "I'm Wes. Glad you could join us."

Felicia hadn't been exaggerating—this guy was gorgeous, and I'd have been smitten if my sexy stranger weren't in the picture. He was younger than us, maybe midtwenties, with broad shoulders and striking hazel eyes.

"Wes is amazing, Nay. I credit him with getting my body back after the twins." Felicia shadowboxed near him, and he blocked her jabs.

*I should learn how to do that.* I made a note to ask Wes later about the self-defense classes Felicia told me he taught. I'd been thinking a lot lately about what I'd do if Davis came back for good. I wondered if knowing how to fight would make me feel stronger and more prepared to face him.

Wes blocked one final jab from Felicia and pulled a stopwatch from his pocket. "You never lost your body; you just decided to change it. All I did was make you do the extra intervals."

"Wes, Naya is my oldest friend. It's her first time, so you'll take it easy on both of us, right?"

He laughed. "That's not what you pay me for, but we'll ease into things, Naya."

"I can handle it," I said, bouncing on the balls of my feet. "Hit me with what you've got."

"Okay. I like you." Wes pointed to a grassy area nearby. "We're starting with Felicia's favorite. Burpees."

Felicia groaned, but we walked the few feet, and she said over her shoulder, "I knew you'd like her. I would have set you up years ago if it weren't for that girlfriend of yours. Katie? Kendell?"

"Kelsey. Soon to be a fiancée, though, I hope. Bought a ring a few days ago." As we congratulated him, color rose on the trainer's cheeks, which was kind of adorable. His affection for the woman was evident. She was probably a nice, uncomplicated person. I wondered what Jake looked like when he told someone about me. If he told someone about me. *And since whatever we were doing might end up being career suicide, would I want him to tell anyone?*

Wes explained how we'd fall to a push-up, then jump back up to do it again with a hop. He demonstrated the move effortlessly, and Felicia gave me a quick raised eyebrow as she eyed his backside. *Thirsty.*

When Wes returned to his feet, he took a step back. "You ready?"

Felicia and I shifted into the position, and we started the workout, falling in sync and grunting as we got back to our feet, time after time.

"These are the worst," Felicia huffed.

"If you complain again, I'll add ten more." Wes counted our reps, encouraging us.

"Tyrant." Felicia only insulted those she loved—well, okay, she insulted everyone, but she was only this way with people in her circle.

I liked Wes, too, and I was already enjoying this workout. I ran every day, but with each push-up and every jump, I got a reminder that I was strong enough to do more. The grass under my hands and the moment of weightlessness when I hopped, the sweat running down my face—I wanted to bottle the feeling.

"I've got ten more in me." I grinned through my breathless huff and ignored my best friend's violent glare.

———

After an hour in the park with Wes and Felicia, I'd collapsed on my couch, exhausted in the best possible way. Wes had already sent me the information on the next self-defense class he was leading, and my friend forgave me for the extra ten burpees . . . eventually. *I'm making plans. I'm going to be okay.*

NAYA: Dear Florence Nightingale: Did you make it home
   safely?

I glanced down at my phone, awaiting a reply to my text to Jake several hours before. Between anticipating messages from Jake and fearing new texts from Davis, each buzz and notification was a double-edged sword. Davis had contacted me a few more times, always with veiled threats or general creepiness, sometimes with a photo or just a reminder he had them. I hadn't blocked him, worried he'd somehow retaliate, making things worse. I also couldn't bring myself to add him to my contacts, so every unknown number gave me pause.

JAKE: Dear Typhoid Mary: Sorry, got distracted with a work thing and forgot to reply. How are you feeling? Sincerely, Nurse Ratched

I leaned back into the couch.

NAYA: Dear Dr. Strangelove: Good. Do you feel sick at all? Sincerely, Patient Zero

JAKE: Fit as a fiddle. I am glad you feel better.

NAYA: I'm still horrified that I ruined your weekend.

JAKE: You didn't. When can I see you again?

NAYA: You left my side like twelve hours ago.

JAKE: So . . . soon?

My stomach flip-flopped as I read and reread his response with the smile of a woman whose fling wasn't over yet. *Do people still say booyah?*

JAKE: Do you own a formal gown?

NAYA: Yes to seeing me soon. No to owning a formal gown. Why?

JAKE: Are you willing to get one? I'm on the board of directors for a charity here, and they're having their annual gala in a few weeks. Want to be my date?

NAYA: Will you wear a tux again?

JAKE: I will. If it sweetens the deal, I promise to do a little dance for you when I take it off.

I chewed on my lip, already opening a travel site on my laptop to search for flights. *To do: Buy a dress.*

NAYA: You *are* a good dancer . . .

JAKE: Is that a yes?

For some reason, visiting him on his home turf felt infinitely weightier than meeting in Cincinnati or him being in Chicago. I couldn't deny the growing feelings for Jake that consumed more of my thoughts than I wanted. Going to North Carolina, to his house, for the sole purpose of being together . . . that meant this was real. That meant I was really risking my professional reputation.

NAYA: I'd love to.

I had to come clean at work.

# Twenty-eight

Joe's anxiety over the president's plans had brought us all into the office on a humid Wednesday morning a few weeks later. We scattered during the summers, so the fact that everyone was there hammered home how serious this was. Joe's voice was his trademark gruff with some added exhaustion thrown in. "I guess the consultants have been examining data for months already."

*So, that one rumor was true.* Jake hadn't indicated anything.

Joe drummed his fingers on the table, color rising on his neck. "I was asked to join a committee that will advise the consultants as a sounding board. We meet next week, and that's all I know."

Anita, one of the senior professors and kind of a legend in our field, piped up. "So, what are we supposed to do?" Her voice was pinched and reedy. I remembered revering Anita as an academic superhero when I was new. She was one of the first women to make big strides in studying math learning and

technology, and I'd hoped she'd be a guide and friend. I was
out of luck. In addition to being brilliant, my colleague was
competitive, self-involved, and uninterested in mentoring. At
the height of rumors spreading about me on campus, she told
me I was foolish to get involved with another faculty member,
and that I deserved the flak I was receiving for being so reckless with my career. At the time, I wanted to lash out and tell
her it wasn't my fault, that he was a monster, and that her blam-
ing me was not how women should support one another. Instead, I'd soaked up her admonitions like a sponge, absorbing
her words and dismissing the idea we'd ever work together or
that I'd ever be in her league.

Joe shrugged. "There's nothing we can do right now except keep writing, publishing, teaching, and doing what we do."

Anita harrumphed, and we all began packing away laptops
and notes.

*No more putting it off.*

"Joe, you have a minute?"

He nodded, and I followed him down the stairs to his office. As we walked the short distance, I ran through what I'd
planned to say in my head, worry prickling at the back of my
neck.

"What a mess," he grumbled, and I wasn't sure if he was
referring to his office filled with chaotic piles of debris or the
situation with the potential cuts. He sat heavily in his chair and
cleared a small space on his desk between us with a brush of
his arm. "Oh, before I forget, Elaine wonders when you're coming over for dinner again. She misses you hanging around."

The thought of Joe's wife, the most organized and orderly

person I'd ever met, made me smile. Early in my career, I'd spent a lot of time at their house, joining the two of them for dinners. In a way, they'd been like a second family. "I'll text her and figure out a night in the next couple weeks."

He nodded. "So, what did you need?"

"I need to tell you something, Joe." His face fell, and I cringed but continued. "One of the consultants. I know him."

Relief seemed to wash over him. "Oh, did he tell you they were coming here ahead of time or something?"

"No. It was a pretty big coincidence, actually. We—uh— we've actually gone out a few times." That felt wildly insufficient to describe things with Jake, but I wasn't sure how else to phrase it.

Joe's eyebrows raised in surprise. "Really? I didn't know you were seeing anyone."

"I mean, we're, um, we've just gone out some. It's not serious." I didn't feel right about that response, but I again didn't know how else to phrase things.

"I don't think it really matters, Nay." Joe echoed Jake's words. "From what I understand, your knowing him shouldn't be important." His words should have comforted me, but I hadn't shared the whole truth. "Don't stress about it."

"I have this sense that our department might be in trouble, and I worry there might be a conflict of interest."

He raised his eyebrows, and I knew him well enough to realize the action meant *what do you want me to say?*

"I wanted to make sure you knew, was all. I worry it will look like we're not being evaluated fairly."

He sighed. "I'll make sure I mention it up the chain if I

think it might be an issue, but for now, I'm not worried. There's nothing wrong with having gone out on a few dates. You're not marrying the guy or anything serious, right?"

That was the time to set the record straight. *We're kind of seeing each other. Just say it.*

Something seized my voice, and I chickened out. In part, I didn't know how to phrase it. *Well, boss, we're sleeping together and texting like high schoolers, and he bought me pencils and sweatpants, so you connect the dots. Then, can you tell me what you come up with?*

"Good, then." Joe shuffled a few papers around, and his attention caught on a Post-it note before he looked up again. "Oh, and I found out why Davis might be on campus. I guess he and the president used to work on some national task force together before Lewis got here. Apparently, they're all buddy-buddy. Maybe Davis is being recruited."

I puffed my cheeks and let the air drain slowly from between my lips. I wanted to be shocked, but I'd never been able to shake away my suspicions that his presence wasn't temporary. I glanced away from Joe, hoping he didn't read the panic on my face.

"I know you guys had a bad breakup. You want to—er—talk about it or anything?" Joe had gone to bat for me on campus, but we'd never talked about it, not in any real way.

Regardless of the cuts, if Davis got hired, I'd have to leave. I wouldn't survive if he had any control and I wouldn't be able to say anything without risking him releasing those photos or God only knew what else. "I'm good, Joe. Thanks for the heads-up."

When I left his office, I stopped in mine to grab a few files

I wanted to review at home. Plucking folders from my desk and dropping them in my bag, I paused to consider what Joe had said about Davis. He'd gotten a good job at State, and it seemed strange he'd be trying to come back. I flipped open my laptop to search for his name. The results populated quickly on the website:

Davis Garner, Business College Dean, and
Caroline Rhodes, Vice President for Research, Considered for Provost

Garner's Record of Scholarship and Service
Makes Him Strong Candidate

Garner Favored as Provost Selection

Rhodes Selected as State's New Provost

I glanced at the text of the articles documenting Davis's attempt to secure one of the most senior positions at State overseeing departments and several centers. He'd been bested by a woman publicly. He must have been furious.

Davis had always loudly declared himself a feminist, calling for equal treatment and touting his many years of mentoring junior faculty members who were women. It was an act. He'd subtly chip away at accomplishments made by female colleagues, and I always wondered if he mentored so he could have a steady stream of women looking up to him. He liked people being reliant on him, especially women.

Publicly, he always complimented my work, said how proud he was that his girlfriend was part of the strong community of women making inroads in STEM. In private, he questioned my research, insinuated I was unqualified, and shamed me for not spending more time on things he thought women should, like fashion, cooking, and housekeeping. Caroline Rhodes getting selected for that position ahead of him would send him to the edge. *Is that why he's creeping into my life again? To control someone?* He hated appearing weak or unwanted. Once, my team beat his at a faculty softball tournament. He'd given me the silent treatment for hours after until he'd pulled up an article I'd recently had published in a less prestigious journal, telling me everything that was wrong with my writing, my research, and me. Then he'd made me repeat back to him all the things wrong with my work until the words started to feel true.

My phone buzzed, and I cringed as I grabbed the device, expecting the unknown number to flash on the screen. I felt his fingers on my skin and shivered before flipping the phone over.

JAKE: Would you prefer flat iron steak or salmon for the gala?

I exhaled a relieved breath, the curiosity about Davis's return ebbing away from the forefront of my mind. I shook my head, willing away the memory of the last time I'd played softball. I had been a good player, and I added *Rejoin the team* to my list. *Assuming there's still a department next year.*

NAYA: You're a fancy date. Steak, please.

Jake replied with a GIF showing SpongeBob SquarePants in a monocle, and I laughed.

JAKE: I only have a few minutes, but what're you up to?

NAYA: Just finished talking to Joe.

JAKE: You'll have to tell me how he took it when we have more time. I can't wait to see you on Saturday.

I considered replying that Joe had taken it surprisingly well since I hadn't told him the whole truth. I decided against it. I had time to tell Joe more when I knew where things stood between Jake and me, and I didn't want to tell Jake more about work. I could keep everything compartmentalized.

NAYA: Will you meet me at the airport wearing a top hat?

JAKE: You want me to meet you in my tux?

NAYA: No, just the top hat.

I sat back in my chair and smiled, rereading the brief exchange. The interlude had momentarily lightened my mood. Still, an uneasiness simmered in me, and I realized this was another moment split between Davis and Jake, as if my feelings about them were two opposing forces: fear and *love*? I minimized the search engine on my laptop and pushed the thought aside, hoping the uneasiness was just paranoia.

# Twenty-nine

I arrived in Raleigh in the late afternoon the day of the gala, and Jake met me at the airport wearing a plastic novelty top hat. He picked me up and kissed me in the middle of the baggage claim. Add some eighties pop song and I was in the last scene of my very own romantic movie.

His lakeside house was a spacious two-story surrounded by poplar trees in a quiet, upscale neighborhood. I knew Jake was successful, but seeing his place hammered home for me what he might have to lose if the Thurmond project went south. His bathroom, like the rest of the house, was clean and orderly. My man liked organization. *My man.* I rolled the phrase on my tongue, testing it out.

The light blue color of the floor-length dress popped against my tan skin and hugged my breasts, revealing what Felicia had said was a tasteful amount of cleavage. It also matched Jake's eyes, which was what first attracted me in the store. I turned again, inspecting the back of the gown before turning to my bloodred lipstick the young woman at the makeup counter had sworn was *fire* with my skin tone. She was right—it was so much bolder than the neutral shades I normally wore, but I loved it. *I'm going to stand out . . . and I'm excited about it.*

I was greeted at the bottom of the stairs by Jake leaning against the kitchen counter, one ankle crossed over the other, checking something on his phone. The outline of his developed shoulder muscles filled out the white shirt in a way that warranted poetry.

"Am I fancy enough to be your date?" I twirled, the dress swishing around my strappy silver heels, as Jake turned. I wasn't worried what he'd think, because I knew he wanted me there, not to show me off, but to be by his side. I grinned as I came out of the twirl, that realization fresh in my mind.

He moved toward me, his hands landing on my waist and his smile mischievous. "Very fancy. Maybe we should skip this thing." He lowered his full lips to my jaw and dropped kisses down my neck as his hands slid over my backside.

"Hey, this dress was expensive. I can't have you tearing it off me."

"Give me more credit than that. I'd ease it off slowly," he said, planting sweet little kisses by my ear before lightly sucking on the left lobe. "And I'd place it gently on a padded hanger before even thinking of pleasuring you. You'd beg, tell me you want me, but I'd say, 'No, Naya, you know this dress is my first priority, and I'll be back in twenty minutes after I run it to the dry cleaner.'"

I giggled and pushed against his chest. "That's all I ask."

Jake brought my hand to his mouth, brushing his lips over my knuckles. "You look beautiful."

I took his arm and let him escort me out to his sleek black BMW in the garage.

"I'm so glad Gladys, the librarian, had to cancel on me," he commented as we pulled on seat belts.

"You two had a falling out?"

"No, she found a much younger man. Can you believe it?"

"Don't hate the player." I enjoyed how he settled his palm on my thigh and rubbed circles as he laughed along with me. "Her loss, my gain, though."

———

We pulled up to a stately mansion as elegant as any place I'd ever been. The redbrick pathway led to stairs nestled between huge white columns, up-lit from behind pristine rosebushes. All around us, women in flowing gowns and men in tuxedos moved into the opulent structure or milled about in the gardens visible from the front of the house.

My jaw must have dropped as Jake took my arm and helped me out of the car, handing the keys to the young valet.

"I'm a little out of my depth," I whispered as we made our way toward the front entrance. That was an understatement. This place could have been a plantation house, and I was surrounded by a lot of very wealthy people.

*Try something new. Check.*

He pulled me closer. "It's easy. Laugh at their jokes, especially if they look rich and ready to donate, take liberal advantage of the open bar, and no matter how amazing the time-share looks at the silent auction, don't bid on it."

"Do you speak from experience?"

"Branson wasn't really my thing." He nodded to another

young man holding the door for us as we entered an immaculate ballroom draped with lush fabrics and filled with sprays of flowers. "And stick close to me. That doesn't have anything to do with navigating the gala; I just like having you close." He dipped his head toward mine, brushing his lips against my ear, his hand resting on my lower back. "I'm glad you're here."

"I'm glad, too." We locked eyes, both grinning, and I slid my hand to his.

The charity was for leukemia research, and the speeches from doctors and survivors moved me to tears. Jake's arm came around my shoulder when he noticed me wiping a tear from my eye, wordlessly offering comfort.

After that, he never stopped touching me. Whether it was his thumb stroking my knee through the fabric of my dress, his arm around my shoulder, or his lips brushing against my temple and cheek, the contact was subtle and sweet. A spark zinged through me every single time.

Once the program was over, we were mobbed by people wanting to talk to my handsome date. Jake seemed to know everyone, and laughed at all their jokes, whether delivered by someone funny or by someone rich.

"You're so good at the schmoozing," I whispered as we left a group of people to head to the dance floor. "I had it in my head you were shy."

Jake chuckled. "Do you think I have them fooled?"

"I think you have *me* fooled."

"You get the real me," he said. "I can be the person out front when I need to, but I much prefer to be behind the scenes or one-on-one."

"You're good at one-on-one." I rested my palms on his

shoulders as we reached the dance floor, and his hand settled on my waist. Around us, couples swayed, their conversation a low hum over the music from the quartet onstage.

"It's a cause I believe in. I started volunteering at hospitals as a Boy Scout, and I never stopped."

That he'd been volunteering to help kids with cancer and their families for a couple decades made the feelings squeezing my heart even stronger. I wasn't ready to acknowledge them or fixate on what flaws of his I had to be missing. Instead, I asked, "You were an honest-to-God Boy Scout?"

"Eagle Scout, actually." His crisp scent filled my nostrils, and I leaned in, noticing the way his eyes crinkled at the mention of the accomplishment. "At first, it was a way for my dad and me to spend time together without all my sisters, but then I got into it. I told you I was a nerdy kid."

I shook my head with a smile. "You're a nerdy adult, but I told you, I like nerds. And you've been volunteering all this time? That's incredible, Jake." I tipped my head up, unsure if I was hoping to kiss him or let all my feelings spill out, but I didn't get the chance to do either.

"And who might you be, pretty lady?" A man with thin white hair and slurred speech approached us at the edge of the dance floor, and I pulled back, startled.

"A little something on the side, huh, Shaw? Haven't seen your *wife* tonight." He swayed, leering at me unabashedly.

Jake shifted, placing more of his body between me and the drunk man. "No, Bertram. I'm separated from Gretchen."

The man looked me over again, and Jake's body tensed next to me. "You're light skinned, but your features sure look colored, or are we supposed to say African American now? I can never keep it straight what you people want to be called. I like pretty light-skinned girls, though." He winked before turning back to Jake. "Didn't think you had it in you, boy."

Jake's eyes flashed, and one hand curled into a fist.

I touched his forearm. *Not worth it.*

Instead, I adopted a cool tone. "You're welcome to just call me Doctor." I stretched to shake his hand. "Naya Turner. Hello." *And "colored"? Seriously? What decade is this guy living in?*

"Bertram Harrison the Third." The old man raised his chin, his voice taking on a more formal blustering tone, though his leering did not abate. That his racist and sexist comments were inappropriate seemed to be lost on him. *Lord, give me the confidence of an old, rich white man.*

Jake pulled me to the center of the dance floor without another word to Bertram Harrison III. His palm rested on my lower back again, our bodies close, as I slid my arm up to his shoulder, my other hand in his. He muttered in my ear, his voice low, posture tense. "That fucking racist—"

"I'm fine. He'll still write big checks for kids with cancer, right? I assumed he was one of the rich ones." I gave a small smile, warmth rising within me at Jake's instincts.

"It's not fine. I mean, he is one of our biggest contributors, but a pig. I can't believe he talked to you like that. I should have—"

"I know. It wasn't worth it, though." The length of our bodies pressed together on the full dance floor, and his hand rested protectively on my lower back while my palm skirted up his biceps. "I'm okay, I promise. I thought I actually handled it quite well."

"You did," he said, his jaw muscles relaxing. "Masterfully.

Certainly better than I would have, but does that happen a lot? People saying things like that?"

I shrugged. "Sometimes. Not usually that overtly. I know others get way worse." Some of the things hurled at Felicia over the years from people made my skin crawl.

"I know Tyson experiences it all the time, but I thought as a woman, maybe . . ." He trailed off after bringing up his best friend, who I was going to meet the next day. "But even saying it, that was a dumb assumption." Jake pulled me against him. "I'm so sorry."

I tried to lighten the mood, to communicate I wasn't holding this incident against him. "He thought I was an escort," I whispered, worried the elegant white-haired couple nearest us would hear. "Is the dress that revealing?"

"No . . ." He glanced over my shoulder and glared, presumably at old Bert, before meeting my eyes again. "He's just an ass. No one else would think that."

"Maybe they think I'm your accountant?"

He took just a moment before he caught on to my playful tone. "Itemize me, baby."

"Your barber?"

"I do like your fingers in my hair."

"Or your nurse."

"So many fantasies . . . I'd make sure they knew you were a doctor, though." He spun me unexpectedly and then pulled me back to the solid wall of his chest.

"That would be very nice of you."

He shrugged with a boyish grin. "I'm a nice guy."

"You are."

"Hey," he murmured into my ear, pulling me to him. The puff of breath spurred on the low-level heat between my legs. "You're dancing with me again."

"I am." I lifted my chin and pulled his lips to mine. "It's not so scary with you."

His gaze was hungry as his grip tightened around my waist. We shared a fleeting, intense look as we swayed with the music, our hands curled together. When we did that, he'd always sweep the pad of his thumb up the middle of my palm, a place I'd never known was an erogenous zone until him. That slow, soft touch felt like something special we shared, like when our hands were linked, it was him and me versus the world. I dragged my own thumb against the underside of his wrist, prolonging the connection but unsure what he was seeing in my face. I wasn't sure if he could tell I was scared of this thing between us.

I broke the connection, moving my thumb off his wrists and glancing away. "Now, we should find that old, racist drunk and hit him up for more money."

"You can't look like that, touch me like this, and expect me to voluntarily talk to that arrogant windbag." He dipped his head to my ear, and I melted into him, my entire body on full alert. "Really, I'd like to get out of here and . . ." His warm breath made me gasp—a small, involuntary sound escaped my lips. "Spend the rest of the night memorizing how every inch of you tastes."

I nodded, wide-eyed, as we started toward the exit, my heart and body open in a way I'd never experienced. I was dancing with him. I was wearing red lipstick. And I had no second thoughts about shutting down Bertram Harrison III. I was living the life I'd put on hold for so many years, the life I'd let fear keep me away from.

I challenged myself to push work and other concerns out of my head, even if just for the night, and nodded. "Let's go."

# Thirty

By the time we pulled into his garage and stepped out of the car, a heady anticipation had coiled low in my belly.

He linked his fingers with mine. "Have I told you how glad I am you're here?"

"A few times."

"Only a few? I've been remiss. I'm so glad you're here."

As we walked, I took in the dove gray walls and framed photos lining the hallway. I paused for a moment to admire one of Jake laughing, splayed out on a green lawn, covered with small children with matching gleeful expressions. "Your nieces and nephews?"

He wrapped his arms around my waist and rested his smooth jaw next to my face. "All eleven. Love those little monsters." I smiled at the photo again, the energy of his family jumping off the wall in such stark contrast to how I'd grown up.

"Is this your grandpa? The one you're named after?" I pointed at a photo of a five- or six-year-old Jake grinning with two missing front teeth and standing next to an older white-haired version of adult Jake. Both held fishing rods.

"Yep."

"You look like him." I trailed my hand over another photo, this one of a young Jake, maybe fourteen, surrounded by four girls. The five of them had arms slung around one another's shoulders, wearing matching green T-shirts. I hardly recognized him. In the photo, Jake was the shortest of his siblings and had chubby cheeks. His teeth were covered in braces, but his eyes were the same familiar blue.

Jake swayed against me and pecked a small kiss at my temple. "Family reunion. We'd go camping every year with my mom's extended family. That was my awkward phase."

"I think you were cute," I commented, letting my body rest backward against his.

He snorted. "You think I would have had a shot with you?"

"Depends," I said, glancing back over my shoulder. "Were your jokes any better back then?"

His body shook with the rumble of his laugh. "Nope."

"I think twelve-year-old me would have still asked you to play kickball." I smiled and stroked my hand over his. "You know, your house is different from what I expected."

"Were you expecting a messy bachelor pad?" He slipped his hands around my stomach, his fingers splayed across my abdomen, the warmth and pressure of his touch through my dress keeping my body at a steady simmer. "Empty pizza boxes? Beer and car posters on the walls?"

I chuckled. "No. It's just very . . . homey."

"I'd love to take credit, but my sister did the decorating

down here. I'm not sure I would have ever thought to hang family pictures."

"Do you miss them? Your family?"

"Yeah. I got this place about six months ago, and Molly and her husband, Chris, came out to help me move. I haven't seen anyone since then, though."

*He never lived here with Gretchen. Thank God.* The idea of being in the middle of their relationship ghosts left me uneasy.

"I told Molly about you." He spoke into my ear as we paused near a photo of Jake and a tall guy at graduation. I guessed that was Tyson.

"You told your sister about me?"

"Of course. And that probably means my entire family knows. We don't do secrets well."

My heart swelled, and an unfamiliar sense of security settled around me. I meant enough to him to tell his family, and I wondered what he'd told them.

"What's she like? That's your twin, right?"

He nodded. "She's tough and doesn't take shit from anyone, especially me, never has. Super competitive, fiercely protective, and funny. She's an orthopedic surgeon. I think you'll like her."

She sounded a little like Felicia. I bet I would, and I didn't miss him saying *I will* versus *I would* like her.

"Um, can we not talk about my family anymore, though?"

I stretched my neck to the side as he swept my hair away. "What do you want to talk about now?"

"I had help downstairs," he said, brushing his lips over the skin below my ear. "But the bedroom is all me."

His lips on my neck warmed me, and I arched into him. "Is that a subtle hint you want me in your bedroom?"

He ground against my backside. "I didn't think it was that subtle."

He turned me and curled his fingers to the nape of my neck. Jake's eyes looked darker, heated with want, and I slid my own hands to his trim waist, trailing along his belt.

I bit my lower lip and locked my eyes with his.

Jake pulled me flush against his growing erection and planted a long, lingering kiss on my lips. We stumbled up the stairs, barely breaking the connection, our mouths and bodies fused. It was a wonder we didn't end up toppling over. In those moments, Jake owned my kisses, his tongue and lips insistent and demanding, and I gave in freely. When we reached the landing, he pressed me to the wall, hands tangling in my hair and pulling me to his face. "God, you make me lose my mind."

The wall was cool against my back, in stark contrast to the heat between us as he kissed me again. His thigh pressed between my legs, the friction a preview at how he could ease the ache there, and I ground against him.

"I want you." He breathed out the words between kisses, his wide palm gripping my ass to pull me closer to him.

I'd never imagined being controlled in this way would make me feel so wanted, but it did. With Jake, it did because I knew he'd hand back control, that he didn't need to own my body to know my body. "Take me, then."

A low groan escaped his lips, and he lifted me, effortlessly, so that my legs could wrap around his waist and my arms around his neck. I scraped my nails along the back of his head and kissed his throat as he carried me into his bedroom, setting me on the edge of the dresser.

I helped his hands through the swirling fabric of my dress, guiding him where I wanted, over my knees and up my thighs to my pulsing center. I reveled at the way his breath quickened when he slid his fingers under the lace of my panties.

"Nay, it's so damn sexy that you know what you want."

Every nerve ending in my body was on edge as he slipped a long, thick finger inside me. His deft movements made me quake, my thighs tense, and my breath hitched.

"More," I moaned, as his lips trailed from my mouth to my neck, planting sweet kisses and playful swipes of his tongue along the column of my throat.

I reached for his belt, but he stopped me, holding my wrist gently.

"I want to get you there first. I love watching you." His thumb moved in tight circles over my compact bundle of nerves, the pressure sending waves of sensation up and over my body, the inevitable peak surging forward.

I repeated *yes* in a harried whimper and he slid a second finger in alongside the first. In that moment, my entire life boiled down to wanting more. More of his body, more of his time, more of his voice, and more moments like this where I felt so good that I couldn't make room for anxiety or fear.

"So perfect," he murmured, thrusting his fingers faster and finding that perfect spot inside me. "I can tell you're so close."

My voice was breathless and desperate as I bucked my hips against his hand. It felt so good, the pressure building, that I was afraid to exhale until his lips met my neck.

"Jake! Jake!" I crashed through the building tension, my body pulsing around his slowing movements, his tongue lapping at my neck. I slumped against him, and his chest heaved even as he pressed his lips to mine.

"I need to be inside you," he groaned, pushing his pants and boxers down. His erection sprung free, thick and rigid, bobbing against his stomach.

I stretched to grip it, wrapping my fingers around him, and his head fell back.

"Fuck," he said before dragging my soaked panties down, the feel of his hands sliding over my legs sending tingles back up to my center.

"Exactly," I said, reaching for him again.

He fumbled with a condom he'd pulled from his pocket, and I smiled in anticipation as he ripped it open.

"I love watching you do that," I murmured, moving my fingers with his.

"You do?" His voice was husky.

"Yes." I rocked up to meet him. The frenzy moving through my body was electric, and after my first orgasm, I was greedy. I watched him roll the condom down his length. "Reminds me how you feel inside me."

"And you like when I'm inside you," he murmured, pressing into my folds, filling me. He gazed at me intently, pupils wide, making his blue eyes appear darker as he slid deeper, so achingly slow.

"Yes . . ." I breathed harder, the words leaving my mouth with desperate exhalations as he built to an even, steady rhythm matching my own. The way he filled me, his ridges rubbing me deep, I dug my nails into his shoulders and was losing control fast. Only, it wasn't just my body I was losing control of. I'd somehow shifted to flirting with needing someone, with craving him. "Yes!" I groaned as his thumb rolled over me with a perfect pressure each time he moved.

His eyes flashed, and he thrust into me harder. "Naya," he growled. He wrapped his arm around me, pulling me to the edge of the dresser, the angle of our bodies shifting.

The way he reacted was exhilarating. I wrapped my legs at his waist, my heels pressing against the back of his thighs. The items on the dresser rattled and toppled with our momentum, and I wondered what we might look like to a casual observer. Two people in formal wear going at it, unable to make it to the bed or take the time to set aside clothing. They'd think we were reckless and maybe a little wild. The thought made me smile.

"You're so fucking amazing," he exclaimed, pumping into me hard, my body shifting to meet him with each powerful thrust.

His words, the sound of his voice, affected me, too. Tension wound in my belly, the delicious friction pushing me closer.

"Tell me what you want." His eyes bored into mine, sending sparks through my body to my heart before pinging between my legs.

I writhed against him as the combination of his thumb and his hard thrusts pushed me to the edge of the cliff, and I was holding on by the tips of my fingers. Jake's eyes locked with mine, and I once again had that sensation of him seeing everything, and in that moment, I wanted him to see everything, to know me inside and out. "You. I need you, just like this."

Our lips met, my muscles coiled, and heat radiated out-

ward from my center. In an instant, I shattered, all the pleasure and intensity flooding my system as wave after wave rolled
through me.

Jake's breath quickened. "Oh, Naya," he panted, pressing
his lips to my neck. He thrust twice more and then pulsed
inside me with the power of his release. He shuddered, mur-
muring my name as our bodies stilled.

We remained entwined, pressed against each other, catching our breath. I was afraid to move, to break the connection,
afraid the way he filled me emotionally might dissipate when
we pulled apart. I wrapped my arms around his shoulders, and
he held me close. I couldn't shake the feeling that that was
where I was supposed to be.

Finally, we separated enough for our eyes to meet again,
and he dipped his forehead to mine. A grin spread across his
face, chest heaving. "I'm so glad you're here."

Jake helped me off the dresser before disposing of the condom.
I took in the room—one entire wall was a large picture window overlooking the lake behind his house; opposite of that
was a king-sized bed adorned with a thick gray comforter. I
gazed out over the water. Even in the dark, it was mesmerizing. The moonlight reflected off the lake in a long, wavering
line.

I thought those few moments of solitude would have been
an opportunity to reset the flurry of emotions, but the way I
ached to reconnect with him was a reminder of how fast I was
falling. I'd never experienced anything like it, and I worried
great sex after such a long dry spell might have skewed my per-

ception. Maybe after not being able to trust someone, I was giving Jake too much credit too early. I leaned against the window frame with the lush carpet under my toes. The memories of his touches lingered on my skin and how his grin made me feel filled my head. *No, this is something special.* It was the *special* I had no idea how to handle.

I spoke over my shoulder, hearing Jake reenter the room. "It's beautiful."

He pressed behind me, wrapping his arms around my waist and dropping a kiss to my shoulder. "Not as beautiful as you."

I rolled my eyes, unable to bite back the grin. "That was so cheesy."

"I can't help it." He'd tossed his shirt aside, and the hairs on his chest tickled my bare back. "The view is why I bought the house, though." He rested his chin near my temple. "There's something really great about waking up every morning with the sun shining in over the lake." His hand continued over my back and ran along the edge of the dress. "It will be better with you next to me."

"Do you ever worry someone can see in?" I stretched my arms to stroke his face.

"Not when it's dark in here. Plus, my property reaches the shoreline. Does it bother you, though? I can close the blinds."

"No," I murmured, my voice a throaty rumble. "I like it."

"I like you." His tongue and soft lips grazed the back of my neck, the pressure of his mouth both gentle and eager.

"Not bored with me yet?"

Jake swept a piece of hair away and brushed his lips along the top of my shoulder. "Never. Do I need to add convincing you to my to-do list?"

"What's on it already?"

When he pulled at the zipper on my dress, the delicate fabric fell to the floor in a gentle *swoosh*. "Getting you out of this dress, for one. Check." He cupped my breasts, reverently, as if testing their weight, and his thumbs swiped over my nipples in languid circles.

"Discover if you're wearing any of your fancy underwear."

"I was. You pulled them off."

"That was on my list, too." His voice was gravelly as he massaged my breasts, moving to roll each nipple and generating a cluster of sparks inside me. "Check."

I squirmed under his touch as he kissed lower down the side of my neck and back up my jaw. "You can't be ready to go again, already," I said with a low groan.

"Not yet, but I can take care of you." He pulled me a few steps away from the window to the edge of the bed, where we fell back against the comforter and he wrapped me in his arms. "Getting you in my bed has been on my list for a long time."

"Check." I ran my fingers through his hair, and he sighed at my touch.

"I can't stop touching you," he said as I gazed at him. "And I don't want to stop. Feeling you, being with you . . . it's like a drug."

"I'm okay with you staying off the wagon," I teased, letting my fingertips graze along his jawline and over his ears. "I think you've ruined me for any other man."

"Good." He smiled, but his intense stare didn't ease into humor. "You know, you're constantly on my mind. I get so damn excited from a simple text." He paused, looking into my eyes. "Nay, I'm not seeing anyone else."

I swallowed. "I'm not, either."

His gaze roamed over my face, looking for something. "I'm . . ." he started and stopped again.

"What?" I asked, softly.

"Do you remember back in Chicago when you wanted to know if I had any fears besides heights?"

"Sure."

"Well, I *am* scared of other things. I'm scared that I'm going to screw it up or you'll do something like Gretchen did, but I'm crazy about you," he murmured into the dark.

His words were moving, vulnerable, open, and perfect. My heart thrummed. In the deepest parts of me, I wanted to confess I might be falling in love with him. "I'm crazy about you, too, Jake." My pulse quickened at the thought, and I veered the conversation to a playful place, unprepared to jump all the way in. "And not just because you give me multiple, mind-blowing orgasms."

He pulled me flush against him. "That helps, though?"

"It doesn't hurt. Were you writing a thesis on the female anatomy for all those years you weren't getting laid in college?"

His chest rumbled against me with his low laugh. "No, but what a missed opportunity. I . . ."

I pictured him hunched over tables in a dusty library, working through the perfect combination of steps. "What? Is there really a story here?" I was getting good at playful and flirtatious, and that ground felt steady, much steadier than wading into the pool of feelings.

"My family does a gift exchange thing at Christmas and we draw names. It started with normal presents, but the goal for years has been to be as funny and inappropriate as possible."

He shrugged. "When I was nineteen or twenty, my brother-in-law bought me a pop-up picture book titled *How to Please a Woman*."

I clasped my hand over my mouth to cover the laugh. "You're kidding me."

"I was mortified. It was quite . . . detailed, and I opened the gift in front of my entire family."

I admired the easy smile that crossed his face as he shrugged.

"But . . . I committed a few pages to memory. Is that weird?"

"Completely. Do you still have the book? I'm very curious."

His laugh echoed off the walls and he squeezed me. "God, Naya, I lo—" Jake stopped himself, then paused for a brief moment, but my face was pressed to his neck and I couldn't see his eyes. I didn't want to believe he was about to say he loved me—didn't want to hope. "I regifted it the next year, and it's been making the rounds since then, almost like a traveling trophy."

"Your family is so weird—it's amazing, but remind me to send your brother-in-law a thank-you card," I said.

"You can thank him yourself one day," he said as I dropped my head to his chest, my arm draped over his stomach.

*One day.* This was another reference to us being together in the future, and not knowing how to define and categorize this relationship made me anxious. If this was something that lasted, what would that mean for the cuts at Thurmond? There were no guarantees my job would be safe, and I wondered how that could work.

I shook away the questions in my head, and we lay in comfortable silence, hands linked over his stomach. His chest rose and fell, the hair tickling the sides of my palm. I'd gotten used to hearing his heartbeat when we lay like this. Even through the medicinal haze of our trip to Cincinnati, I remembered how comfortable the steady beat had made me feel. I looked up at him. "You never told me. When we were in Cincinnati, did you enjoy the movies?"

He chuckled. "Um . . . how sure are you that you like me?"

"Eighty percent?" I joked, squeezing his hand. "Why? Didn't like them?"

"I couldn't get through the first one," he admitted.

"What?" I lifted my head to meet his eyes. "Seriously?"

"I tried! I did, but you were asleep by then and . . . it was just so silly."

"I'm in shock, I really am. How is that even possible? I don't know if I can seriously be with someone who doesn't like *Star Wars*!" I exclaimed, hitting his chest playfully, though he caught my wrist in soft hands.

"Are you seriously with me?" he asked, picking up on my words.

"Not if you can't get through one of the best movies ever made," I teased, but his expression remained serious, so I continued. "But otherwise . . ." I let my hand rest over his heart. "Maybe. Do you want to be?" I finished, my voice unsteady.

He searched my face. "Of course I do." His fingertips grazed my cheek. "I want us to be exclusive. I want to admit that I already added a note on my calendar that May seventh is the day I met you, and, yeah, I want to be seriously in this with you."

I didn't know how to respond other than making another joke, but he kissed me tenderly, pulling my lower lip between his, slowly sliding his fingers into my hair. The kiss was like salted caramel, and I didn't have to respond.

We parted, our faces close together. "Long-distance is hard, I know. And my ex told me I worked too much, and didn't communicate enough, and she was right, but I'll try. I will be better with you." His eyes grazed over my face earnestly.

"Well," I started, tracing my hand over his chest. "I . . ." Nervousness crept across his expression.

"You'd have to give the movies another try," I deadpanned.

He didn't miss a beat and pulled his hands from me. "I guess it's not meant to be, then." He looked away before flashing a large smile at me and kissing me again, his arms wrapping around me.

"What about work?"

"We'll figure it out," he said in a low voice. "Seriously, Naya—Carlton and I put some checks and balances in place, like I promised. I'm not part of the team reviewing your department. We can also keep it quiet until this is all over if you want. Would that make you feel better?"

I weighed his words while longing for his fingers to move against my skin again, for him to distract me with his touch. "So, you're my boyfriend?"

"Do you want to go steady?" His lopsided smile filled me with butterflies.

"Is that what it's called for adults?" I asked, nervous and comfortable—it was a strange and conflicting ball of emotions. "I'll require use of your letter jacket."

"Maybe I do have you fooled if you think I had a letter jacket." He laughed, his head tipping back. "Are you really going to make me watch *Star Wars* again?"

A yawn escaped my lips. "Definitely."

He returned my yawn and smiled sleepily at me. We snuggled together, our naked bodies pressed close to each other. I fell asleep enveloped in his arms, the moonlight over the lake pouring into the large picture window.

# Thirty-one

Jake's friends strode toward our table the next morning. Both men were tall, one tanned and slim with blond hair and the other with skin a little darker than mine and a shaved head. On the drive over, Jake had assured me that his friends would like me. I tried to repeat that in my head; the gravity of meeting people close to Jake, of really being part of his life was scary. My gut reaction was to retreat, but it was too late, so I took a deep breath and smiled.

"I'm Eric." The blond reached out to me. "This is my fiancé, Tyson."

"Sorry we're late," Tyson grumbled. "*Someone* refused to leave until the puppy was perfectly settled."

"Naya," I said, shaking his hand. "You have a puppy?"

"A ten-week-old golden retriever."

Tyson eyed Eric with an affectionate exasperation. "She's a dog. She didn't need the perfect white noise setting and six blankets to be alone for a couple hours." He looked to Jake for support. "You're with me, right?"

Jake held up his hands. "I am not getting in the middle again."

"I think I read somewhere that white noise can help puppies relax in new environments," I offered. "What's her name?"

"Bandit." Eric beamed like a new father, pulling out his phone to share photos of the little golden fluff ball. I'd wanted a dog since I was a kid, but my mom was allergic, and then I'd stayed so busy with work, it never seemed like an option. My heart lurched looking at photos of the puppy as some people's did looking at baby pictures. I still didn't have time, especially since I'd committed to a long-distance relationship less than twelve hours earlier, but maybe I could start volunteering. *To do: Check out the humane society website.*

"Anyway, we're celebrating," Tyson said, draping an arm across the back of Eric's chair.

Jake raised an eyebrow, peeking up from his menu. "Celebrating?"

Eric's energy was contagious, and I liked him immediately. "The first time in forever you brought a woman with you to brunch."

"I brought my sister that one time."

"That doesn't count, Romeo."

I tried to jump into the conversation. "Do you all work together?"

"I see you've been talking about us nonstop, Jake," Eric said after the waitress returned with coffee and a tray of mimosas.

Jake shrugged. "How could I do justice to meeting you in person?"

Tyson's assessing glances made me want to double-check I'd combed my hair or that I hadn't accidentally put my shirt on backward.

"I actually work with his dreaded ex, and these two met in college." Eric glanced between Tyson and Jake expectantly, using his hand to motion for them to begin speaking. "Tell the story. You know you want to."

"We were roommates freshman year, but we became friends when Tyson lost a bet," Jake began with a laugh.

"A bet?"

Tyson's expression softened. "With a guy on our floor. We bet we could beat him and his roommate in *Mario Kart*."

"*You* bet a guy on our floor and sprung it on me when I got home from class one day," Jake added. The telling of this story seemed choreographed, as if they'd told it hundreds of times before, like an old married couple.

"Long story short, Jake didn't tell me he sucked."

"*Mario Kart* and basketball, huh?" I said, turning to Jake.

"You've seen him play basketball and you still like him?" Eric asked.

Jake shot his friend a playful glare. "I'm good at badminton. Does that count for anything?"

I was, again, struck by Jake's comfort with having his short-comings out in the open and his ability to joke about them. I couldn't help but spend a moment making the comparison to Davis, who would go to any lengths to make sure he didn't look bad, including throwing me under the bus.

Jake's smile was easygoing before he shifted his gaze to Tyson. "Anyway, we lose and then I learn the terms of this bet—"

Tyson shrugged. "Losers had to join the ballroom dance club for a month. I really didn't think we could lose. I didn't realize Jake spent so much time playing because he was trying to figure out how the controller worked."

"After I threatened to kill him, we became good friends . . . and decent dancers." Jake squeezed my shoulder.

I turned to Jake. "So that's where the sweet moves come from, huh?"

He shrugged one shoulder. "It was actually fun. I stuck with it for a while."

Eric closed his menu and beamed. "I wish Tyson and I had a story that cute."

"Our story is fine." Tyson rolled his eyes again but stretched to plant a sweet kiss on Eric's cheek. "Jake and Gr—" Tyson stopped, eyes flashing to Jake. "We met through Jake."

"You met at Thomas's wedding?" Eric leaned forward on the table.

"Same trip," Jake said after returning Tyson's pointed look with a slight head nod.

I took a drink from my mimosa, as I did my best to ignore the exchange between Jake and Tyson. "I was waiting to meet friends who ended up having to cancel. I found myself talking the ear off a stranger in a bar." I reached for his hand. "Enter, Jake."

"Wait, wait, wait," Eric interrupted. "You met in a bar? I need a moment to process that."

I must have looked confused as I contemplated my misstep. *Isn't meeting in a bar normal? Did I inadvertently share something embarrassing?* I'd been so concerned with figuring out how not to make a fool of myself, I hadn't stopped to think about the location.

"That came out wrong," Eric reassured. "It's just that Jake is not overly social."

Tyson came to his friend's defense. "Babe, you make him sound like a hermit."

Eric gave a plaintive *c'mon* expression, which Tyson returned with *be nice.* Eric's attention shifted to me. "Okay, Jake is shy. It's hard to imagine him approaching someone in a bar, is all. Is that better?"

"You know I'm sitting *right here?*" Jake asked, finishing his drink.

"It's not a bad thing. You've always been that way, right? Last time she visited, your sister told me that back in the day, your parents bribed you to ask a girl to prom." Eric's eyes lit up as he started the story, and Tyson stifled a laugh, his fist covering a grin.

"You have to remind me to thank her for sharing that," Jake muttered.

"What were you bribed with?" I squeezed his knee under the table.

"Oh, that's the best part!" Eric exclaimed.

Jake interrupted. "It's not that interesting."

"Now I really want to know."

"He got to go to math camp if he asked her."

Jake hung his head, a grin across his reddened face. "You know, I am still trying to impress this woman."

"Oh, believe me, I'm impressed. I've never dated anyone who went to math camp. Did the bribe work?"

Jake laughed. "Well, sort of. The girl said no. I met some-one at the camp, though. My first kiss was there."

"I have such a great picture of this," Eric exclaimed. "I'm imagining sweat bands, tube socks, and graphing calculators."

Jake addressed Tyson, whose smile cracked from behind his hand. "Are you sure you want to marry him?"

"More often than not." Tyson nodded, a flash of adoration for his fiancé crossing his face. "But I guess you'd be the man to calculate the exact ratio."

The three of them had this wonderfully comfortable rap-port, and I felt increasingly at home as part of the foursome. Jake rubbed his thumb across the nape of my neck as he laughed along with his friends.

"So, you were the mack-daddiest of all the studs at math camp?" Eric asked.

"Well . . ."

"Oh no." Tyson chuckled.

"*She* kissed me, but it still counts."

"So, *she* was the mack-daddiest of all the studs at math camp. That makes more sense," Eric corrected. I was positive he and Felicia would get along.

Jake pinned Eric and Tyson with a mock-pleading look. "I thought maybe, *just maybe*, you would tell stories that make me look good. What was I thinking?"

Eric turned to me. "He does all kinds of charity work, talks to his mother regularly, and makes a mean chicken cac-ciatore. His fashion sense is above average, and he paid for his secretary to go on a Caribbean cruise with her husband as a Christmas gift last year." Eric took a sip of his mimosa. "He's generous to a fault, loves kids, and is really smart, but he's not allowed to attend math-related events anymore because the combined impact of all of the panties dropping at his impressive nerdiness throws off the calculators."

Jake flipped off his friend. "I get the microphone at your wedding. Remember that." Jake stood and asked Tyson, "Can you keep your better half from telling more embarrassing stories about me until I get back from the bathroom?"

"He *is* a good guy," Eric said when Jake was out of earshot. "And he hasn't seemed this happy in a while. He's into you."

Heat rose on my cheeks. "Well, I'm pretty into him, too."

Eric smiled, but Tyson's expression was more guarded. "Just don't fuck with his head, okay?"

I was taken aback, and stammered, "I–I, I don't plan to."

"Not that we think you would, but Jake's family to us." Eric's voice was smoother, and he shot a pointed look at Tyson before returning his gaze to me. "I said he was shy earlier? That's not really the right word. He's just nice. So, just don't take him for granted. That's all we're trying to say. His ex did a number on him."

I opened my mouth to say something that would reassure him and myself that I could be a good partner. Of course, our decision the night before to make ourselves an official "us" had me questioning if I *was* ready and if I really would be a good girlfriend. I knew I wouldn't cheat on him, but I had no idea if I was whole enough to be a true partner. That we were going to keep the relationship under wraps until the review of Thurmond was over made me feel slightly at ease. I'd have time to practice, to get it right, before anyone in my life was watching. Before I could form any of that into a coherent response, a woman's voice interrupted our conversation.

"Eric?"

Both men glanced over their shoulders. A woman waved as she strode toward our table. She was tall and slim with loose blond hair in waves, a Marc Jacobs bag slung over one shoulder, and an iced coffee in her perfectly manicured hand.

"Speak of the devil," Tyson muttered under his breath.

"Behave," Eric chided.

"I thought that was you." The low, kind of smoky voice sounded familiar. "I popped in for coffee and saw you over here. I had to come say hi." She smiled at Tyson and Eric, showing perfectly straight, white teeth behind plump, glossy lips.

Tyson sat straighter. Eric cocked his head to the side with a pleasant, if somewhat cool, expression, but it looked forced. *Who is this woman?*

"How are you, Gretchen?" Eric's gaze trailed to me for a moment, and my expression must have shown that I knew the name.

*Why did I never consider the possibility we'd run into her?*

"Oh, I'm great," she said, a chipper note to her voice. She didn't seem to register Tyson scowling at her and shot me only a cursory dismissive glance. "Heading into the office for a few hours. Have you seen Jacob? He's been ducking my calls since my brother's wedding."

Eric pressed his lips together and shrugged.

"He'd call you back if he wanted to talk to you." Tyson cast his gaze to the side, arms crossed over his chest.

She cocked her head to the side. "Always nice to see you, Tyson."

"Go to hell," he returned under his breath, and Eric shot him an exasperated look.

If the woman was surprised by Tyson's harsh words, she didn't show it. Her eyes narrowed, and one side of her mouth turned up. "You never liked me."

"Cheaters rub me the wrong way."

"Half of the gay men in Raleigh rubbed you the wrong way before I introduced you to Eric, so be nice." She cast a sweet look to Eric, who pinched the bridge of his nose.

"You're both adults," he muttered from behind his hand.

"He started it. Anyway, can you tell Jacob to call me if you happen to—" She stopped, her gaze flicking up. "Oh, well here he is now." Her tone changed, an iciness forming below the sweet surface.

Jake stopped short before sitting. "What are you doing here?"

"Well, hello to you, too. Eric and Tyson were protecting you from me, apparently."

Jake wrapped his arm around my shoulder, and she seemed to notice me for the first time, a spark of shrewd assessment spreading across her face, and her eyes flicked to his hand on my shoulder.

*Did he do that for my benefit or hers?* I wasn't sure if I should feel like a stage prop or a support structure.

Her pretty blue eyes narrowed slightly, and she seemed to be working through a problem in her head.

Somewhere deep in my body, the urge to rise and strike pulsed, to fight for what was mine. I shoved it down when Jake spoke again, his voice even.

"Do you need something, Gretchen?"

"You've been avoiding my calls. I want to meet. Some night this week?" She glanced at me again but said nothing.

"But I'm sure you've been *busy*. I'll have our secretaries set up dinner."

"I think the lawyers can handle everything."

"If I told you once, I told you a thousand times," she began, brushing a strand of blond hair back off her neck in the most delicate way imaginable, "if people could just talk to one another, Eric and I wouldn't make so much money. You never listen to me."

Jake's jaw tightened, but he didn't respond. I wondered if that was frustration at her saying it or guilt at it being true.

She shifted her catlike gaze again. "You should know he never listens, but I'm being so rude." She stretched her hand in my direction. "I'm Gretchen Vanderkin-Shaw. I was the woman at this table once upon a time." She laughed, a breathy, humorless sound. "It's been a while now, I guess." Something flashed across her face, breaking through the mask of quick-witted confidence. She looked sad, and I had a moment of sympathy for her. I'd only heard Jake's side of their story, after all, and it was probably painful to see him with someone else. Her veneer reappeared quickly, though, the flash of sadness replaced with cool skepticism. "Anyway, who are you?"

"Naya," I said quickly, trying to infuse confidence into my voice. "I'm visiting from Chicago."

Jake's posture was casual, but his entire body tensed. "My girlfriend, Gretch."

Her brows lifted, surprise curling her expression. "You're the woman from the hotel, aren't you?"

I stammered inside my head, trying to think of how to answer. *Why, yes. I'm the one you heard screaming through the walls while your soon-to-be-ex-husband repeatedly went to town on me.*

"I see. How nice. Well, then, I'll leave you to your . . ." She paused, her gaze slipping back to Jake's hand on my shoulder, which tightened. "Breakfast."

She spoke again before I could think of something to interject. "We'll have dinner soon, Jacob. See you at the office, Eric." She waved and turned on her heel. "It was nice to meet you, Nora."

*What the hell just happened?*

The table was silent as Gretchen walked away. Tyson's expression darkened, Eric rolled his eyes, and Jake took a long sip from his water glass muttering something incoherent under his breath.

"Well," Eric said with a heavy exhale in my direction. "Now you've met Gretchen."

"She seems . . ." I tried to think of the right words, glancing up at Jake, whose expression gave nothing away. Turns out I didn't have to.

"Like a self-important nightmare," Tyson finished.

I cracked a small smile. *Yeah. As much as I avoided demeaning other women, that fit.*

"Change of subject," Eric demanded, then asked, "What do you do, Naya? Jake said something about teaching?"

Tyson's gaze moved back to me, not interrogating, but I still felt he was cautiously gathering information, like a protective older brother. No wonder, if that woman was Jake's ex.

"I'm a professor; I specialize in math education, particularly how technology can enhance math education for students whose first language isn't English. What about you?"

Tyson's face instantly softened, and his eyes brightened. "I'm a teacher—"

Eric cut him off. "His fourth graders love him."

Jake looked down at me. "Your big research project is with fourth graders, isn't it?" It almost felt like Jake was bragging about my work, and it warmed me through and through. "You'd be into the project, Tys. Tell them about it, Naya." He and Eric listened intently as Tyson and I talked about teaching and learning math, and I felt more at home at this table by the minute.

"How long are you in town? Has it been very hard living so far apart?" Eric asked, plucking a piece of fruit from his plate, his sensible egg white omelet already decimated.

My order of chicken and waffles was less sensible, but delicious. I was stuffed.

"I'm leaving early on Monday morning. Quick trip," I responded, ignoring his question about long-distance relationships.

"We're going to the office so I can give her the grand tour," Jake added.

"The woman flies across the country to see you and you take her to work?" Eric gave Jake a deadpan expression, and Tyson raised an eyebrow.

I'd wanted to see his office and where he spent so much of his time. Like me, Jake had shared that his office often felt like home. We'd Skyped several times when he was working late, and I'd entertained myself with more than one fantasy about pushing the neatly stacked folders off his big desk and taking a break from work together. "All my idea," I chimed in.

"If that's true, you may have found your perfect woman," Eric mused.

# Thirty-two

Like it did almost every night, the tone warbled to indicate our video call was connecting, and Jake's face flashed across my screen.

"Hey, you."

I stretched out on my couch with my laptop on my knees, and my heart did a funny dance at the sound of his voice. "Where are you tonight?"

Jake traveled so often, I usually didn't know where he was on a given day. I wondered how people had families with jobs like his. I bet he would be one of those dads who returned from every trip with something for the kids and me. *Whoa, where am I going with this?*

"Have you ever been to Tempe?" He sounded tired, and his white dress shirt was rumpled.

"I can't say I have. Tell me about Tempe."

"It's hot," he sighed. "I arrived this morning to meet with a prospective client, and it was over a hundred degrees already."

He sat back on the bed in his hotel room, loosening a sage green tie and undoing his top buttons, his hands scraping the five-o'clock shadow covering his jaw.

*My boyfriend is sexy.* Even though it had been a month since my trip to North Carolina, the term "boyfriend" still felt strange, like a word in a foreign language.

Jake had made one more weekend trip to Chicago, and we'd managed to escape my apartment long enough to watch Fourth of July fireworks. It had been three weeks since I'd seen him, and I missed the way his breath felt against the back of my neck when we fell asleep. I was beginning to feel listless, looking for ways to fill my time outside of work. I started volunteering, Felicia and I worked out with Wes once a week, which was fun, and I'd enrolled in one of his self-defense seminars, but it wasn't enough to take my mind off missing Jake, worrying about my job, and avoiding contact with Davis, who I hadn't run into again, but who was periodically texting.

"How was your day?" I asked.

"I may have to ask you to bail me out of jail," he grumbled.

"Why are you flirting with the law?" I carried the laptop into my bedroom and settled on the bed.

"Gretchen won't let up. I'm ready to just give in to whatever she wants, so she loses her excuse to call me." He sighed and leaned back.

My jaw clenched at the mention of his ex. I wasn't a jealous person, but I'd searched for Jake's wife online in a moment of weakness and immediately regretted it. In addition to being the perfect physical specimen I'd encountered at the diner, Gretchen Vanderkin-Shaw was also, apparently, brilliant. A magna cum laude graduate, a law degree from an Ivy League school, and a partner in a law firm by thirty-five, she also had a philanthropy record that probably rivaled Jake's. She'd been honored for her work to build pipelines for women of color practicing law, and in any other circumstance, I might have been excited to meet her. In this reality, she was basically the exact person I least wanted my boyfriend to be married to. *Though, ideally, your boyfriend isn't married at all.*

"What happened?"

"She's been going on and on about us being on the *same page* about our split." He raised his fingers to make air quotes. His speech got faster as his frustration rose. "I don't want to have dinner. I don't want to talk to her."

"That sucks," I answered honestly, but something felt off. It took a lot to rile Jake.

He shook his head the way he did when he wanted to move on from a topic. He never wanted to talk about Gretchen. His expression flashed exasperation for a moment before resignation took over. "Is it weird to talk to you about this? I feel like this is dangerous territory."

I adopted a soft tone, trying to infuse some humor. "If I end the call in a fit of rage, you'll know for next time."

His lips tipped up in a grin. "I bet you're cute in a fit of rage. Do you stomp your feet and pound your fists?"

"No, since I'm not seven. I would eviscerate you with my razor-sharp tongue, though."

"Sounds sexy." He smiled boyishly.

"Well, tell me what's going on," I said. "Maybe you'll get lucky."

Jake groaned. The screen froze for a second, the image of

him running his fingers through his hair still visible. "Meeting isn't out of line. I'm probably being a jerk avoiding her calls. It's just that she keeps pushing boundaries."

My hackles went up. "What do you mean?"

"She's always flirting with me, touching my arm, or referencing old inside jokes like we're still together."

I remembered her demeanor in the café and eavesdropping on them at the hotel, and a flash of possessiveness tore through me. I wondered if he ever missed her. I knew he'd never be unfaithful to me, but I couldn't blame him for thinking of her. She probably never needed to google how to flirt. I nodded, unsure what words would come out if I spoke.

"She just keeps right on acting like we'll be getting back together. Like this isn't real." His brows furrowed, and he was continually rubbing the back of his neck. "I mean, *she* was the one who cheated on *me*. I'm trying not to be a dick, but c'mon."

*Would you still be happily married now if she hadn't cheated?* It was the question wedged in my mind.

"This is weird," he added, probably taking some meaning from my silence. "I shouldn't have said anything. We don't need to talk about our exes."

"It's on your mind. We should talk about things on our minds." I fought the grimace of my own hypocrisy, not mentioning or even hinting at my own past and Davis's reappearance.

He stepped out of the frame on my screen. "I'm still here, just want to change," he said from off-screen.

"I'm sorry you have to deal with it, and that someone broke your heart like that."

"Well, kind of." His voice carried across the room before

he returned in just his boxer shorts and a T-shirt. Getting comfortable on the bed, he put on his reading glasses. I loved how cute he was in them even though he grumbled that needing them made him feel old.

"What do you mean?"

"I don't know if she broke my heart, exactly." Jake squinted and shook his head. He looked like a flustered puppy, but I schooled my expression.

"I hated that she cheated—I was embarrassed. Hurt and angry, and I felt betrayed, but I wasn't heartbroken."

"How does that work?"

"I told you I was a late bloomer?"

"Sure." I examined Jake's face as he blew out a breath slowly.

"When I was younger, I practically took up residence in the friend zone. No one ever wanted to date me, plus I'd usually been too unsure to ask anyone out. My confidence took some hits."

I leaned back against my pillows and nodded.

"Anyway, I met Gretchen after I got my MBA, and she was pretty and smart and interested in me. We were compatible and got along. We were both involved in the community, and we wanted the same things. She seemed like a woman I *should* be in love with, but there was just never that spark. But things were fine, and I told myself I didn't need fireworks, that maybe that didn't even exist in real life. I assumed that getting along would be enough." He knitted his brow and glanced off the screen.

"But it wasn't?"

"It was. For a while." He worried his lower lip with his

front teeth. "In retrospect, I didn't love her, not as much as I needed to, not like I should have. That's how I rationalized working long hours and not taking the time to talk to her about real things. I'm man enough to admit that." Jake rolled his shoulders and glanced up at the ceiling. "When we were together it wasn't fun. After a while, we didn't laugh and intimacy became a task, like emptying the dishwasher or doing laundry. She pulled away. I pulled away. I shouldn't have been so surprised when I walked in on her and the neighbor. When I'm with you, I feel so connected, like it's just you and me in the world. It was never like that with her."

Jake scrubbed a hand over his jaw. "At the time, all I could think was I still wasn't good enough." His voice trailed off, and his shoulders slumped. "I was feeling sorry for myself, but I was in a dark place before I met you."

My heart broke for him. "What Eric and Tyson said at brunch; it makes more sense now."

"What did they say?"

"They were looking out for you. They wanted to make sure I was for real."

"You're so for real." Jake pulled his lips to one side, and I wished I could reach through the screen to kiss him. "I'm not sure I've ever actually shared all of that with anyone. It's kind of embarrassing."

"Don't be embarrassed." I tucked my hair behind both ears. "What happened? Did you try to work it out, or . . ."

He released a slow breath. "She wanted to. Said we should go to counseling."

"But you didn't?"

He brought his elbows toward each other, his hands shifting to the back of his neck. "I didn't see the point. I couldn't envision ever trusting her again. At that point, I couldn't imagine trusting anyone, you know?"

I did know. Not for the first time, I wondered if it might be time to tell Jake the truth about my past.

"We'd been fighting a lot about starting a family," he explained. "It had always been a someday thing, and all of a sudden that changed to a never thing for her. She said she was too deep into her career to risk it by having kids. I didn't expect her to give up her career, though. I offered to stay home or cut back my hours, or that we could look into adopting an older child, but she got to a point where she refused to even discuss it.

"Anyway, after that, she said if I agreed to staying married, to forgiving her, she'd give in on having kids, even though she didn't want them, like that was something she could just barter."

His expression was rigid, a deep crease visible between his eyebrows.

"That hurt more than the cheating, her thinking about a child, *our child*, in such a transactional way. For me, it was a sign we didn't really know each other, so I told her that was it for me. After that, it was amicable, I guess."

I nodded. "I'm sorry that happened to you."

His face relaxed, the crease disappearing, and he shrugged, dropping his arms to his side. "It was for the best, in the end." He scrubbed his hand over his jaw before speaking again. "Do you want kids someday?"

I should have anticipated the question, but it caught me off guard. "I think so. Not . . . yet, but someday. My job is pretty demanding right now." *But I might not have it for long, as you know.*

His expression remained the same, but did I see his eyebrows dip, just a fraction of an inch? He was intently looking at my face, and I glanced off-screen. We'd been careful, always using condoms, but an accidental pregnancy was not something I could handle.

*To do: Research birth control options.*

I changed the subject, uncomfortable with the nervous energy rising in my stomach. "So, Tempe today and Boston Thursday?"

"Then, to see you." He smiled, breaking the tension. "Not that I don't love staying in bed with you, but do you want to do something with your friends when I'm there?"

Deep down, I was afraid they wouldn't see all the special things in him I saw. I was a little afraid they might see things I was missing, the way they might have with Davis if I'd let them spend more time together. Early on, after meeting Davis a couple of times, Felicia questioned what I saw in him, and after that, I made excuses for them to not be together. Felicia grew increasingly suspicious, and eventually, I stopped seeing her or Aaron at all. By that point, I knew they'd figure it out, so I withdrew. Eight months pregnant with the twins, my best friend barged into my apartment a few weeks after Davis and I broke up. His campaign to destroy me at work was in full swing, and I was on the verge of quitting when she demanded I come clean, and then held me while I cried like we'd never been apart. I was falling hard for Jake, and if Felicia told me she didn't trust him, I didn't know what I'd do.

"Maybe," I said, noncommittal. "Let's play it by ear."

"I can't wait to—"

My phone rang on the bedside table, cutting him off. I picked it up to silence the ringer when I saw the name. "Sorry, hold on, it's Joe." Jake nodded and waited for me. It was odd for Joe to be calling at all, let alone this late.

"Hi, Joe. What's up?" The feminine sob on the other end of the line was a definite sign this was not Joe.

"Naya? It's Elaine." His wife's voice was shaky.

"Elaine, what's wrong?"

"Joe had a heart attack three days ago. He's recovering from bypass surgery, and they're cautiously optimistic, but can you come to the hospital tomorrow? He's beside himself about something related to work. He's been asking for you."

My heart rate slowed incrementally. "Of course. I'll be there." Elaine gave me the information, and we hung up with a plan for me to visit in the morning, my mind still trying to cobble together an image of Joe—sturdy, grumpy, tough-love Joe—lying in a hospital bed.

"Are you okay?" Jake asked, his eyes meeting mine through the computer screen.

"Joe had a heart attack." My voice felt distant, as if disconnected from my body. I shook my head, willing my thoughts to come back together. "He wants to talk to me about work."

"Something going on?"

"I have no idea."

# Thirty-three

Joe looked so small under the fluorescent lighting, with monitors beeping and tubes running to and from his body. "It's gotta be you, Naya." He'd waved away my questions, and I'd sat and let him talk about work, because he'd said it relaxed him.

"So, will you take my place?" Joe wanted me to replace him on the president's advisory committee that would be a sounding board for Jake and his team.

*Warning!* flashed in my head in big neon lights.

"Joe . . . you know I shouldn't." I waffled between bringing up Jake or not with Joe in this condition, but I couldn't let him push for this without all the facts. "I'm still seeing that guy, the consultant. It wouldn't be right."

"Nay," he croaked, attempting to straighten in his bed before realizing he couldn't. "You're the most ethical person I know. I'm not worried about this."

"It would still look bad. I think someone more senior

should represent us, Joe. This isn't like the reception. This is making big decisions, and I don't have tenure yet. What about Anita? She loves this stuff."

"Do you need me to explain why Anita shouldn't represent us? She will fight change tooth and nail. That approach will not work here, not with this president." He gave me a level stare. He wasn't wrong. "I need someone who can play the game, and the president wants some pre-tenure voices in the room, anyway."

I agreed when he threatened to come back to work and do it himself. Joe would go to bat for me, no questions asked—he had, time and time again. I couldn't let him stew about this or try to rush his recovery by going back too soon. I agreed to take his place and hoped he couldn't see through the false confidence in my voice. *To do: Figure out how to divulge my conflict of interest without making myself a liability or causing Joe more stress.*

—————

A week later, I sat at a long conference table in the president's suite. I tapped my fingers on the mahogany and glanced around as the room filled. No one spoke. They chose seats and tried to look busy, everyone on their phones.

JAKE: Stop worrying. It will be fine.

NAYA: How did you know I was worrying?

JAKE: I know you. Maybe picture everyone in their underwear.

JAKE: Although, I'm not sure the image of Flip in tighty-whities is going to ease your mind.

NAYA: I dunno. He's not bad looking for an older guy.

JAKE: Whatever makes you happy. Tell me about it later.

JAKE: The meeting. Not your, I assume explicit, fantasy about
    Flip in skivvies.

I smiled to myself, took a deep breath, and stilled my fingers. *It doesn't matter that I'm one of the youngest, least-experienced,
and lowest-paid people in the room. I am qualified to be here.*

Jill from the accounting department walked in and shared
a brief smile with me, but she took one of the few available
seats on the other side of the room near Doug. He'd been a
good friend of Davis's and was a member of the president's cab-
inet. Though he'd never done anything specific to me, their
association gave me the creeps. President Lewis made eye contact with each of the twenty people around the room as he
spoke. "Welcome, everyone. Thank you for coming."

I settled back into my chair. *Here goes nothing.*

"We'll have a few others joining us, but let's get started."

Fifteen minutes later, we'd been given our charge. We
were to speak candidly with the consultants about our opinions on some early findings they'd unearthed. President Lewis
concluded by saying, "I can't promise you'll all be happy with
every decision, but it's important to me you are here."

I glanced down at my agenda. I'd told Jake about my spot
on the committee, and he'd offered to tell Flip about our relationship, but I knew I should be the one to do it. I planned
to talk with him about the conflict at the end of the meeting.
His secretary had indicated he would have fifteen minutes, and
that I should walk with him back to his office before he left
the country on a fundraising trip. I figured that would give me
time to exit gracefully if he removed me from the group.

The imposing wooden door swung open with a loud creak,

and all heads turned to stare at the latecomer sauntering in. He was tall, in his late forties, and wore an expensive-looking suit with a sharp red tie. *No, no, no.* I was afraid to look up to his face, but it didn't matter. I'd recognize that cocky swagger anywhere.

He took the chair across from me, pulling materials from his briefcase. My body went cold, and my foot bounced at full speed under the table. There was no quick way out of the room, and his proximity triggered an urge to run.

The president stopped to ask Davis to introduce himself.

"Sorry for my tardiness. I am Davis Garner, formerly—" He paused for a minute as his eyes met mine across the table. His eyes flicked down and up over my chest. "Former professor in the business school. I'm in administration at State now."

Around the room, some murmured hello and others gave him wide smiles, and the president continued with a nod. I tried to face him, but my gaze wandered back to Davis, who was eyeing me with his head tilted.

The president spoke for another fifteen minutes, providing context for what would be asked of us before opening for questions from the group. I noticed Davis thumbing at his phone. A chill ran through me and lingered as I felt my own device buzz in my pocket. I didn't dare pull it out for fear of what I might see on the screen.

I packed my things quickly. I wanted to get to the president before he was mobbed. I even got to my feet, but was stopped by a hand on my arm.

"I'm surprised to see you here. I thought it would only be senior people." The smug, clipped baritone of his voice hadn't changed.

I closed my eyes for a moment and took a deep breath before I turned. *He can't hurt me here. Be professional and get the hell out.* "Hello, Davis."

"You look good," he said, scanning my body again, this time moving down to my black high heels and all the way back up.

I turned to face the president again, but before I could speak, Davis spoke up. "Flip. So sorry I was late, but it's great to see you!" He smiled warmly at the president, who returned his smile and joined us. The warmth between them only chilled me further—I had no idea what game Davis was playing.

"Glad you made it," the older man said, clapping Davis on the shoulder. "And you're Naya Turner, right? Taking Joe's place?"

I nodded, extending one slightly trembling hand. My voice had gone somewhere, I wasn't sure where, but I couldn't find it.

"She's come a long way from the little student who followed me around," Davis joked with the president.

"Ah, so you're an alum as well as a faculty member?"

"I—uh—no." I figured out Davis's game, and I mentally scrambled to reestablish my footing. "We met a year after I started working here. I was never a student here." *And I never followed this asshole around.*

Davis tipped his head to the side. "Are you sure? I could have sworn . . ." He tucked one hand casually in his pocket and scratched his chin with the other, as if trying to recall something important.

"Quite sure."

"Oh well," Davis said, jovially. "You still look just as young as you did back then." He rested a heavy palm on my shoulder, and I bit back the instinct to knee him in the groin while pulling away, creating more space between us. "Shouldn't we all be so lucky, right, Flip?"

The two exchanged a laugh, and my pulse beat in my ears. *Great. Years of work to build up my reputation, and he makes me sound like an eighth grader with one comment.*

When someone pulled the president's attention from us, Davis leaned closer to me and whispered near my ear, "Did your legs look this good when you were following me around?"

His breath made my stomach churn.

I opened my mouth to respond, but he flicked his eyes over my body again and then back up to my face before I could. "We'll catch up soon, pretty girl." He winked, leaving me slack-jawed and feeling like I needed to shower.

"Flip, can I steal you for a minute?" Davis stepped around me and led President Lewis toward the door.

The older man paused and looked over his shoulder. "Dr. Turner, I know you wanted to tell me something. I'm late for a flight—please just email me." He smiled and waved before leaving the room with Davis. I should have asked for a brief minute, or at the very least, I should have said something, but my voice had gone into hiding again, and I had no idea how to craft the email saying what I wanted to say. *Maybe I'll just wait until he's back in the country and we can meet in person.*

# Thirty-four

When I escaped the room, a bead of sweat trickling down my back and no closer to admitting my relationship with Jake, I unlocked my phone to see two texts from Davis.

UNKNOWN: Good you aren't asking questions. You're much more appealing when you stay silent.

UNKNOWN: Let me know if you need reminders on how to do that.

Pressing my lips together, I gripped the phone to my chest. *No. No. No. No.* Davis being involved in this project meant a whole new array of sharp objects was dangling precariously over me. He wouldn't hesitate to suggest cuts to spite me or the things I cared about. Worse, if he ever found out about me and Jake, he'd try to destroy their company. I knew he would. Davis took any inch of power and control and stretched it to his advantage. He warped the truth and cornered people until they bent to him. I couldn't let him corner Jake.

"That goddamn, fucking, shit-eating motherfucker!" Felicia's reaction was exactly what I needed to hear as I drove away from campus after the meeting, up to and including this string of expletives. This was a situation where I needed mutual outrage.

"Exactly."

"Who does that? What is his deal? Does he have a small dick? It sounds like he has a small dick."

I laughed, despite wanting to cry. "He's definitely got something to prove." I clenched the steering wheel. "Ugh, and the way he looked at me, Fel? I wanted to throw up."

"What are you going to do?"

My frustration was a throbbing pressure point between my eyes. "I have no idea. The president said to email him, but I already have to tell the man I'm sleeping with one of the consultants. I don't want to complain at the same time that the external committee member he hand selected is a lecherous creep. Oh, and someone who I also used to sleep with. I can't put that all in writing, let alone dredge up everything from back then—I don't think anyone would believe me. It's been too long. They'll think I should just be over it by now."

"Nay, you're not over it. Who cares about *should be*?"

I nodded, wishing she was right but also fighting back tears, because I could see people like Anita shaking their heads and telling me it was my fault. If I could put up with him on my own, I wouldn't have to face more of their judgment. "No, it's too late for that."

"But if they knew about Davis and what he did—"

"I just have to deal with him. I did it before. I can do it again." *I hope.*

Felicia's silence spoke volumes. She disapproved of my solution. "Are you going to tell Jake?"

"No." I didn't want to chance him intervening and things getting worse, and I knew he would intervene. "I'm not telling anyone else."

"You sure?" Felicia asked. "He should know, Nay."

I'd managed this alone for so long, I didn't know *how* to tell Jake. The idea of coming clean, sharing every shameful thing with him, turned my stomach. Telling him I was still allowing it to happen was out of the question. Felicia was right, but something held me back, some deep-seated urge to keep myself protected. "I'm sure."

"Goddamn, fucking, shit-eating motherfucker," Felicia muttered on the other end of the phone.

# Thirty-five

Jake flew into Midway on Saturday night, and I greeted him with a sign reading "Captain Calculus." It had been a few days since the meeting, and I willed myself to pack away the wild array of emotions I was feeling. That was a little easier the moment I saw Jake, and thirty minutes after stumbling through the door of my apartment, we huddled together, on the rug next to my couch.

"You should remind me of all the reasons I should only recruit clients in Chicago." Jake toyed with the hem of my skirt. The same skirt he'd pushed up my hips when he'd pulled me down on top of him.

"You didn't get this kind of welcome in Boston?" I teased, tickling at his ribs.

"This is a uniquely Chicago greeting." He trailed his finger down the side of my face, then added, his voice softer, "I missed you."

His eyes took in every inch of me, every curve and flaw, until I glanced away.

He gently pushed my chin up so my eyes met his again. "Why do you do that? Every time I look into your eyes, you look away."

My cheeks heated. "I don't."

"You do."

"Just a habit, I guess."

"Did some horrible boy in middle school tease you in a failed attempt at flirting and make you wary of male attention?" A grin emerged on his face.

"Would you go beat him up for me?"

"Of course. Unless he's a really big guy now, in which case I would write him a strongly worded email."

His smile faded back into a serious expression. "Does it bother you? I can try to stop."

"No."

Jake stared at me with this intensity sometimes, like he could see into my head.

"It's nothing," I insisted.

He remained silent but continued to rub his thumb over the back of my neck in long, slow sweeps. He'd told me about his past; perhaps Felicia was right, and it was time to be a little brave.

"I'd been at TU for a year as a new professor. I was young, green, eager. Anyway, I met this guy, another professor; he was older, good-looking, well respected on campus." I tried to think back to how I'd initially seen him. "We started dating. And it was good." I paused, gazing down at the floor, trying to remember the signs I should have seen in those early months. "For a while it was good." I glanced up, but Jake's expression was inscrutable. "We were together a little over two years, but he wasn't always kind; he—"

"Did he hurt you?" Jake's muscles tensed.

"He . . ." I touched his forearm, bracing myself for the admission and deciding how much to share. "He wasn't kind. He could be aggressive and . . . cruel."

"Did he hit you?"

I dug my nails into my palms, remembering the rough shoves into walls, the sting of slaps, and how I'd curl up into a tight ball in his bed when he'd finished. "It doesn't matter."

That shame I'd internalized over the years was a chill spreading across my back like the scrape of long, bony fingers. I didn't want to be a victim, especially not in front of Jake, so I pushed the thoughts aside. I shuddered, hoping he wouldn't notice, hoping I could keep the emotions tucked away until I was alone.

He held me tighter, though—of course he noticed.

"Sometimes he hit me and . . . other stuff; it was a long time ago."

Jake looked away from my face, a muscle in his jaw ticked, and his hands had balled into fists at my sides as he seemed to struggle with what to say.

My stomach knotted with his reaction. The last thing I could handle was pity on his face or confusion about why I'd stayed with Davis so long. I didn't know the answers. I'd convinced myself it wasn't abuse. I was educated, and I thought I knew better, so what was happening was something else. I'd thought it would get better, and when it didn't, it was too late.

I'd started to believe his lies, that I needed him. By the time I stopped believing the lies, I believed the threats.

"I finally ended it. I was terrified, but we were in a public space, and I just said I was done." I didn't tell Jake how I'd been so anxious beforehand I'd been sick in the bathroom and almost chickened out, that when I actually said the words, that I was leaving, my voice had been broken and shaky and I'd braced for him to strike.

"What happened?" Jake asked the question like he didn't want to know the answer, voice thick and gruff.

"He told me he'd hurt me, humiliate me, and that I'd regret it. I thought he meant physically. Somehow, he knew killing my career would hurt me more than anything he could do to my body. So, that's what he did."

Jake nodded more emphatically, his gaze returning to my face. "That's why you're so concerned about your reputation at work."

I nodded, deciding not to tell him about the texts. The photos and messages were too real a reminder of what I'd been through. "He took every opportunity to use the power he had to make sure people thought the worst of me. He shared my phone number and photo on some website for people looking for kinky sex. These guys kept harassing me, and I had to change my number. I'm pretty sure some of my students found out." I rubbed my hands over my upper arms. "It was bad. He left campus a year later, but the damage was done. I was a joke . . . and I was always looking over my shoulder. It was like he was still controlling me without touching me."

I locked eyes with Jake, and he nodded, urging me to continue, his fingers lacing with mine. I took a deep breath, pushing myself to say the thing I'd feared all those years, to show vulnerability. "When you look at me like that, I feel like you can see . . ." I gulped in a series of shallow breaths, glanced down at our hands, and then looked back to his face. "Like you can see everything, and . . . I'm ashamed."

Jake pulled our linked hands to his face and slowly kissed each of my knuckles. Finally, his voice cut into the tension. "It's not your fault. Please don't feel ashamed. I don't know if I see everything, but when I look at you, I see so much. If it's in my power, you'll never feel helpless like that again."

Those memories had been replaying in my head for so many years, I couldn't imagine forgetting that helpless feeling. I knew if I told Jake that Davis was on the committee, Jake would try to fix the problem, and there was no way for him to do that without everything becoming more complicated. I worried I'd already said too much and he'd figure out it was Davis. When he didn't ask, though, I didn't say a word, instead choosing to let that part of the story remain untold. I would tell him eventually.

# Thirty-six

"C urry Palace is up the street, or we could go Italian if you want."

The next evening, we were sprawled on my couch trying to decide what to do for dinner. My feet were resting in Jake's lap while we watched a rerun of *Law and Order*. All of it felt so incredibly *couply* and domestic, part of me wanted to snap a selfie to remember the moment.

I should have.

"I could go for some lamb vindaloo. That would mean we'd have to get up from the couch, though." Jake rubbed his thumb over the arch of my foot, and I let out a low moan.

"Good thing they deliver."

"Clever girl," he said with a wink. Just then, his phone buzzed on the coffee table and he glanced down. His expression lost its playfulness. "Sorry, it's Carlton. Let me take this real quick." He slipped onto the balcony.

As the glass door slid closed, I got up to find the menu in

a kitchen drawer, where I thumbed through the embarrassingly large stack of carryout menus. My kitchen was pitifully under-utilized, and I couldn't claim skill with anything beyond boiling water and toasting bread. It might be nice to be able to spend time in the kitchen, versus always going out or digging through takeout menus. *To do: Learn to cook.* I smiled, imagining his surprise if I whipped out an apron. *To do: Learn to cook Jake's favorite meal.*

I was still grinning and thinking about my plan when I noticed him pacing and running his hand over the back of his neck while holding the phone to his ear. He gripped the railing of my balcony and looked out over the city intently for a few moments before coming back inside.

"Something wrong?" I asked.

He let out a heavy sigh and sank back onto my couch, patting the cushion next to him. "I need to talk to you about something. Two things, now, I guess."

I wrapped my arms over my stomach and abandoned the menus on the counter. *No good conversation ever starts like that.* "What's going on?"

His voice was earnest, and I tensed. "I was going to tell you last night, but we started talking about everything and it didn't seem like the right time, but then Carlton called . . ."

"Tell me what?" My mind raced at full speed in twenty different directions. "Is this about work? You know something?"

"Yes." He paused, leaning forward, his forearms on his knees. "We're meeting with the president on Monday to go over our initial findings."

I nodded, urging him to get to the point before my heart jumped out of my chest.

"What is it?" The blood in my face drained. "Are you recommending my department gets cut?"

His brow furrowed. "We're not making any hard recommendations, yet."

My entire body pinged with anxiety. "You're making a *soft* recommendation my department be cut?" I raked my fingers through my hair as I stood. *This is one of the few programs in the country where I can do the work I want to do, and I'm so close to tenure.* The possibility of having to start over left my chest tight.

"You know the education departments have struggled," Jake reasoned, his tone like the one you might adopt to calm a screaming child or an agitated dog. "From a financial standpoint, there are issues, and the institution is shifting focus to business, engineering, areas like those. Teacher education is outside that. That can't be a surprise."

Had I expected him to go to bat for me? Part of me had. In the back of my mind, I'd assumed he'd look out for me, even though I had been the one to specify that we should keep the office and the bedroom separate.

I stood, pacing. "We're not cogs in a machine. It's not all about revenue."

Taking a deep breath, he responded in an even tone, blue eyes trained on me. "It's not *all* about revenue . . . but it's *somewhat* about revenue. You know that."

I opened my mouth, fists balled at my sides. "Yes, but—" I expected him to interrupt—I was used to men interrupting—but he just watched me. "But you can't reduce education to money. It's so much more than that. It's the creation of knowledge; it's young minds finding purpose. We need teachers."

"A university is still a business. It takes money to introduce those young minds to purpose, and the department is a drain on resources. It's naive to think otherwise."

*Condescending. Now he sounds condescending.*

"I'm not naive," I spat back. "I know revenue is involved. I'm not stupid."

"I never said you were stupid." His voice remained even, resigned, almost pitying, and it sent a surge of fire through me. "Naya, you're acting like I was the one who decided all this. And even if I was, it would still be the right decision. I'm sorry, but that's just the reality." He looked up at me from the couch, his expression plaintive. "I wanted you to have a heads-up, is all. We've looked at a ton of data, and your department is in trouble."

My fingernails dug into my palms, and my lips pressed together.

"Can we please just talk about this?" he asked, his voice low and steady.

"We are talking."

"Calmly?" He paused for a beat. "This is my job, Nay."

The slate gray walls of my living room were closing in. Jake inhaled deeply, and the crease between his eyes deepened. "I don't want to fight with you."

"This is everything I've worked for. We're talking about my livelihood and my passion." I sounded frail and chastised myself, but I wanted to fight. The old me would have stayed quiet, but I'd spent too many years with my fists tucked away, and I wouldn't be left defenseless again. "I'm sorry if I'm being too *uppity* for you, but you can't just drop this and expect me to roll with it."

His chest heaved, eyes flashing. "You're acting like I . . . I don't know." He closed his eyes, pressing his thumb and forefinger between his eyebrows, trying to take control of his own emotions. "Like you thought we would just ignore real problems." His calm demeanor began to crack, an edge bleeding into his voice.

My heart thrummed in my chest, and tears stung the backs of my eyes. *He's right.*

I'd been trying to engage Joe and others in conversation about our shortcomings to no avail, but hearing Jake say it was like an elbow to my solar plexus. I swallowed hard and blinked.

"Can't you put the smallest amount of trust in me to not screw you over?" His eyes caught something on my face and softened. He reached for my hand, but I shrugged away.

"You just *told* me you were going to screw me over."

Jake groaned and scrubbed his palms over his face, frustration etched in every muscle. "Why are you being so unreasonable? I'm not screwing you over. That's not what I said at all. I wanted you to know the way the wind was blowing. Can you please just *listen*?"

"Don't talk to me like that." What upset me was knowing the person I wanted most to think I had it all together was witnessing and identifying all the cracks, and he didn't understand why that was such a big deal. I'd never seen him angry, and seeing his neck redden and his features harden brought back old fears.

"Talk to you like what?" His voice was edgy, notes of frustration lacing each word.

I walked toward my bedroom, ignoring his question.

"Dammit, talk to you like what?" He repeated his question and tried to tug me back to face him.

"Like a condescending asshole." I shrugged away from his touch, shuddering at how much Jake tugging me made me think of Davis.

"Unbelievable," he muttered, linking both hands behind his neck, his biceps tensing. "I'm not being condescending; I'm just trying to give you information."

"Telling me I don't understand condescension is condescending."

"Nay, I know what you do is valuable. I tell you all the time how much your work impresses me, how important I think it is."

I swallowed back tears, because he did say that often. I thought back to brunch with his friends and how he'd told Tyson and Eric about my research, but I wondered if he'd really been listening when I talked about my career and what it meant or if he'd just been appeasing me.

He hung his head at my icy stare, squeezing his eyes shut and muttering, "This is not how I wanted this conversation to go."

I balled my hands at my sides. "I'm sorry I didn't follow your script, but I get upset when someone I'm fucking tells me what I do is worthless."

At my statement he stiffened. "I didn't ever tell you that. And I'm just"—he motioned between us—"someone you're fucking?"

A stony silence hung between us.

*You're so much more than that.* My body tensed, but a part of me wanted him to feel as unsteady as I did . . . and I didn't answer.

Hurt flashed across his face before he adjusted his expression to something resolute. "You know that's not true." He stepped forward, and I backed against my doorframe. "And this guy who hurt you, who messed with your head? I'm so sorry—so angry—you had to deal with that, but I would never hurt you. Never. How do I get you to realize that I'm not like him?"

"I know you're not like him." Jake was so far from Davis, they were barely the same species, and yet, I couldn't stop holding my metaphorical fists up to protect myself from the next blow, because, for the first time, Jake was angry and pointing out the things in my life that were wrong. "I know you're not like him," I repeated, as much to myself as to him.

"Then why are you acting like this news is aimed at you? I *know* it's not good news, but it's not personal, Naya. I get it feels personal, but you have to see it isn't."

I understood everything he was saying, and I wanted to agree, to sit down rationally and talk through what was coming, but every time my mind leaned in that direction, I remembered my lowest points with my ex. I was so far into the hole I'd dug, I couldn't see a way out. That helplessness was the sensation crawling over me as I stood in front of Jake, tears threatening to fall. I wanted to sweep it away, but the memory of that darkness surrounded me.

*And it always will. That's the real problem.*

My voice cracked. "Because I'm broken, okay? I'm a broken goddamned mess. It's been years and I can't let it go and I am sick to death of being scared. And the job we're talking about is the only place I'm worth a damn, and if I don't have that, I don't know what I am." I gulped in a breath. "I'm fucked-up, Jake. I've been trying to hide it from you, but I can't lose the only thing I'm good at, the only place I matter. I'm broken, but I have this one thing, this one place, where I feel whole."

Jake's face was horror-struck, his features frozen. He tried to pull me into a hug, but I shied away. Pity bled into the edges of his expression, and my stomach soured. "You matter to me. We can fix—"

"You can't put me back together."

He raised his voice, trying to talk over my interruption. "I'm trying to say we can fix—"

I exploded at him. "I'm not some problem you can just fix!"

When he slapped his open palm against the doorframe, the sharp crack of skin against wood filled the space and I jumped back, the hairs on my arms standing on end. "Damnit, Naya. I'm not trying to fix you. I'm trying to tell you I'm in love with you!"

He pulled his hand back as if the wood were hot, realizing the power with which he'd hit the frame, the violence in the act. "I'm sorry." His voice softened. "God, I'm sorry. I didn't plan to yell that and scare you. I didn't even plan to say it yet, but I am head-over-fucking-heels in love with you, Naya." He raised his palms, slowly bringing them to my face as if giving me the chance to push him away. When I didn't, he cupped my face gently in his hands. "I love you."

*He's in love with me.*

*I'm overreacting.*

*"Sweetheart, you're overreacting, just like always."*

*He's in love with me.*

I slid my hands to his wrists, and his expression shifted to something resembling hopeful—not a smile, but the tension dissipated, and he searched my face before meeting my eyes.

"Naya, I . . . You're not broken. I want you to feel whole. I want you to feel whole with me. You're perfect. You're everything." His fingertips were warm against my skin. His voice was almost a whisper. "Will you say something?"

*Calm down and say it back. I love you, too.* I wanted to say it, more than anything, but I didn't. I couldn't.

"What was the second thing?" I asked, my voice small.

"What?"

"You said you had two things to tell me. What was the other one?"

*Just tell me the second thing doesn't matter. Give me a reason to let this go.*

His face blanched.

*No. No. No.*

"When Carlton called . . . it was to let me know he let it slip to President Lewis about you and me when they had lunch yesterday."

My mouth dried, and I closed my eyes. My hands fell from his wrists. "He let it slip. What does that mean?"

Jake spoke quickly, the words spilling out. "Lewis wanted to know why we'd structured the process the way we had, with the two teams—he was curious—and Carlton mentioned we were in a relationship. He assumed Flip knew, that you or your boss had told him. I thought you had, I swear."

*Damn it!* This was my fault, and it was too late.

Jake reached for my arm, and I whipped it away and pressed my palms to my eyes. "I told you, I fucking *told* you this would be an issue, and you wouldn't listen." The rage was stirring inside me, but I had nowhere to point it except at Jake, who stood in front of me, crestfallen. "You kept telling me it would be fine, it would be okay, and now, look. It's not okay and it's not fine. Do you have any idea how bad this is? Not only am I going to lose my job or be put in a corner somewhere, my reputation will be in the garbage, again. And your company—"

His expression was muddled between frustration, sympathy, and affection. "I'm not worried about my damn company right now. This isn't us, Nay. This is work. Can we . . ." His gaze moved to the ceiling before his palms slid down to my shoulders, then down and up my arms. "I'm sorry I didn't take it as seriously as you did. But, God, can we just stop and talk it through? We can work it out together. I know we can." He locked eyes with me. "We can, Nay. Please."

I wanted to melt into him, to rest my head against his hard chest and listen to his heartbeat. I wanted all those things, but I couldn't shake the feeling that falling for him was what had landed me here. The years of sacrificing everything for work were about to be meaningless, again, because I let myself get wrapped up with a guy. *But he's not just a guy; he's the guy.* That was worse because I'd promised to never put a man ahead of my career, and here I was.

His brows dipped, and I almost leaned into him before my spine straightened and I jerked away. *Years.* I'd rebuilt my career from the ashes of Davis's slander. I cursed myself for ignoring my gut telling me this relationship was wrong. There I was, standing in front of the man I loved, hearing it might all burn down again.

*Sweetheart, you're overreacting, just like always.*

"This may be your *work*, but it's my *life*. It's everything I've worked for. It's everything I've sacrificed for. It's my whole life."

The pain was recognizable in his eyes and the way the muscle in his jaw ticked. "Your *whole* life?" His voice was shaky, and his shoulders, normally so square, slumped forward. "Aren't I part of your life, Nay?"

I held his stare, and I knew he was flashing back to his wife cheating. Guilt and shame mixed with my anger and worry. I needed to protect him and to protect myself. "We started out as just sex. We should have left it there. Temporary."

"We had a connection from the first time we met, and you know it. Did you hear me just tell you I'm in love with you? You're all I fucking think about. I love you, and I know you care about me, too. Why are you doing this?"

I held myself rigid, afraid as soon as I moved, I would break.

When I didn't respond, his body tensed. "I don't think this is about work at all. This is you getting scared and running away. It's what you do." His voice flattened, and his words were sharp and bitter. "You did it the first night we met. Every real thing I know about you I've had to pry from your tight hold. And I let you hold me emotionally at arm's length, because I knew you were worth it, figured someday you'd really trust me, and I thought we'd gotten there. When does it stop, Naya?"

I squeezed my eyes shut again, trying to block everything out and keep myself in this moment. My heart pounded, and my mind spun. Jake's accusations, Davis's threats, the idea of packing up my cluttered little office. All the worry expanded, pushing everything else out of my head. "I can't do this. I'm sorry. I'm sorry, but it's not worth the risks." I walked into my bedroom, closing the door behind me and flipping the lock before the tears came.

"What does that mean?" Jake asked from the other side of the door. "Naya, what does that mean?" He banged on the door repeatedly, frantically, but I didn't answer.

I couldn't face him. Eventually, he stopped knocking, though I could hear him sitting on the other side of the wood.

Hours later, closer to a croak than anything else, his voice came from the hallway. "I'll go. I'll give you space. Will you lock the door behind me?"

I leaned my forehead against the door inside my bedroom and said, "Yes."

JAKE: I'm at the Marriott. Please call me.

JAKE: I'm sorry I lost my cool—can we talk?

JAKE: I love you. I need you.
JAKE: We can figure this out.

JAKE: Dammit, will you respond?

JAKE: I'm going out of my mind. It's been four days. Talk to me.
JAKE: Please?

# Thirty-seven

When I needed someone to take my side, I could always count on Felicia, no matter what. She was my "ride or die." But when I needed a voice of reason who wouldn't hesitate to disagree with me, Aaron was my man. That's how I found myself, a week after my fight with Jake, sitting on the floor of their living room with Chinese takeout.

I'd texted Aaron and said I was on my way over with beef and broccoli and egg rolls. I offered to keep him company while Felicia and the kids were at her dad's place in Florida for the week, but I knew he saw through my ruse. He initially eyed my hair, piled in a messy ponytail, and my paint-stained sweatpants without comment, but it didn't take long for him to ask.

"So, what's going on? Or did you get dressed up to hang out with me?" He sipped from his bottle of beer, eyebrows raised.

"I'm sorry my clothes don't meet your high standards."

Aaron wore his usual, jeans and a T-shirt. The shirts spanned decades—tonight, it was one from college I knew Felicia had been attempting to throw away for years. "I never care what you wear . . . but *you* usually do." He set down his drink. "Seriously, what's going on? Is it work? That guy? Felicia told me you had a fight." He let the heavy silence push me to talk.

I launched into the story, telling him about the president's committee, and Davis's texts, and my fight with Jake. When I was finished, I dropped my head into my hands.

When I looked up, Aaron's expression was concerned, his words measured. "Davis has been texting you?"

*Shit.* I hadn't meant to reveal that. "I don't want to talk about the texts. Fel doesn't know that part yet." I eyed Aaron's doubtful expression.

"What has he been sending you?"

"I'll deal with it, I just . . . I can't right now, Aaron."

"Nay . . ." He set his bottle aside and leaned forward. "Is he threatening you? Do you need the police? Please don't shut us out again."

"Seriously, it's fine. It's not a big deal. Please drop it."

"Okay. For now." He sighed after a beat. "But I don't like it." He set his beer aside and shoveled a forkful of fried rice into his mouth and chewed. "So, you've just been ignoring your boyfriend?"

I nodded, gazing at my feet. "I don't think he's my boyfriend anymore." He hadn't messaged me in a couple days. I couldn't blame him. How long had I expected him to keep trying to reach me when I didn't respond?

Aaron stayed quiet but was nodding again, his lips pursed.

"Am I being unreasonable?"

"I get why you're hesitant and that the work thing is complicated, but it sounds like you are. Nay, what do you want to happen? Let's go step-by-step."

I dropped my head back to my hands in exasperation; leave it to a math teacher to lead me down a rational path. "I have no idea."

"Yes, you do."

"I want my career. I want to be at TU and keep studying, writing, and teaching in a place I love."

"And . . . what else?" He nudged my foot with his before taking a bite of rice.

"I want him. It's been so long since I had someone I could count on—I mean, other than you guys. Someone who cares about me. I wanted that." I didn't tell Aaron that Jake had told me he loved me. Even when I was admitting everything, sharing that felt too personal—it made my screwup so much bigger.

"That's called a relationship."

I smiled through my cloud of despair.

"Adults have them sometimes. You may be familiar with them from seeing movies and reading books."

I searched for something to throw at him but had nothing within reach. Instead, I stared at the stained carpet from my seat on the floor and cringed. "Your carpet is in dire need of replacement, by the way."

"Don't change the subject. But yeah, the carpet's bad. Blame your three favorite kids." He took an audible deep breath and looked from the carpet to me. "Nay, there's no sugarcoating it. You screwed up." Aaron ticked off examples on his fingers.

"You kept the relationship a secret at work, you blamed this guy for things that seem way out of his control, and you refuse to talk to him about it."

I covered my face again. I'd already known that.

"But," he added, "if he's into you, and it sounds like he is, then you can fix it." He held my gaze. "Unless . . ."

"Unless what?"

"Unless you don't want to fix it. You've said for a long time you're happy alone. Did you mean it?"

"It *is* easier to be alone. You and Felicia have this perfect relationship, but most people don't have that. Most people get dicked around."

"Eh, we're nowhere near perfect, and you're aware of that because she tells you everything." He fixed me with a knowing look, hands tucked behind his head. "I screw up weekly, and living with your best friend, the love of my life, is not always a picnic, but that's normal. People are imperfect, so relationships will always have flaws."

I nodded.

"Anyway," he said, not taking my bait, "how is it easier?" He paused, raising his eyebrows expectantly, but began again when I delayed answering. "Let me take a stab—you're worried that every guy will treat you like Davis did, and this guy—"

"Jake," I interjected.

He nodded. "Okay, *Jake* will do the same, so you want to cut him off before he has the chance to hurt you. I get that, but at some point you have to trust someone, right? And," he continued, nudging my shoulder, "yes, it sucks he told you your job might be in trouble, but you knew that already, right?"

I mumbled a reluctant confirmation.

He revved up for his next points. "And, here's the hard truth, Nay: The thing you're scared of is that he *might* end up being a dick."

I turned my head to give him a skeptical look. "That isn't helping—"

"I don't know the guy, but the possibility exists that he could break your heart, betray your trust, or steal your car. He might also be a good guy. From what Felicia's told me, he sounds like someone who could be really good for you. You won't know until you get out of your own way, give up on this idea of perfect, and give him a chance to love you, flaws and all."

I eyed him skeptically, unwilling to admit he was right. "Why do you think he loves me?"

He gave a wry smile. "I'm sure you're an all-star in bed, Nay, but no guy is going to log the miles and time this guy has just to get laid. There has to be more to it."

"Maybe," I mumbled, since the memory of Jake's *I love you* and the pang of loss were inextricably bound.

"And you love him, too. That's clear. So, give him a chance."

"It's not that easy," I protested.

"No, but it's not that hard." Aaron took a drink from his beer. "Just let him into your life."

"I did let him in."

Aaron cocked one eyebrow.

"I did!"

"Why haven't we met him? He's been to visit you a bunch of times, right? You don't have that many close friends, Nay. Why haven't you introduced us?"

He was right, of course. Jake had even asked if I'd wanted us to do something with my friends, but I'd always demurred.

"Okay, I get what you're saying."

"Now we've agreed I'm right, as I so often am, what are you going to do about it?"

I looked up at the ceiling and asked myself the same question.

*To do: Figure out what the hell I want.*

———

I mulled over my conversation with Aaron as I lay in bed later that night. I'd opened my text window twenty times to attempt a reply to Jake, but after how I'd acted, I needed to say something perfect. It had been days since he'd last messaged me, and everything I tapped out seemed insufficient. I checked flight times, wondering if a grand gesture, surprising him in North Carolina, would be better. But he traveled so often, I might show up to his doorstep only for him to be in Kansas City or Portland.

I took a deep breath and opened the text window again.

NAYA: Hi.

Three dots blinked immediately. My heart somersaulted into my throat, and my stomach dropped. The wait felt interminable, and the dots disappeared and didn't come back. After a few minutes, I couldn't take the wait anymore. Maybe making him laugh would break the thick layer of ice.

NAYA: Gladys, I hope this isn't too awkward. Is Jake at
    your place?

NAYA: Can you tell him I miss him?

Nothing. I refreshed the window, hoping to see the moving dots. *He might be away from his phone. Maybe he's trapped under something heavy. Maybe he's on a date.* I ran through every horrible scenario, and my anxiety was on ten. I refreshed the window again, tapping my fingers against the side of my phone, nerves on edge. Finally, the moving dots appeared on the screen, and I held my breath.

JAKE: funny.

JAKE: U miss me?

NAYA: I do.

JAKE: you suck at showing it

I winced. He'd never said anything so curt before, even during our fight.

JAKE: soyour talking t me now?

He was always so precise, even when texting. The typos worried me.

NAYA: Are you ok?

JAKE: Do yU care?

JAKE: I told you I love you andyou Stoppd talking to me

JAKE: no NOt ok. drunk tnite tho.

Jake rarely had more than a drink or two, and I hadn't seen him drunk since the first night we'd met.

NAYA: Jake, I'm so sorry.

JAKE: Fr what?

JAKE: Ignring me fora week or for being so goddam scared

JAKE: Its what you do. You gt scared then you run.

NAYA: We should talk when you're sober

JAKE: Why? When i'm sober will you stil care more abt work than me?

NAYA: I never cared more about work than you.

JAKE: liar. Thats wht I get tho. I cared abt work too much to realise my wife was fuccking the neighbor

JAKE: And I fell inlove too fast with the 1st woman I met

JAKE: Tyson said slow dwn but nope, I was so sure, sosureyou were The fcking love of my life.

NAYA: Jake, can we talk tomorrow? I don't think you mean this.

JAKE: I mean it. Just wouldn t say it to u sober

JAKE: I told you I love youu and you said itwas jst sex. Do you know what that felt like? Like all iam to you is a hard dick?

NAYA: You're not. I'm so sorry for everything. We can fix this.

JAKE: You mde it very clear you dont want to fix anything.

JAKE: I get you got dealt a shitty hand, but Im a person. U cant just throw me away and pick me bck up latr whn u feel like it

JAKE: Why do wmen think thats allowed?

NAYA: Jake, please. Can we talk tomorrow?

JAKE: No. I'm done tyring to talk toyou.

JAKE: U ignored me fr a week lk I meant nothing. you said ur broken, but maybe you r just heartless.

My breathing stuttered and my stomach clenched at the biting words. *He's right.* Regret swept through my body, and I clutched the phone. He had it right, and I replayed the argument, knowing how I'd flown off the handle. It hadn't been about him or even the job; I'd felt unsteady again. But I was so screwed up, I'd just kept putting it on Jake, and he deserved so much more. I swiped my hand across my cheek and bit back a sob, moving my wet thumb over the screen of my phone. I should have typed *I love you*. I wanted to, but I couldn't make my fingers move to form the three short words. It was too much, and maybe he was right.

NAYA: I'm sorry.

JAKE: You want temporary. You g ot it.

# Thirty-eight

"Y ou know I love you, but you look like shit." Felicia opened the front door and wrapped me in a hug. "How are you?"

"I'm fine."

"Bull, you've been a puddle of sad since everything went down."

"This is the first time you've seen me."

"Am I wrong?"

She wasn't, but I wasn't planning to admit the amount of time I'd spent rereading old text messages from Jake and crying. At night when I couldn't sleep, I replayed every moment we'd spent together, searching for every clue that being apart was the right thing. That didn't stop me from creeping on his social media.

The day before, there had been new content, and my stomach flipped, seeing him tagged in a photo, a selfie reposted by Gretchen dated seven years earlier. The two were smiling and sitting at a candlelit table. Jake was holding the camera while Gretchen kissed his cheek. They looked kind of perfect together. The caption read *Going out for Italian food with this guy tonight. Not quite the same as the honeymoon in Florence, but I'll take it #TBT.* I remembered how much he had avoided this meeting, how being around her put him on edge. *But he agreed to go to dinner, so maybe not anymore.* I'd added *terminate social media connection with Jake* to my list but immediately crossed it off, knowing having no connection with him would be worse than seeing things like that on his feed.

I put on my coolest, most confident-sounding rational professor voice. "I'm fine."

"You don't have to be," Felicia shot back. "You trusted a guy for the first time since Davis, and no matter what you say, that was a big deal and I know you're not fine."

"All right, I'm not fine, but it's too late now, right? I screwed it up."

"Did you try to call him?"

"No," I answered simply, though I had begun to call him a bunch of times. My pride stopped me from hitting the button to dial. I didn't think I could handle hearing him say the things he'd texted me, no matter how much I missed his voice.

"Why not?"

"I don't want to talk about it, Fel." I sighed, exasperated. "Can I just get that sleeping bag I asked to borrow?"

Her slow sigh told me she was debating whether to let me get away with the subject change. Her audible inhalation communicated that I was off the hook for now. "C'mon. It's in the living room."

"Thanks."

"Are you going camping or something?" Aaron asked from the floor of the living room, where he was building Lego towers with the kids.

"We're going to this retreat site in the woods, and we'll be in cabins. It's for that committee I'm on." I settled into an armchair across from my friends, pulling the sleeping bag to my chest.

Aaron cocked an eyebrow.

I shrugged. "The president has a thing with being out in nature." We were supposed to be giving feedback and answering questions the consultants had come up with during their review. *That won't be at all awkward.*

"Maybe it'll be fun. I'd have fun watching all you nerds trying to survive while roughing it." Aaron planted himself on the other end of the sectional.

Felicia, perched on the arm of the couch, scrubbed her fingers through Aaron's hair playfully. "You realize you're a high school math teacher and not a cattle rancher, right, honey?"

"Yes, but I go outside, sometimes." Aaron laughed, propping his feet on the coffee table. "Will your guy be there? John?"

"Jake—why do you never say his actual name?"

"Because it bugs you. Will he be there?"

"Yes." *Two days in the woods with a man who's seen me naked. Scratch that, two men who have seen me naked.* "Davis, too."

"Naya!" Felicia sat upright, concern coloring her expression. "You never said he was going to be there. Are you okay being that close to him?"

Aaron shot me a pointed look from across the room, and I knew he'd kept his promise to not tell Felicia about the texts, but he wasn't happy about it.

I tucked my knees to my chest, choosing to stare at the kids and not my best friend. "I don't really have a choice."

# Thirty-nine

I searched the parking lot for Jake before climbing out of my car, but I didn't see him or Carlton in the assembled group outside the main administration building. I did see Jill across the lot and hoped I could stand with her while we waited. Since we were both on this committee, I'd hoped Jill and I might get to know each other better. At thirty-three, I found myself adding *make new friends* to my list, which was humiliating, but throwing myself into work and hiding out had also meant not making time to socialize. I hadn't sunken to googling *how to make friends as an adult* yet, but I saw the search in my future, especially since I was single again.

I stretched for my tote, which had shifted in my trunk.

"I still can't believe you're here." Davis's voice behind me was like a bouquet of dull knives and tin foil, and set my nerves on edge.

I took a moment to close my eyes and collect my nerves

before turning to face him and instinctively taking a step backward. *Breathe*.

"Well, you knew I would be . . ."

"It's cute when you trail off like that. It's wonderful that you don't care if people see you as inarticulate."

I felt exposed standing so close to him in this wide-open space. The flashy red sports car parked nearby with the custom license plates—NO1DR—was his. I'd been so busy looking for Jake, I'd missed it. He used to tell people it was a joke, him nearing middle age—no wonder he'd drive such a flashy car. He actually chose it to read "number one doctor." The car had changed in the years since we broke up, but the plates remained the same.

He chuckled, a grating sound. "I meant since news about you screwing the consultant is out. I figured you'd slink off somewhere."

I clenched my jaw and remained silent, my heart tripping to get out of my chest, and I hoped my shock didn't show.

His lip curled in a half smile. "Oh, Flip asked my opinion on it. He really trusts my judgment." His eyes trailed down my body, and goose bumps rose on my skin. "You're smart enough to know where your strengths are. It's a bold move, I'll give you that. I just didn't know you had it in you to be so calculating."

He reached across me and plucked the tote from my hands before I could stop him, his forearm grazing my breast, making me recoil. "Allow me." He leaned against my car, my bag over his shoulder. I stepped back, but unsure who in the milling crowd knew what, I was desperate to avoid a scene.

"It won't work, though, pretty girl. He can't save your job.

I could, though, if I was so inclined." His voice held the same rogue confidence it always had. He laid a hand gently on my shoulder, and I flinched and shrugged it away. "It's been a long time."

Davis smiled—it was a rueful gesture. His hand returned and his thumb stroked the side of my neck. A cold flash ran through me. Over his shoulder, I saw Jill eyeing us, her normally cheerful expression turned into a frown. *Does she know?* She looked away quickly, and my face heated. Behind her, I saw another cold stare. Jake's expression was impassive, but he was staring at Davis and me. When he looked at me, he always seemed to see so much, so I hoped he'd read my expression for what it was, even from that distance, but he didn't.

I jerked back, but the damage was done, and Jake had turned away.

"Don't be like that. You know I get what I want in the end." Without another word, Davis pushed off from the car and strode toward the assembled group; he was still holding my bag, leaving me to follow along behind him like a lost, scared child.

I ducked into the back row of the van, hoping others would seek spaces with more leg room and I'd be left alone for the drive, but I'd miscalculated. Davis crawled into the back next to me, claiming the rest of the bench seat, his legs and arms spread wide. He leaned close to my face as he fumbled with his seat belt, and his hand brushed the outside of my thigh. "Didn't think you'd get rid of me that easily, did you?" He said it under his breath, the consonants hard and cold, even in a whisper.

My mind screamed *say something, move to a different seat, or slap him,* and I tried to remember Wes's voice from my self-defense class, but my body retreated to old reactions. I flinched, goose bumps rising on my arms. From the front seat, Jill shot cutting glances in my direction, and a familiar sense of help-lessness filled me as this cycle seemed to be starting again.

We turned out of the parking lot, and Davis said in a voice loud enough for most passengers in the van to hear, "So, Naya, feel free to ask me about anything you don't understand when we get there—I'm happy to help." The two people in the seat in front of us smiled at Davis over their shoulders—two of his former cronies—and they all exchanged pleasantries.

His voice lowered, and I was sure the others couldn't hear it over the sounds of the road and their own conversations. "You can beg, too. I liked it when you begged."

I recoiled, curling into the smallest possible amount of space I could take up on the seat. "Leave me alone, Davis," I muttered. I wanted to strike him or punch him, to hiss at him. Everyone would hear, though. Above all, I wanted to fly un-der the radar, as I had done for years, and sink into the seat.

"You're blushing. You remember." To anyone observing, his expression would have looked professional, collegial, maybe even engaging, like we were discussing my research or his re-cent golf outing. A flash of heat glinted in his eyes when he referenced my humiliation, though; a glee that jumped from his dark irises. "Good," he said in a hushed, cold voice filled with malice.

I shook my head, shifting away from his touch while a chorus of *react* and *you're stronger than this* rang in my head.

*To do:* . . .

I had nothing. I didn't know what to do.

# Forty

We arrived at the site and crowded into a meeting room. All around us were large windows that looked out over a path leading through the forest to the lake beyond. With fifteen of us squished around a table designed for twelve, elbow room was at a premium, and the smell of coffee and a variety of colognes and perfumes filled the small space.

My breath caught when I spotted Jake at the head of the table with Carlton. All my thoughts scattered, and my body responded to him on instinct. *He looks good. Does he miss me? He needs a haircut.* My fingers itched to stroke the curls at the nape of his neck. *What did he think when he saw Davis touching me? Did he sleep with Gretchen? Be professional! He looks good.* His eyes met mine for a millisecond and then darted away. *Does he hate me?*

I sought Jill in the crowd, to explain what she might have thought she'd seen between Davis and me, but she stood near him, eyes down, and didn't meet my gaze.

Two things about the weekend became clear as we introduced ourselves around the table: It would be difficult being around Jake and insufferable being around Davis. I struggled to remember what I'd ever seen in him, and the fear and disgust I'd felt in the van extended, for a bit, into sheer annoyance.

Davis's chest puffed out, and he somehow took up more room at the table than anyone else during his rambling introduction. When I spoke, Carlton nodded and smiled, as he had with everyone else. Jake gave a curt nod without glancing up from the sheet of paper in front of him, where critical notes required his full attention. *Well, what did I expect?*

Jake and Carlton and their two staff members were there to listen to our opinions and experiences and ask questions, to help them interpret all the data they'd collected. After an hour, the dull ache in my stomach was joined by a low throb in my temple. The headache wasn't about Jake.

For the fourth time, Davis had repeated something I'd just said and claimed it as his own idea. For years, I'd let him convince me he was smarter and more capable, but it was evident here that he wasn't.

My gaze shifted to Jake every time he did it. I hoped to see a reaction, amusement at Davis's ridiculous behavior or outrage on my behalf, an eye roll or a sympathetic glance. He didn't react at all, short of a few shared looks with Carlton.

*Stop expecting anything.*

When I disagreed with two colleagues, saying that promotion policies disproportionately favored people in science and business, Davis chuckled.

*That asshole just laughed at me?*

He addressed his comments to the head of the table, where President Lewis, Jake, and Carlton sat. "Unlike Drs. Smith,

Bradley, and Carmichael, Naya doesn't really have much experience with those policies, having not yet earned tenure herself."

I clenched my hands in my lap and swallowed the sharp retort building. It wasn't fear of Davis building this time, though. I didn't want to make a scene. *Don't react to him. It's not worth it.*

"It's a complex process, and not everyone understands the fine nuances of it, especially those with so little experience."

*Don't give him the satisfaction of reacting.*

"It's just your opinion, and of course, Naya, you're allowed to have it," Davis said, turning to me, his face drawn into something resembling pity. "It's great you're jumping in!" He might as well have been reaching across the table to pat me on the head.

I seethed at his condescension and cut my gaze to Jake again. *You see this, don't you?*

He didn't look at me, his eyes remaining on his notes.

I didn't want him to say anything. I didn't need him to fight for me, I just wanted him to recognize what was happening, to meet my eye and see that my fears were justified.

Davis kept speaking. "But in my experience, the policies are heavily skewed in favor of faculty working in science and business. Those in English, philosophy, political science, and other liberal arts are left behind. In my extensive experience, it holds true at TU. Now, I—"

*Be professional. Be professional. Be prof—fuck it. It's not like things can get worse.*

I interrupted him. "That's what I said, Davis." My voice was clear, loud, and confident. I clutched my fists under the table and willed my voice to remain steady. Though, my confidence hedged when no one nodded in agreement or said a word. Instead they all stared at me, all but one person.

"Excuse me?" Davis's cocky smile faltered, a crack appearing in his Master of the Universe mask.

*Deep breath.* "You demeaned my lack of experience and then repeated my point." I glanced around at everyone. *Had no one else noticed he'd been doing this all day?* Faces around the table were frozen, and Jake finally looked at me with a steely expression.

Davis's eyes narrowed, then he chuckled again. "I'm not sure I know what you mean, Naya. I was simply contributing to what Drs. Smith, Bradley, and Carmichael were saying." He smiled at the man to his right and added, "So sensitive!"

I unclenched my fists—I didn't need to fake my confidence anymore. The anger at his condescending tone was a prod pushing me forward. I wasn't scared; I was pissed.

"Surely you can think of a few original things to say. Stop rephrasing my ideas and claiming them as your own."

Davis's face reddened, and his eyes narrowed slightly.

President Lewis interrupted. "Let's break for now. Dinner will be down by the lake." He turned. "Dr. Turner, a word in the kitchen?" Everyone else made their way to the front door to head to the picnic area by the lake. Davis's eyes were trained on me, but he followed the crowd toward the door, all of them avoiding looking at me. Jill made eye contact briefly, but the cold and distant expression from earlier remained.

*Stand up for myself. Check. But not one of my best decisions.*

Jake didn't look up from his notes, but I thought I saw a muscle in his jaw tic, and the hand resting on the table was in a tight fist.

Davis's glare made the hairs on the back of my neck stand on end.

*I guess it got worse.*

---

President Lewis plucked a coffee mug from a cupboard.

Most people had filtered out of the building toward the lake, and the muffled voices faded.

*I'm going to get fired.*

He held out the pot before filling his mug, but I waved it away. "So," he said, leaning against the counter. "We haven't had a chance yet to meet one-on-one since you took over for Joe." His voice and posture were light and friendly, casual even, as he sipped the black coffee. "Thank you for doing that, by the way. He has a lot of faith in you."

*I made a big mistake.* I'd hoped to raise a rallying cry for the women around the room to stand up and be heard, but then no one rallied. I'd made a fool of myself in front of the president of the university. The same president who knew I'd slept with his highly paid consultant.

"Thank you," I answered. "President Lewis, I'm—"

"Please, call me Flip." He smiled, taking another sip from his cup.

"Flip, I should apolog—"

He stopped me again, interrupting with such grace I couldn't take offense. "Do you know how I got that name? When your real first name is Archibald, it doesn't seem you'd need a nickname, right?" He chuckled to himself. "Archibald came from my dad losing a bet with an old army buddy. My mom was fit to be tied, but there it was."

I nodded, brow creased. *Where is he going with this?*

"But 'Flip'? All my doing. When I was in college, I wanted to impress a young woman. I thought doing a backflip off the porch of my fraternity house would be the way to get her attention." He smiled, wistfully. "Those ideas sound so logical when we're young, don't they?"

I tilted my head and smiled politely.

"Needless to say, it didn't go well. I broke my arm in two places, and the first guy to get to me, some guy just walking by, called me 'Flip.'" He chuckled and ran his hand over his left arm. "Hurt like a sonofabitch, I'll tell you. But the nickname stuck."

"That's a . . . good story," I said, unsure of the proper response.

"It is." He laughed.

I stepped away from the counter—standing straight was better for an apology. "But, President, er, Flip, I need to apologize for what happened in there."

"Do you know what else is interesting about that story, Naya?"

*Is he not noticing me speaking?* "What, sir?"

"I did impress the young woman, eventually. Hell, she agreed to marry me before the cast came off. And the guy who gave me the nickname? Been my best friend for over fifty years. And between you, me, and these four walls, I think I've made it as far in my career as I have because my name stands out in a pile of resumes. Not many Flips around."

I pressed my lips together, trying to suppress a smile.

"Sometimes things that seem dumb, stupid, even dangerous at the time—hell, things that most certainly *are* dumb, stupid, and dangerous—sometimes they work out. And sometimes those bad decisions? They end up being the most important decisions we ever made. Especially when you have a good head on your shoulders to begin with." He eyed me over the rim of his coffee cup.

*Touché, Flip.* I nodded slowly, wondering which of my dumb, stupid, and dangerous decisions might end up being my ticket to happiness.

"To address the elephant in the room, I would have liked to know about the relationship between you and Mr. Shaw. I've shared that with him, and I'm telling you. I'm disappointed you kept it a secret."

I glanced away. "I'm sorry I didn't disclose it. I know I should have."

He nodded. "I imagine you do. These things can be complicated, but I still think you're an important voice in these conversations. In the future, please speak up. If you'll give an old man leeway to say so, you're good at it.

"As for what happened in there?" He took a sip of his coffee, then dumped the rest in the sink. "It's commendable that you stood up for yourself. And it needed to happen. Those old boys' club rules don't apply anymore, and I'm sorry I didn't step in myself. I will do better. Would you like me to speak with him?"

I shook my head. I appreciated his offer but didn't want to give Davis chances to spin more lies.

President Lewis patted me twice on the shoulder and said, "I don't think we need to discuss anything else." He left the room to join the others at the lake. The screen door clicked as he exited the building.

# Forty-one

*Okay. That went better than I thought.*

Flip walked away from the cabin toward the tree line, beyond which was the lake where everyone had gathered for dinner. I needed to get down there before they came looking for me, but first I wanted to take a few minutes to collect myself before seeing Jake. I stepped out the door but headed in the opposite direction, into the woods. With Davis by the lake along with everyone else, I could finally take a deep breath. The early-evening sun cast everything in a muted light, and I focused on the crunch of sticks and loose dirt beneath my shoes before sitting on a large boulder in a clearing. Talking with Flip had made me feel better, more in control. I loved my job and had worked hard, but I realized as I inhaled in the fresh air that I'd been using my job as a hiding place.

*To do: Review my tenure materials. I can't have real power in this place until I earn it, and I'm ready. I've done everything required to be promoted.*

*To do: Invite Jill and other early-career women to start a club or organization, some space to connect with one another.*

*To do: Get Jake back.*

I'd been considering what I could say to him to make things right and how to choose the perfect words and ultimately realized the perfect words would be the ones I opened my mouth and said out loud. *I need to be honest with him.* I took another deep breath and stilled my nerves, calling up every reserve of confidence I had. *I'll find him. I'll beg him to listen. I'll grovel if I have to.* I turned to the lake when footsteps sounded behind me.

I whirled around.

Davis laughed, a dry, grating sound. "Did you *tell on me?*" His voice was low, menacing, and he approached me quickly. "Convince Flip I was being *mean* to you?"

"I didn't say anything about you, okay?"

He advanced, making me step back. "You know if you do, you'll regret it. It would be so easy to share a photo or two. I'm sure your boyfriend will have plenty of time to look at them after we fire his company for unethical conduct. Maybe I'll convince Flip to bring suit against them for the lost time and resources."

My pulse raced as I took another step back, the snap of twigs under my feet, the distant sound of the birds suddenly louder. "I'm not going to say anything to Flip. Just leave me alone, Davis."

He ignored me, holding up his phone. I couldn't take back the photo, like I couldn't take back the years of manipulation. I had to live with the consequences of both. The bruises he'd left on my arms, the hateful words he'd said, and the violence he'd threatened weren't in the photo, just in my memory, and I couldn't take that back, either.

*I will not cry in front of this asshole.*

"I'm not having this conversation with you, Davis." I used my most detached voice and tried to move around him, though he blocked my path and stepped forward, edging me closer to a tree. He'd always used his size to box me in, to make me cower, but I was so sick of being scared. My adrenaline surged.

"You want to leak the photos?" I stopped backing up and stood squarely in front of him. "Then do it. I'm done with your games and your threats. I'm done with you hanging this or anything else over my head. You don't get to control me anymore. You can't hurt me now."

His smirk froze in a mirthful grimace. The scent of his cologne assaulted my nostrils. I'd loved the smell of Polo before meeting him, but after we split, it turned my stomach. A moment later, when I pushed at his chest, trying to get around him, he backed me against the tree.

As soon as I hit the bark, my synapses fired in all directions and I tried to remember what I'd learned from Wes. I was tired of being scared, but fear coursed through me just the same.

"This tough-girl attitude doesn't fool me, and I can *definitely* still hurt you. I can hurt your boyfriend, too. Or do you even care about that? You were always selfish. Selfish and stupid. What did you think you were doing in there, talking to me like that?" His voice was icy, and his eyes cruel and dark.

"Get out of my way, Davis." I lunged, but I couldn't get leverage with him so close, our chests touching.

He ignored me, adopting a soft tone one might use with a

small child, grazing his finger along my cheek. "You're not in charge of anything that's happening here, pretty girl. Just like back there."

I jerked away. "Don't call me that, and get out of my fucking way or I'll—"

"You'll what? Scream? Everyone's gone. No one would hear you. Anyway, who would they believe, Naya? They all respect me, and they know you're just a dumb bitch with an agenda to ruin me."

Everyone at the retreat did know him. And almost all of them had been around when he began his campaign to discredit me. Even Jill had looked at me like something dirty since seeing Davis touch me in the parking lot. The tears welled, and I struggled to keep them at bay. My heart pounding was a stark contrast to the peaceful, still woods around us.

"You won't do anything," he sneered. "And you'll think twice before trying to make me look stupid again. Do you understand?" He was closer now, too close. I fought the urge to cower and nod. That's what he wanted.

"You didn't need any help to look stupid." I straightened. "And this isn't about me. I know you were beat out for the position at State by a vastly more qualified woman. This is about that, about your pride and your precious ego, but I'm not your damn punching bag anymore. I'm not your anything."

His eyes flashed. He gripped my arms and shoved me backward again. Bark dug into my skin, and I stared up at him, my eyes wide and my breath short.

"Shut the fuck up," he hissed. "You're nothing. You're inconsequential." His grip on my shoulders tightened.

*No one would hear me . . . and he knows it.*

*Jake.*

*No one can save me.*

He touched my face again, a slow, rough drag of his index finger down my jaw before gripping my chin. I froze, my eyes darting around the small clearing—everyone else was at least a mile away. Davis tilted his head and squinted, leering at my chest and then back up.

"Get off me!" I pushed him, panic rising in my voice. I clung to the fact he couldn't do anything too extreme because of where we were, and that we'd have to join everyone later. *He's too smart for that. Isn't he?*

"Davis, let me go!" I tried to wriggle free, but he was stronger, his pelvis against mine, hands moving down to hold my arms.

"You aren't in charge here." His voice was low, and his fingers dug into my skin.

I tried to knee him and failed, only grazing his thigh.

"That shit back there, you don't get to talk to me like that, ever. You think you know about Caroline Rhodes? You two have one thing in common—both stupid bitches getting by because of what's between your legs." His eyes were dark, and his expression crazed. He rarely let go; even when he was hurting me, humiliating me, he was controlled and put together. I worried, for the first time, that he wasn't weighing out the possibility of getting caught.

"Davis," I pleaded. "Let go of me."

His face brightened, and he sneered again, the resulting expression a horrific mask. "You scream, and everyone will know you're the helpless child I told them you were. Misinterpreting a friendly hug from a colleague, tsk–tsk, Naya . . . Not that they'd hear you, anyway." He dropped his other hand, yanking at his belt.

I closed my eyes.

*This isn't happening. This isn't happening. This isn't happening.*

I had no choice but to scream and hope someone could hear me. It would happen just like he said, and I'd be ruined all over again.

*Helpless.*

*A victim.*

But he didn't get to win, not this time.

"Let me go!" I screamed and used my whole body to push him back.

He grabbed a handful of my hair, wrenched my head back, and slapped me hard across the face. Flashes of light dotted my vision as the pain registered. With all he'd done, he'd never hit me in the face. It had always been somewhere that could be hidden. At that, one thought blared in my mind. *He's out of control.*

"You think you can fight me? That girl in the picture, the girl who needed to be told what to do, that's the real you."

I shook my head, finding no voice. I started to retreat into myself as I had all those years ago, to fold into the smallest possible space where I could block out what he was doing.

I remembered Felicia and Aaron saying, *We'd love to see the volume go back up.*

Wes's words from my self-defense class filled my head. *If you can't do anything else, use your voice.*

Then there were Jake's words. *I love you.*

I wasn't the same person I'd been three years ago. I'd rediscovered my own strength, and I deserved better than this. *I don't have to fold. I can fight and I can save myself.*

I screamed as loud as I could in his ear, and he clamped a hand over my mouth. Fighting my instinct to pull his hand away, instead I wriggled an arm free and jammed the heel of my palm up into his nose like Wes had taught me. The crunch was satisfying, and he grabbed for his face as blood gushed down his chin. Before he could retaliate, I kneed him in the groin with all the strength I could muster and shoved him away from me.

My breath came fast, and a primal rage coursed through me. I knew I should run, but I wanted to go on the offensive, to kick him or punch him again. In that split second of indecision, he grabbed me, his hand viselike around my wrist. He was unhinged, his face contorted in a gruesome snarl, blood running from his nose. "I would have been nice, but you had to push. You always had to fucking push."

My heartbeat thudded in my ears, but Felicia and I had practiced—we'd done the move over and over again in class and out, so clamping down on his hand and twisting until his extended arm was behind his back and under my control was natural. Forcing him to his knees in front of me was almost instinct. My mind whirred at conflicting and crashing thoughts— how much I loved feeling strong, how much I hated being even remotely like him, how he'd hurt me for so long, and what he'd wanted to do to me in that clearing. "You're damn right, I fucking push." I sucked in another shallow breath, applying more pressure as he tried to shift away. "I push back now, and you don't ever get to push me again."

"We heard screaming—what's going on here?" Jake's partner, Carlton, ran up the path flanked by Jill and Davis's friend, Doug. They stared at me wide-eyed, three mouths agape, and after a moment, I released my hold and Davis scurried from me.

"What the hell happened?" Carlton stepped between us.

Davis held up his bloody hands, palms out. "She's crazy," he exclaimed. "She just went nuts and attacked me."

Still standing in place, the three looked between us, but all I could do was shake my head. I couldn't get enough breath, and my pulse thrummed, but I stuttered, "He attacked me."

Davis again gestured to his face. "Doug, you know me, man. I'd never do that. She's lying."

Jill continued to look at me, worry and something else etched on her face. *Empathy? Judgment?* She stepped nearer to me, asking if I was okay, but I could only shake my head. The power that had been surging through me dissipated, and my hands began to tremble, my legs feeling wobbly. The full impact of what he could have done, what he wanted to do, hit me, and tears sprang into my eyes.

She looked from me to Davis, her shoulders squaring. "She's not lying," she said to the other two men. "He would . . ." Jill glanced at Davis again. "She's not lying."

Doug and Carlton exchanged a look, and Carlton talked hurriedly into a phone.

My heart thundered, sweat ran down my back, and I was numb, as if I were outside of my body. I pulled at my shirt, trying desperately to put it back in place. Smears of his blood ran down the front, and a button was missing. They all stared at me.

Three more people rushed into the clearing, and everyone was talking at the same time. I shook, unable to still my hands.

*This isn't really happening.* The sting of my cheek from his slap and the scrapes along the backs of my arms from the tree couldn't be explained away. *He hit me. He was going to . . .* Tears pricked behind my eyes, and my breathing was fast, too fast. The ghost of his touch on my body turned my stomach, and my head spun.

People were talking in hushed tones all at once, and the sound was overwhelming, a dissonant clatter in the stillness of the woods. It was blocked out when two solid arms circled me.

I took a gulping breath, inhaling as deeply as I could.

*Sandalwood.*

Jake's familiar voice was thick with emotion as he spoke close to my ear, cutting through the chaos. "Are you hurt? What happened? Did he . . ."

"No, I—" I tried to take a breath, but instead I sobbed, unable to finish the sentence. He pulled me tighter against his chest, his chin on my head. Everything seemed to come out at once in a steady stream of tears—the fear of Davis hurting me, of losing everything I'd worked for, of losing Jake. Also, the knowledge that I'd fought back, finally, after all the years of hiding. I'd fought.

"They're all going to know about us."

"It doesn't matter," he said, his voice rough. He ran his hand over the back of my head, stroking my hair. "You're safe."

"Really, guys. This is not what you think. Doug, c'mon . . . you know me. She was into it and then just went off." Davis's voice crawled up my spine, and I shuddered.

Jake whipped around, and his body seemed to grow taller

and wider as every muscle tensed. The hands that had been stroking my back moments before balled into tight fists at his side.

Carlton stepped between the two men, putting a meaty
palm against Jake's shoulder, stopping him from lunging toward
Davis, who stood ten feet away near Doug.

I didn't recognize Jake's voice. It was menacing. "You
should think very carefully about what you say, because if you
open your mouth again, I will finish what she started and
break your fucking jaw."

I couldn't see Jake's face, but something in his expression
wiped the sneer clean off Davis's, and he slumped against a
tree, hand held to his injured face.

Jake wrapped me in his arms again, wordlessly.

"He's not worth it," I said into his shirt as he stroked the
back of my head, his fingers threading through my hair.

"You are."

# Forty-two

T hank you, ma'am." The officer finished taking my statement, tipped his head, and walked out to the parking lot.
They had Davis in the back of a police cruiser, but he would
probably have a good enough lawyer that he'd be out in no
time and spinning his lies. He'd continued to spout we'd been
fooling around and that it had gotten out of hand.

I gingerly skimmed over the cheek that was tender and
swollen. I could only imagine what I looked like, my face bruised
and arms scraped, tear tracks on my skin. Someone had handed
me a clean T-shirt, and I clutched it, anxious to get the blood-
stained fabric off my body, but unprepared to be anywhere alone
where I could change.

"Need this?" Carlton held out a blue ice pack and sat in a
chair across the table from me.

I thanked him, pressing the cold plastic to my face. "I
didn't thank you for, um, for—"

He shook his head. "I'm sorry we didn't hear you sooner."

Carlton and the others had been on their way back to the cabin to grab something when they heard my screams and ran. I gripped the ice pack as an involuntary tremor ran through me, remembering the moments leading up to their arrival.

"Is Jake still here?" I asked in a shaky voice. When the officer started to take my statement, Jake had stepped out of the kitchen. I wondered why he hadn't returned.

"He didn't want to leave you alone, but I made him take a walk before he did something he'd regret and ended up in jail himself." Carlton was surprisingly soft-spoken, not at all the jovial front man I'd seen in the meetings. "Not that I blame him. If what happened to you happened to the woman I love . . . I don't know." He shifted his gaze to his wedding ring. It looked worn, the gold dull from years of wear.

"Oh, we're not, um, together anymore."

His eyebrows ticked up, a note of skepticism in the shift of his eyes. "I'm not sure that really matters."

The president had canceled the rest of the retreat. I'd cringed when I heard, sure my colleagues would be angry that they'd come all this way only to go back home, but no one complained, not in front of me, anyway. The flash of taillights and the crunch of gravel came through the window as one of the vans departed.

I dragged my eyes from the glass to find Carlton eyeing me intently, concern in his gaze. "Jake will take you home in our rental, if you want. I can ride with Flip."

As if on cue, Jake stepped through the door.

It took a little over an hour to travel from the retreat site to my apartment. Immediately after we pulled away from the site, he reached across the center console. I wondered if he might try to take my hand, but he froze midair and dropped it to the gear shift. We spent the drive in silence, listening only to the sounds of the road around us and the robotic voice on the GPS. I glanced at his profile; his jaw was firm and his eyes focused on the road. The space between us seemed endless as we drove, parked, and rode the elevator to my floor.

My fingers shook as I tried to unlock my apartment door, and Jake tentatively stepped beside me, taking my keys gently and unlocking the door.

He was so stiff and careful not to touch me, like he didn't know if it was allowed. After the door was open, he fiddled with his watch and looked away from my face. "Do you want me to call someone for you?"

I shook my head without saying anything.

"Okay, then I'll . . ." He rested his hand on the knob, then hesitantly stepped out the door and looked down the hall. That shift, that movement of his eyes, tripped something in me. Emotionally frayed and physically exhausted, I took control again, but this time to reach for what I wanted.

"No. Jake, wait." I stepped forward and touched his arm. "Will you stay?"

He swallowed, and his gaze traveled over my face, pausing on the bruise on my cheek.

His forearm was warm, and the familiar act of touching him gave me more confidence. I reached for his wrist.

"Please?"

It took him a moment, but he slowly laced his fingers with mine and pushed the door closed behind him. His movements were still cautious and deliberate.

I didn't break eye contact and stepped toward him, but it was Jake who closed the distance between us. He pulled my body to him, wrapping me in his arms again and blocking out the world.

"Naya," he said in a ragged voice that unfurled from deep within his chest, his breath heavy over my ear. He kissed the side of my head roughly. "I didn't know . . ." he said into my hair. "I was ready to kill that bastard, to wring his neck."

Jake kissed my temple again, a peck. Then another. "I wish you'd told me it was him."

Under my palms, the cotton of his T-shirt was soft over his pectoral muscles, and he held me close. For the first time in hours, I relaxed my muscles, leaning against him. I wanted someone to hold me who I could trust to not let me fall.

"I would have . . . I don't know, but I would have done something." Brushing his lips near the top of my ear, he dropped a third kiss, and I molded my fingers along his jaw. Counting the kisses was a way to keep time, to keep myself in the moment. He exhaled heavily as my fingertips grazed his hairline. He touched his forehead to mine and brushed his lips to the tip of my nose.

I turned my head to meet his lips, seeking the familiar pressure. He hedged for a moment, then his mouth opened to mine. The kiss was soft, slow, and sweet. I tried to say everything I hadn't verbalized with my mouth. That I was sorry, that I needed him more than I could admit, and that I loved him, too. Unable to find any of the words, I sank into him, and he cupped my cheek.

He held my face in both palms. "I—"

I shook my head, reaching to nip at his lower lip. His kisses left me grounded in a way I hadn't been since Davis attacked me, and I didn't know how else to show him he was what I needed, who I trusted.

He gently pulled his body from mine, tipping his head away. "Naya, wait."

*I am good with words. Why can't I find any of the right ones?* I let my hands trail back down his chest, my fingers splayed. I didn't know how to communicate that I didn't want anything except contact. "Please, don't leave."

He exhaled heavily and searched my face. "I haven't stopped thinking about you." His fingers flexed at my waist. "I couldn't even look at you in the meeting. I wasn't sure I could handle it, but all the while that monster was just a few feet from you. God, it turns my stomach." His brows pinched and his jaw tensed again. "I accused you of looking away, and I did the same thing. I'm so sorry, Naya. I'm so sorry. I should have paid more attention."

I clutched the fabric of his T-shirt, taking in his pained expression. "Don't apologize. You didn't know." Desperation rose in me, an almost frantic need to convince him. *I don't want to be alone.* "I've screwed everything up, Jake. With us. Just let me prove to you I'm worth another shot."

"Naya." He shook his head slowly. "You don't have to prove anything." He moved from my waist to cup my cheek, avoiding the tender side of my face. "You're always scared people will be disappointed. What I texted you? I'm so ashamed I said those things. You didn't deserve that."

What he'd said during our last text exchange came back to me. Fifty times, I'd reread the message where he said I was scared. That maybe I was broken.

"Right now, I want to wrap you in my arms and protect you from everything." His brows dipped. "But you don't need me or anyone else to do that."

Tears slipped down my cheeks, and he wiped them away with his thumbs. I opened my mouth but didn't have the words. *He's right, about all of it.*

"I don't know what that means for us, and I'd never ask you to hash that out after everything that happened today. For now, I just want you to feel safe, and I'm not going anywhere if you want me here."

I nodded, untangling my fingers from the fabric of his shirt. "Okay," I said in a voice just above a whisper. "I want you here."

He nodded and kissed my cheek, a soft peck at my temple, before wrapping me in his arms again.

# Forty-three

Four weeks later, I sat in my office on a Thursday afternoon, preparing for classes to begin.

The return of the students would give campus the energy and life that made me excited to be a professor. The summer had been a whirlwind, and there was something to be said for returning to normal. Of course, not everything was normal.

Davis's assault had dredged up emotions and memories from when we dated. I rarely slept well, but recently I hadn't been sleeping at all, and every unexpected noise or sudden movement left me quaking, startling awake prepared to fight. Davis had been charged, though the lawyer I spoke with said it would likely be reduced and assisted me with an order of protection. Looking in the mirror, I could see that the large bruise had faded but been replaced by puffy eyes and dark circles. I'd finally admitted to myself that I couldn't handle it all alone anymore, that maybe I'd never really handled it at all.

*To do: Make an appointment with a counselor.*

Out the open window, the cool breeze swept through my office, and my phone buzzed on my desk.

JAKE: Is there such a thing as a groomzilla?

NAYA: Eric?

JAKE: Tyson.

NAYA: Really?

JAKE: He's in charge of the cake—it's his one job. Best man = my job, too.

NAYA: It doesn't sound like such a hardship.

JAKE: Do you want to do the next four tastings with him? Why are there so many bakeries in this town?

NAYA: Enjoy some frosting for me.

Jake had returned to North Carolina two days after the retreat, promising he'd come back anytime I wanted. We'd shared a long embrace, he'd kissed my cheek with soft, promising lips, and then he was gone.

He still loved me. He hadn't said it, but I could feel it in how he touched me, how he looked at me. I was scared, though, and I wasn't sure how to fix it. The night he left, he'd texted.

JAKE: How are you?

NAYA: I'm ok. Felicia came over.

JAKE: Good.

The next night he'd sent Thinking about you and I'd responded with Good night. Same the next night. Clutching my phone like a teddy bear before bed, I looked forward to the messages, and they came night after night without fail.

Finally, I'd initiated an exchange. Good morning. I'm thinking about you, too. Since then, we'd traded short good morning and good night messages every day, periodically sharing small parts of our day or updates. Things weren't back to the way they were, but they were within sight of normal.

Before leaving the camp, Jill had approached me, squeezed my shoulder, and we'd exchanged a knowing look. Away from the rush of the moment in the woods, I recognized the flash of shame wash over her expression. It was a look I knew so well, but I'd never looked for it on someone else. I wanted to reach out, to tell her she didn't have to endure him, that she wasn't alone, but I didn't have the words, and people surrounded us. I squeezed her hand, which I hoped conveyed everything I didn't want to say in such a public space. I hoped she found her strength sooner than I'd found mine. We hadn't talked yet, but I knew we would.

A second retreat with nine different departments was scheduled for mid-September, obviously minus Davis. I was nervous about the announcements the president was going to make and what would happen to our department, but I'd decided if push came to shove, I'd start somewhere new. I could do it, and it would be fine. I was cautious but breathing easier than I had in a long time around my peers. I'd been given an out, an offer to not attend the second retreat, but that felt too much like Davis winning. I declined the offer to skip it.

On top of everything else, I would see Jake, and we'd made plans to meet somewhere private after the first day's meetings. Our texting was sweet and friendly, but we hadn't talked about us. I longed to see him and ached to kiss him, but also worried our connection was too badly damaged and that he wouldn't want to repair it. I had a couple of weeks until I'd know, but luckily they would be filled with the busy beginning to the semester.

A knock at my office door interrupted my thoughts. I glanced up to see someone I never would have expected: Quinton or Quenton, fist poised against the doorframe. He stood before me in green seersucker shorts, a polo shirt, and his signature boat shoes.

"Dr. Turner? Do you remember me from your Intro to Learning class? Quinn Sterling. Do you have a minute?" *Quinn. Damn, I was so close.*

"Sure, come in." I motioned to the chair on the other side of my desk, and he dropped into it. "What can I do for you?"

His gaze skittered around my office, down at his shoes, and back to me. "I wanted to, um, to ask you about, like, what we learned in class last semester." He toyed with his sunglasses, which were perched atop his product-laden hair.

"Sure. Anything in particular?"

"Well, I had to do community service this summer."

My attention caught on the *had to*, which made me envision Quinn in an orange jumpsuit.

*Not his color.*

"And we helped with, like, um, this summer school program in the city for, like, poor kids. I didn't want to do it at first, but then, it was, um, it was cool." He took his sunglasses off his head, then put them back on, fidgeting.

"That's great," I commented, trying to sound pleasant and reassuring.

"And, um, the kids had a hard time doing, like, totally basic math, like multiplication and shit—er, stuff—but they loved video games." He relaxed a little, letting his hands drop to my desk, and he leaned forward. "And I remembered you talking about that in class."

"Sure, gamification can help kids get excited about math."
*He was paying attention when I talked about my research?*

"Yeah! This one kid really didn't get it. We didn't have anything fancy, it was, like, a really poor school, but I brought in my tablet, and we found this free app, and like, we played these games and it totally helped him. It was really cool. I felt, like, really good about myself."

I smiled. *I'm proud of the little shit.*

"Anyway, I liked doing it a lot, and I was wondering if you could help me do it, like, for a job." His dispassionate, too-cool-for-school mask was gone, replaced with genuine curiosity and vulnerability.

"To be a game designer?"

"No. A teacher."

I could have been knocked over with a feather. "Definitely."

"I don't know a lot yet. It's, like, new still, but using games to help was cool. My major is marketing, but can you help me, um, switch or whatever? This seems way more interesting." His expression was hopeful, and I couldn't stop my smile from widening.

"I'd be happy to help, Quinn."

When he walked out thirty minutes later, I shook my head. If someone else had been in the room, I would have given them a wide-eyed *did-you-see-that?* A sense of professional wonder filled me like a balloon, and I wished I had someone to tell.

NAYA: The strangest thing just happened.

JAKE: Yeah?

# Forty-four

President Lewis stood at the front of the main lodge in a TU sweatshirt and jeans. I glanced around the room, wishing there was anyone near me who would share my incredulity. *Is our seventy-year-old university president wearing skinny jeans?* The people to my left and right, including my stuffy colleague Anita, looked unperturbed. Joe would have at least given me a raised eyebrow, but he was still recovering and on strict orders from Elaine to step back.

We'd departed early that morning from the parking lot outside the main administration building, piling into a charter bus. Professors from nine departments settled in awkwardly, stilted conversation buzzing through the vehicle as people whispered about "Camp Job Search" and "Retreat to the Unemployment Line." I'd wanted to ask Jake a hundred times what to expect, but everything between us still felt fragile, so I'd held back, even though we'd made plans to meet up that night by the lake to talk.

Flip walked across the front of the room where forty of us sat in folding chairs. "Thank you all for being here. I know we've been tight-lipped about this, and I appreciate the trust you've placed in me and this process." Despite his grandfatherly tone of voice and an impressive ability to pull off wearing those jeans, the room vibrated with anxiety. "So why are we here? Put your minds at ease; this is not 'Camp Pink Slip' or any of the other colorful nicknames you've heard.

"I wanted all of you here as we figure out how to move forward with the consultants' recommendations. There will be cuts, but none of your programs are in that position."

I let out a breath along with the rest of the room before Flip spoke again.

"Not yet, anyway."

The older man kept speaking. "The boys from the consultation firm will walk you through it, but before I sit down, know this—" He paused, and I admired his bright white tennis shoes that looked fresh out of a box. "Many of you know I don't go in much for *traditional*. I like to shake things up. I think that's why the trustees hired me, and I'm sure that, someday, that's why they'll fire me." He smiled, eyes crinkling, and a chuckle moved through the assembled group. "But until then, it's my job to make sure TU is the best damn university in the country, and you're all going to help me make that happen."

My muscles unclenched, and a surge of air left my lungs—my job was safe. I could keep studying and teaching the things I loved.

Carlton and Jake walked to the space just vacated by Flip. Jake wore a pale blue polo shirt and dark jeans. I loved him in blue, and I wondered if he'd worn it for me. I bit the inside of my cheek, attempting to suppress the myriad of emotions I felt in the moment.

"Thank you, Flip," Carlton said. He explained that they had placed all departments of the university into four categories along the axes of success and potential. As Carlton spoke, Jake illustrated on a nearby whiteboard, drawing the four quadrants.

"And we didn't measure success just in dollars—we included notoriety, reputation, and student enrollment, among other factors," Jake chimed in over his shoulder.

"First, we had the high success/high potential programs—your cornerstones that are doing well. Think of accounting and engineering. Second, low success/low potential programs—unpopular programs not doing well. Those are easy to move forward on." Carlton motioned to where Jake had scrawled on the board.

"Next, high success/low potential programs. This is more complex. Take, for example, a program that brings in lots of money, but for which there is little recognition for research or few job opportunities for graduates."

Some heads around the room nodded, everyone piecing together where their department fell. I was surprised when Anita nodded and leaned forward.

*This might be the first time in twenty years she's been interested in something someone else is saying.*

"Now we get to all of your departments, which fell in the last quadrant—low success/high potential programs; what we're titling 'stalled programs.'" The room met him with a stony silence, expecting more explanation.

I desperately tried to focus on what this meant for my job

and not on the curve of Jake's shoulder blades as he turned to add something. "Your nine departments are here," Jake said, pointing to the fourth quadrant. "All have a high potential for impact—job prospects are good for graduates, faculty could bring in big research dollars, and the potential for solid enrollment is high; unfortunately, successes aren't there yet. In terms of TU's goals, your departments are stalled, and we will work together to push them forward."

*To do: Tell Joe we're safe.*

Jake scanned the crowd as he and Carlton took questions about the model. He held my gaze for a moment, the corners of his lips tipping up, before focusing on a woman asking a question two rows ahead of me.

"Let's get to work," Carlton said, clapping his hands together before breaking us into small groups.

# Forty-five

Hours later, the sun was low in the sky, casting the lake and surrounding woods in a shadowy, warm glow. We'd been released from our work, and most of the crowd had joined Flip for dinner in the camp's dining center. I'd ducked out, the sloppy joes doing little to entice me. Instead, I grabbed a granola bar from the kitchen and trekked toward the lake where Jake and I'd agreed to meet. I was early, but I figured I could find a spot and run through what I wanted to say.

I'd been sleeping better and talking with the counselor about all the things I'd kept buried for years. It was so much harder than I'd anticipated, but every time I left her office, I could pick up one or two more pieces of myself, even if just to hold them for a few minutes.

As I neared the shore, the broad shoulders were easy to recognize. Jake sat on the sand, his back to a group of Adirondack chairs. He'd come early, too. I held my breath, admiring the way the wind blew his hair askew—it was a little long for him, like the night we'd met. His legs were stretched in front of his large frame, and he was reading something on his phone while he waited.

I closed my eyes and inhaled the fall air, and then slowly exhaled, willing myself to step forward, despite the urge to turn around. With the counselor, I'd figured out running and avoiding was a tactic I'd used to stay safe, but one that had become routine for me in every other facet of my life. With another slow inhale and exhale, I pulled my phone from my pocket. I'd thought a lot about how I would start this conversation, how I'd jump into everything that needed to be said to get us back. I missed him, but I missed me *with him*, too. When we were together, I didn't worry I wasn't measuring up or feel like I was always guessing what he wanted. I knew what he wanted, and it was me.

*Now or never.*

NAYA: Knock-knock.

Still hiding along the tree line, I watched his body language carefully. I imagined two expressions on his face: the relaxed, playful grin I'd come to know so well and the pained, pinched grimace from our fight. Jake's head remained dipped over his screen, but his posture relaxed.

JAKE: Who's there?

NAYA: Doorbell repairman.

He laughed, the sound carrying to the tree line, where I bit my lip and smiled.

JAKE: Do people still say LOL?

NAYA: IDK

His chuckle was quieter, more subdued, and faded into silence before he checked his watch and my phone buzzed again.

JAKE: I figured you'd be early. But I figured you'd get a little
   closer than those trees. Still coming over?

NAYA: Do you still want me to?

JAKE: That's a silly question.

Jake pivoted to face me.

My breath caught in my throat as he looked up and smiled.
It was a small, closed-mouth smile, but the expression was soft
and kind. "Yes, I want you to come talk to me."

He patted the ground next to him, tilting his head.

I'd accused him of hurting me, I'd ignored him, and I'd
shown I didn't trust him at the first bump in the road. Jake had
been so gracious, more than I deserved, but he'd have every
reason to write me off. Instead he was patting the sand and inviting me over, which said so much about why I needed him
in my life. I lowered myself to sit, our elbows inches apart.

Slipping his phone into his pocket, Jake rested his forearms
on his knees.

We sat in silence, both taking in the sight of the water, and
I stole quick glances at his profile.

His voice broke the silence, the low rumble stirring something in me. "I liked the joke."

"I thought you might." I wrapped my arms around my
knees and rocked, my feet sinking into the sand. The silence
fell between us again, but it wasn't uncomfortable, just unfin-
ished. I toyed with the ring on my middle finger, deciding where
to begin.

Jake spoke first. "You're nervous?"

"A little," I admitted.

"How did it go with the counselor?" he asked.

"Really good, actually." During one of our brief texts,

I'd shared I was going to see someone. "I should have done it years ago."

"Good."

"How was the cake tasting?"

"I can now tell you the pros and cons of fondant."

I chuckled, and we fell back to silence; the breeze moving through the trees and the gentle lapping of the water were the only sounds. It was so strange to sit next to him again, next to the body with which I had become so familiar, but with so much distance between us. *Can't we skip ahead through this awkward part and be us again?*

"Listen," Jake said, his voice low. "I've been thinking about you a lot."

I remembered how tightly I'd gripped his T-shirt in my entryway the night Davis had attacked me, how desperate I'd been for connection.

He ran his long fingers through his hair. "I know you can't just flip a switch and trust people. I've been reading about what survivors go through, and I get it now, or I'm starting to, I think. I was asking too much of you and demanding more than you were ready to give."

My stomach and heart traded places, and I slid my clammy hands over my thighs again, noticing Jake's glance following their movement. His lips were pressed together. I remembered those lips on mine and down my body, and I felt flustered and inarticulate. My mouth opened to speak, and I had no idea what would come out.

"There's no switch to flip, and I *am* scared."

He turned to face me, his expression inscrutable and his gaze intensified, those blue eyes searching my face.

"But I don't want to be." I took another measured breath and continued. "We had something good, and I blew up at you and it wasn't fair and . . ." I searched for how to end my confession with something sweet and endearing. I drew a blank, and goose bumps rose on my arms.

He nodded, his chin dipping almost imperceptibly.

"It was inexcusable to just walk away and ignore you, to make you feel disposable, because you're the furthest thing from that." I gave up on finding the perfect thing to say and let everything out. "And, I should have told you about my ex sooner. I was embarrassed, and I didn't realize how much he'd taken up residence in my head. I have a lot of work to do on myself still, and I didn't want you to feel like you had to put your career at risk to save me. I still don't want that for you, so I understand if—" I stopped short.

His kiss was full of gentle sweetness, a hint of hunger and want. Our tongues met, sliding over each other's, and his fingers brushed the sensitive skin near my ear. We pulled apart, just an inch, and he pressed his forehead to mine.

"Please don't finish that sentence," he said, cupping my face in both of his warm palms. "I don't want an if." He pecked at my lips between statements. "Nay, I would risk anything for you. Don't you know that? And you have to believe that I know what you do is valuable. I always have."

Another tinge of anxiety ran through me. "Our program being safe, was that you?"

"I would have pushed for it, but I didn't have to." He noticed something on my face and hurried to clarify. "I would have pushed because it *should* be safe, despite our initial findings. Your program *is* high potential, and everyone on our team agreed once we shifted to the current model. What you do matters, Naya. It's worth fixing what's broken in your department."

He stared intently into my eyes, and I didn't look away. "And *you* matter. To me, you matter more than anyone."

His lips hovered near mine again; his touches were just as soft and his tongue as intent as before, but this time our physical connection was hard-won. When Jake told me I mattered, I wanted to be the person who deserved those words.

His voice in my ear was the only sound I cared about. "You're . . ."

"Getting better at flirting?"

"What do you mean?" His forehead fell gently against mine as he laughed. "Your flirting skills have always been impeccable."

"You must have forgotten how I got sick while attempting to have a one-night stand with you."

Jake's grin widened. "That was definitely memorable, but only a guy who was already falling for you would have texted you the next day."

I laughed, blinking back the tears welling in my eyes. "You texted me that night."

"Exactly." He cupped a cheek with one hand. "One night would never have been enough."

The puff of his breath touched my cheek, and a grin formed on my face, mirroring his. I opened my mouth to speak, but voices behind us stopped me. Our eyes widened, and we parted quickly as the group of faculty members from the dietetics department emerged from the trees, waving in our direction. I waved back, and Jake stifled a laugh, dipping his chin as they moved toward the dock as the sun began to set.

Jake slid his fingers across the ground between us, rubbing a thumb over my knuckles, the grains of sand rough between our skin.

"Have you checked everything off of your list?" he said finally as the group settled near the dock thirty feet from us. His voice was deep and low; our only physical connection—our fingers in the sand—felt like being naked with him.

"Yes. But now I've added new things." I wrapped my arms loosely around his waist. "I want to learn to cook, travel, learn Spanish. I want to run a marathon and start volunteering. I took a couple self-defense classes, and I think I might try kickboxing."

"Where will you start?"

"I'm planning on you teaching me to cook, to begin with. I hope the relationship can survive."

"I think at this point, we can survive anything." He swept a fingertip over the underside of my wrist.

"Jake, can we start over?"

"No," he said, glancing over my shoulder at the group. "Let's just . . ." His lips brushed by my ear. "Keep going."

I closed my eyes against the torrent of emotion and the shudder of pleasure his quick touch evoked. "It shouldn't be this easy."

"I doubt it will be," he said, resigned. "I work too much, and I know you do, too. And we'll have to figure out how to be together when we live so far apart." He looked over the lake, his expression a little sad. "It's probably going to be hard."

It terrified me I wasn't going to be interesting enough to sustain the connection between us. I was worried he might walk away from me or I'd try to push him away again. I paused, thinking back to my sessions with the counselor.

*I need to pay attention to how much this self-doubt creeps in.*

I followed his gaze across the water, our fingers mingled in the sand between us. "I'm nervous, but not as much as I would have thought."

"What do you mean?"

"I can't think of anyone else I'd want to try with." I angled my body to his. "It's taken me too long to say it, far too long, but I'm in love with you, Jake . . . toe-curling, dancing-in-public, don't-care-who-knows-it, point-out-I-snore, and tell-me-another-joke in love with you."

*Trust a man. Check.*

His eyebrows dipped, a grin spreading across his face.

"Say something . . ."

He smiled, his blue eyes bright and dancing as he stroked a finger down the back of my hand.

". . . well?"

He glanced over my shoulder again. "I was waiting until the dietitians were distracted." He brought my fingers to his lips, kissing my knuckles sweetly and holding my hand to his face. "And, for the record, I'm in love with you, too. Phobia-facing, pun-making, you-had-me-from-day-one, I'm-never-letting-you-go-again in love with you."

"When I imagined you saying that, I pictured fewer dietitians," I whispered back.

"I always assumed there'd be a gaggle." He laughed, and, like that, it seemed we were back to where we'd been, making each other laugh and forgetting the rest of the world.

My spine relaxed in a way that made me realize how stiffly I had been holding myself. "Is 'gaggle' the technical term for a group of them?"

"I'm not sure. I'll have to ask next time I'm at the library. Man, that will be awkward with Gladys, though."

"It's a hard life you lead," I said.

"Not really." He shrugged, his fingers slipping from my skin, the trace of his touch lingering on my nerve endings. He smiled at me, his eyes almost twinkling in the sunset. "It seems I have it pretty good right now."

A slight breeze picked up, but it didn't diminish the warmth between us. I had nothing to add to my list in that moment, but it felt like a whole world of things I *could* add had just opened up.

# Epilogue

The cut of the pants and the way the jacket framed his shoulders left me in awe every single time. *I wonder if Jake would agree to wearing tuxedos around the house or while mowing the lawn.*

The ceremony took place on the top of a mountain overlooking a lush valley, and the smell of gardenia and lavender filled the air. Jake stood at the altar, his features bathed in the sunlight of the hazy North Carolina morning. His gaze moved to mine, and he smiled, the one just for me, before he turned back to face the happy couple.

Jake handed the ring to his best friend. They exchanged a tight hug before Tyson faced Eric and the officiant walked them through their vows.

I dotted a tissue at the corner of my eye. Jake glanced my way and winked—he'd been the one to give me a small package of them, even though I'd insisted I wouldn't cry.

The ceremony was followed by cocktails while the couple took pictures in front of the stunning vista with their wedding party. Standing in this jovial crowd alone would have made me anxious a year before, but sipping the drink, I enjoyed the moment.

The last year had been a whirlwind. Davis was convicted but didn't receive any jail time. He hadn't tried to contact me, though. He'd stayed away from Jill, too. When we'd finally talked, she'd shared that her experiences had been like mine. We cried and shared, and it was horrifying and affirming to know someone else going through a similar healing process. We'd become close, and between her, the counselor, and Jake, I felt like I was finally moving out from Davis's shadow.

I'd made progress on my list, and Jake and I started adding things to a new one together with the myriad of changes we made at work, me earning tenure, Jake's traveling, and more weekend trips between Chicago and Raleigh than I ever would have thought manageable. We'd gone to Seattle to see his family at Christmas. I'd fretted over the third degree I was sure I would receive from his four sisters, but they welcomed me into their circle like I'd always been there. After the new year, we went to my small hometown in Iowa to see my family, and we'd visited my grandfather, and I told him I was done auditioning. I was signed up for an intensive Spanish-language course for the spring, and couldn't believe I'd waited so long. I was excited.

With as much as he traveled anyway, Jake decided to work based out of Chicago, and that plan was finally coming to fruition. I never got better at flirting, but it seemed I'd never have to do it with anyone else, so I stopped worrying. We'd spent the last three days packing up his house on the lake to prepare for his move to join me at our new place.

*Buy a house. Check.*

My phone buzzed, and I pulled it from my clutch.

FELICIA: The boys and Emily want to know when Jake can come over to play.

FELICIA: Aaron does, too.

NAYA: Aww . . . he has a crush on my boyfriend.

AARON: I only asked if he'd be back in time for poker this week.

NAYA: There's nothing to be embarrassed about. He's cute.

Arms wrapped around me from behind as I stood at a high-top table, sipping a mimosa. "If that's Felicia, can she tell Aaron I'll be back in time for the game?"

I grinned and tapped out the reply assuring Aaron he'd have his date for poker. Jake fit into our group like he'd always been there. He'd won over Felicia immediately, clinching it when he volunteered to babysit. Aaron and he just clicked. I think Aaron liked having another guy around. Felicia's trainer, Wes, had started hanging out with us more often as well, and all of a sudden, I had this widening circle of people. It was kind of amazing.

"You know, day drinking is a great idea for a wedding," Jake whispered into my neck, pulling me to him. My blue chiffon sundress caught in a slight breeze and swirled around me as I set my phone down and faced him.

"Agreed." I laughed, and he took the glass, planting a playful kiss along my jawline. "How is the happy couple?"

"Eric loves having his photo taken—he's in heaven. Tyson loves Eric and is tolerating it. I was released into your care," he said breezily, and I wondered if some alcohol was part of the wedding planner's technique for cajoling wedding parties.

"I'll do my best to keep an eye on you."

"I'll keep an eye on you, too," Jake said with a boyish grin, setting the glass aside and wrapping his arms around my waist.

"Worried I'll get ornery?" I asked, wrapping my other arm around him.

"I like it when you're ornery." He planted a quick kiss on my lips and tasted like champagne. We swayed to the music playing from across the lawn, and his grip tightened on my waist. "But I like you all the time." He flashed a smile again. "Except when you leave dishes in the sink instead of putting them in the dishwasher right away. We're gonna fight about that."

"That, and how you squeeze from the middle of the toothpaste tube." I rubbed my hands over his shoulders.

"And the toilet paper should roll from the top—"

"You're always going to be wrong about this. Bottom."

"I can't wait."

"You can't wait to fight?"

Jake gripped me tighter and lowered me into a playful dip. "I like making up with you."

*I can't wait, either.*

"Hey, cut it out. *Way* too much PDA," Tyson said from behind us as he and Eric approached, hands clasped.

"That's impossible," Jake returned, smiling at the couple and dropping his lips to mine. "How can I not publicly display my affection for this beautiful woman?"

I gave both grooms hugs. Tyson had warmed up to me once Jake and I reconnected, though I was back on thin ice for taking his best friend a thousand miles away. I kissed him on the cheek.

I gestured around the space. "The ceremony was so beautiful. I cried."

"I knew you would," Jake said, pulling me to his side.

"It turned out well," Eric said in a rare moment of humility about this event he'd been planning for a year. "And the cake looks good," he said, taking Tyson's hand.

Tyson stretched to bump fists with Jake. "All those tastings were worth it."

"If you say so," Jake countered. "It meant a lot of extra time at the gym and every baker in the city thinking we were a couple."

"That one woman who insisted we practice feeding each other!" Tyson's face lit up when he laughed like that.

Jake shared his laugh. "Hey, I was willing to play along so you could practice."

"I know how bad your aim is, man. The cake would have ended up on my shoulder or the hood of my car." Tyson turned to Eric, and his smile softened. "Besides, there's only one person I ever plan to share my cake with." He pulled Eric to him with an adoring expression. "So, no practice necessary."

Eric beamed at his new husband before addressing me. "And you've been warned about Jake's potential bad aim, Nay," Eric said. "If you bring him cake tasting for your wedding, maybe bring a poncho."

I chuckled but eyed Jake nervously, though he was exchanging a look with Tyson I couldn't read. I never wanted to push, knowing how badly his marriage to Gretchen had ended. We were happy the way things were. We planned to be together, had vaguely discussed starting a family, but I honestly didn't know if he wanted to be married again, and I was okay with that.

When the grooms were pulled away by Tyson's grandmother, I asked Jake, "What's up with them trying to push us down the aisle?"

He bent his head to my ear, his warm breath on the delicate skin behind my earlobe, and whispered, "I was thinking we'd pick the cake together."

I turned abruptly and looked up at him in surprise, my eyebrow raised. "What?"

"I have experience now, but you love cake more than anyone I know." Jake circled his arms around my waist again, and I tried to decide if he was joking or proposing, scrutinizing his grin.

He must have seen the question in my face. "Oh, I'm not asking you to marry me, if that's what that face means."

"Good to know." I wrapped my arms around his neck.

"I didn't bring the ring with me, so you'll have to wait and see what I have planned."

My jaw dropped, and I again tried to read his tipsy expression.

He waggled his eyebrows and planted a playful kiss on my mouth, my face still turned up in surprise. "Don't worry. For now, I can't wait to fight about the toothpaste, check things off our list, fall asleep with you every night, and wake up with you every morning."

*Sounds good to me.*

## AUTHOR'S NOTE

Naya found her happily ever after at the end of a long and winding road. If you or someone you love is, or may be, experiencing intimate partner violence, information and resources are available nationally and through agencies in your local area when you're in a safe place to access them.

---

### NATIONAL DOMESTIC VIOLENCE HOTLINE

thehotline.org
espanol.thehotline.org
1-800-799-7233
1-800-787-3224 (TTY)

## ACKNOWLEDGMENTS

I come from a long line of strong women. I come from homesteads in Colorado, and the Jim Crow south, from sweet potato pie and aebleskivers, from traveling the world, and from love that stood the test of time. Thank you to the generations who fought so I could flourish. My grandmothers were both writers, something I knew little about until after they were gone. Thank you for raising strong, loving children who became strong, loving adults, so I might become one as well.

To my parents: You've encouraged me to write, to reach, and to achieve from day one. I'm sorry I accidentally sent you an early copy of this novel full of the sex scenes I thought I'd redacted. You've shown me what love and a strong relationship looks like for over thirty years and across three continents. Thank you to my brother for always cheering me on and promising to listen to an audio version of this book, provided I am not the one narrating. To Amanda, Mike, Melissa, Jean, Bruce, Barb, Tim, Aretha, Allison, Kaitlin, all my aunts, uncles, and cousins, my niece and nephews, and my friends, thank you for listening to me talk about this book for years.

For my husband and Tiny Human—squeeze hugs. You two are my world and my everything, and I love you. Also, Tiny Human, you can NEVER read this book.

It's a gift to work with strong, funny, and kind publishing professionals. Thank you to my incredible agent, Sharon Pelletier, for believing in this book and in me. Thank you also to Lauren Abramo, Kemi Faderin, and Mike Hoogland at Dystel, Goderich & Bourret, and Kristina Moore at Anonymous Content.

Thank you to my phenomenal editor, Kerry Donovan. Your support, insight, and guidance have meant the world to me. Also thank you to Tara O'Connor, Dache Rogers, Bridget O'Toole, Natalie Sellars, Mary Geren, and the rest of the Berkley and Penguin Random House team for bringing this novel to life.

Robert Fulghum said, "We're all a little weird. And life is a little weird. And when we find someone whose weirdness is compatible with ours, we join up with them and fall into mutually satisfying weirdness—and call it love—true love." Thank you to all my weird friends, especially two of you. Bethany, who was my first friend in college, has been my best friend for decades, and will be my sister always. Thank you for always cheering, always reading, and always joining me in ordering dessert, even though you never finish it. Finally, I'm the taller one. It's in print now. I win.

Allison Ashley—you're stuck with me for life. You are my go-to critique partner and I am forever in your debt for the advice, brainstorming, countless reads, unwavering support, and late-night humor. I trust you implicitly with my first ugly drafts and can't imagine being on this journey to publishing with anyone else. You're my person.

Robin Ridenour, you taught me to be a better writer. I have appreciated your humor, kindness, encouragement, attention to detail, and storytelling. Thank you also to Kat, Alex, Ron, and everyone at Scribophile who helped me improve. TeamCarly, the best writing group around, has been a constant source of support and encouragement. Thank you to Katie, Haley, Emily, Brian, Tera, Jenn, Ann, Pat, Tara, Sheri, Nicole, Michelle, Crystal, Maggie, Jessi, Susan, Kristine, Kathi, Mitzi, Racheal, Nadine, Salem, Joyce, Som, Alissa, and all the other friends who agreed to be early readers and shared their time and suggestions.

Penny and Greta slept at my feet during every step of this book's creation, from those first stumbling paragraphs through final edits. Thank you to the best and the worst dog in the world for keeping me company. You've both earned treats.

Continue reading for a special preview of

# THE FASTEST WAY TO FALL

by Denise Williams, coming in Fall 2021!

# Britta

I hustled down the hall, late and waterlogged. *It would rain today of all days.*

With a graceless slip on the slick tile of the conference room, my umbrella sprayed water into the air and I hit the floor with a surprised cry. My skirt rode up my thighs as the box of donuts skidded across the polished wood floor, coming to rest by my boss's Louboutins. Around me, conversation stopped, and I lingered in a cocoon of awkward silence.

Normally the box was empty and stuffed in the trash before our boss arrived, already full from her kale smoothie or whatever Paleo-adjacent, keto-friendly organic breakfast food was trending. Everyone would enjoy the treat and I'd maintain my status as popular coworker, but the rain had other plans for my reputation and dignity that morning. Maricela's manicured fingers slipped under the table to pick up the pink box.

"Britta, you made it." Claire's sickly sweet voice broke the silence, and a chuckle went around the conference table. She sat back in smug satisfaction.

That's what I told myself, anyway. From the spot on the floor next to my dripping umbrella, I couldn't see anything except her impossibly high heels. For a fleeting moment, I wondered how good their traction was and if she might have her own run-in with the slippery floor.

"I like to make an entrance," I mumbled, clambering to my hands and knees before trying to stand without flashing the entire staff of *Best Life*, the millennial-focused lifestyle website where I'd worked as an editorial assistant for four years.

"Britta, are you okay?" Maricela Dominguez-Van Eiken looked like a person who'd run a lifestyle empire. Back straight, dark hair curled and cascading, a perfectly organized planner settled perpendicular to the newest iPhone and a rose gold water bottle. She'd built *Best Life* from the ground and turned it into a lucrative, trendsetting company designed to help people live well. Kale smoothies aside, she had impeccable taste and just seemed to have her life together. *What's that like?*

I rubbed my knee and rotated the wrist I'd landed on, catching Claire's smirk from across the room. *Just a little mortified.* "I'm okay. Sorry I'm late."

She nodded and passed the box of donuts to the person on her left. It began a slow rotation around the room, pair after pair of hungry eyes lingering on the treats as my colleagues waved their hands to pass. No one would take one after she demurred.

"It's February first." She tapped her index finger to her collar—her *impress me* gesture. At the beginning of each month, Maricela sought new ideas from the entire team. After four years, I *needed* to stand out. I was a good writer, but I'd never gotten the chance to flex those skills for *Best Life*. I wondered if I might be able to contribute more to the world than recommendations for face creams or the inside scoop on whether escape rooms were over.

"I have an idea," I chimed in and raised a finger. All eyes, once again, landed on me. "There's a new app called FitMe that's been gaining popularity. Unlike other apps that focus just on tracking weight loss and counting calories, this one has real people serving as coaches and the experience is very individualized." I kept an eye on my boss, who loved the intentional marriage of technology and human interaction. I wouldn't have been surprised if she had a secret "tech+people" tattoo somewhere on her body. "What if I join and document my journey? I'd talk about the app, but also everything I'm going through as I reach fitness goals."

I didn't have to look around the room to know I was the only one who'd be described as plus-size. If she liked the idea, I was the one person who could write it. I learned early in life I was supposed to be ashamed of what my mom called my extra fluff and my sister called my fat ass. It wasn't until I got to college that I started to accept that I was fun, smart, and . . . fat, and that last one wasn't the only thing that defined me. When I found FitMe, my wheels started turning with this idea. I was positive the unique perspective I could bring plus the human-and-technology integration was a sure winner.

Maricela was nodding again but had moved her finger from her collarbone to tap her chin.

*Shit, she hates it.*

"Thank you, Britta. I'd like to see something more original than a weight-loss piece, though. I'd want a stronger connection to wellness, with there being so much body-shaming in the world already. Bring us the next idea, though." She called on someone else, and I squelched the urge to sink into my chair and hide. It wasn't the first time I'd had an idea shot down—everyone had—but I'd been positive it would be the bump I needed to earn a place on the staff as a feature writer. I glanced across the table at Claire. She'd made no secret of her goals, and with one position available, we'd both been trying to stand out. Hopefully she didn't have some great idea to pitch.

Claire caught my eye, her expression pensive, before she tapped at something on her phone, and I turned my attention back to the discussion about homemade face masks and aromatherapy yoga mats.

After graduating from college, I'd hunted for jobs, desperate to prove to my family that my English and journalism double major wasn't a one-way ticket to unemployment. I was confident I'd find a job where I could write stirring pieces that would change minds and hearts. I was wrong, and I jumped at the editorial assistant position at *Best Life*. Four years later, I'd learned not to roll my eyes. Though we generated a lot of helpful and insightful content, we also spent a lot of time discussing things like aromatherapy and yoga mats. Some days, it felt like I'd veered so far from my original plans of being a writer, I wasn't sure I'd ever get back.

"Great idea. Put together a plan for road testing the masks and let's get it up for part of the Valentine's Day Alone series. Britta can assist." I'd zoned out, but a senior staff member flashed me a big smile. I'd have to figure out what I missed later.

"Anything else?" Maricela looked around the table and paused at Claire's raised hand.

"I have one," she said, her voice even and annoyingly casual. "It's a different angle on Britta's idea. There is another app which is just starting to add coaches. I could join that one while Britta joins FitMe, and we'd do the project together, broadening the scope to focus not only on changing bodies but on the entire fitness experience."

I looked to Maricela. *Please let her finger be traveling to her chin.* No such luck, it was still tapping at her collarbone. She was interested in Claire's spin. "What sets this second app apart? How would dual participation improve upon the idea?"

Claire's shoulders squared. "The app is a lot like the others out there, but they take a different approach. It's called HotBody. Their campaign is about being hot while being able to rock the body you're in."

Our boss' finger drifted toward her chin as her lips pursed. "This is an interesting take, but I don't love the visual of a thin woman writing about being hot and a plus-size woman writing about getting fit."

A hundred responses flew through my head, all landing somewhere between tears and declaring I would write about being hot, too. Luckily, my rival spoke before I did, and with a more measured tone than I'd planned.

"On the surface, I agree. However, there's a unique take here. Or rather, a very common take. I *am* thin, but I have my own body image issues. Don't we all?" She glanced around the room where most of the women and a few men were nodding. "And I'm comfortable writing about it."

I nodded and leaned forward, resting my arms on the conference table. "And I love seeing women who are big and happy with their bodies. I love reading stories about people deciding to make a change and losing a bunch of weight. Both can be inspirational, but neither are my story. Plus-size and fat people can be interested in exercise and fitness without necessarily wanting to change themselves. I think I could tell that story and I think it would land with our audience."

Maricela glanced at her notes, finger hovering between her chin and collarbone.

Claire joined me again, our impromptu tag-team approach seeming to work. "The project would be about the relationship with one's body. And if the apps are focused only on looks or only on weight loss, we'll point it out, so readers know. I think it's a win-win."

Maricela glanced down at her tablet, and after a few taps and swipes, she smiled. "Okay, put together a plan. Let's try it."

As we moved on with the agenda, Claire eyed me coolly, clearly conflicted about the idea of sharing the spotlight but also knowing this could be the way one of us found ourselves on the writing staff. We'd been in competition since we started, both eager to do well and stand out, and both ready to move up at *Best Life*.

She was a good writer and when she spoke about her body, she sounded genuine. I swallowed, realizing the extent to which I'd have to step it up and make myself vulnerable. Despite my impassioned plea, I didn't actually much care about exercising. I assumed I'd have to eat better and go to the gym for a few months to do this project, but I wasn't wanting or expecting something paradigm-altering to happen. Still, if I got it right, it would be big for my career, and I could fake it long enough to make the project work. Nothing was going to get in the way of success with this project and earning that spot as a feature writer. In that spirit, I flashed a wide grin at Claire.

*Game on.*

**Denise Williams** wrote her first book in the second grade. *I Hate You* and its sequel, *I Still Hate You*, featured a tough, funny heroine, a quirky hero, witty banter, and a dragon. Minus the dragons, these are still the books she likes to write. After penning those early works, she finished second grade and eventually earned a PhD in education, going on to work in higher education. After growing up as a military brat around the world and across the country, Denise now lives in Iowa with her husband, son, and two ornery shih tzus who think they own the house.

Ready to find
your next great read?

Let us help.

**Visit prh.com/nextread**

Penguin
Random
House